BIRTHRIGHT

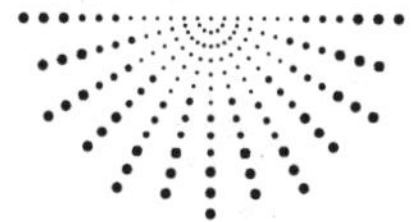

ANNA MARKLAND

BIRTHRIGHT

By

ANNA MARKLAND

COVER ART BY DAR ALBERT

BIRTHRIGHT by Anna Markland

Book V, The Montbryce Legacy, Anniversary Edition

www.annamarkland.com

"Two loyal brothers must cope with afflictions that render them unmarriageable and, in their minds, unfit for love. Two sisters, also afflicted and locked in the attic of a manor home their entire lives, cope with freedom and, in their minds, the undeserved love offered them by these noble men. The story takes an unusual and heart-touching approach to the stories of these four people, then weaves it with a tale of court intrigue and malicious intentions that has readers sitting on the edge of their seats in fear for the lives of these endearing characters."
Connie Flynn, author of ***The Dragon Hour.***

In honor of my grandson Adam,
already a handsome young man.

And in memory of my beloved Topaz.

Hear no evil
Speak no evil
See no evil
~Ancient Wisdom

MORE ANNA MARKLAND

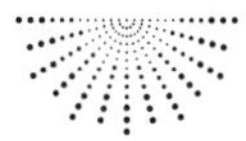

The Montbryce Legacy Anniversary Edition (2018)

I Conquest—Ram & Mabelle, Rhodri & Rhonwen

II Defiance—Hugh & Devona, Antoine & Sybilla

III Redemption—Caedmon & Agneta

IV Vengeance—Ronan & Rhoni

The Montbryce Legacy First Edition (2011-2014)

Conquering Passion—Ram & Mabelle, Rhodri & Rhonwen (audiobook available)

If Love Dares Enough—Hugh & Devona, Antoine & Sybilla

Defiant Passion-Rhodri & Rhonwen

A Man of Value—Caedmon & Agneta

Dark Irish Knight—Ronan & Rhoni

Haunted Knights—Adam & Rosamunda, Denis & Paulina

Passion in the Blood—Robert & Dorianne, Baudoin & Carys

Dark and Bright—Rhys & Annalise

The Winds of the Heavens—Rhun & Glain, Rhydderch & Isolda

Dance of Love—Izzy & Farah

Carried Away—Blythe & Dieter

Sweet Taste of Love—Aidan & Nolana

Wild Viking Princess—Ragna & Reider

Hearts and Crowns—Gallien & Peridotte

Fatal Truths—Alex & Elayne

Sinful Passions—Bronson & Grace; Rodrick & Swan

Series featuring the stories of the Viking ancestors of my Norman families

The Rover Bold—Bryk & Cathryn

The Rover Defiant—Torstein & Sonja

The Rover Betrayed—Magnus & Judith

Novellas

Maknab's Revenge—Ingram & Ruby

Passion's Fire—Matthew & Brigandine

Banished—Sigmar & Audra

Hungry Like De Wolfe—Blaise & Anne

Unkissable Knight—Dervenn & Victorine

Caledonia Chronicles (Scotland)

Book I Pride of the Clan—Rheade & Margaret

Book II Highland Tides—Braden & Charlotte

Book 2.5 Highland Dawn—Keith & Aurora

Book III Roses Among the Heather—Blair &Susanna, Craig & Timothea

The Von Wolfenberg Dynasty (medieval Europe)

Book 1 Loyal Heart—Sophia & Brandt

Book 2 Courageous Heart—Luther & Francesca

Book 3 Faithful Heart—Kon & Zara

Myth & Mystery

The Taking of Ireland —Sibràn & Aislinn

The Pendray Papers

Highland Betrayal—Morgan & Hannah (audiobook available)

Clash of the Tartans

Kilty Secrets—Ewan & Shona

Kilted at the Altar—Darroch & Isabel

Kilty Pleasures—Broderick & Kyla

THE DWARF AND THE GIANT

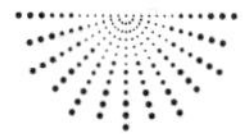

BELISLE CASTLE, NORMANDIE, 1100 AD.

"At my birth, the midwife believed it her sacred duty to murder me."

Standing proudly in the gallery of Belisle Castle—the only home he had ever known—Denis de Sancerre paused in his oft-told tale, enjoying the warmth of the flames from the hearty fire at his back. The heat chased away the early autumn chill creeping into his aching bones.

Eyeing the familiar banners wafting in the warmed air in the rafters, he adopted his usual story-telling stance—hands on hips, legs braced—and took a moment to relish the predictable open-mouthed stares. The faces of his listeners and almost imperceptible nods unwittingly betrayed their understanding of the midwife's intentions. He always wondered who among his rapt audiences would have led the mob gathered to dispatch him to Hell.

When he deemed enough time had passed, he continued. "Imagine. A babe not only dark and twisted, but a hated Angevin to boot. Only the strident entreaties of my mother's maid and the intervention of Antoine de Montbryce ensured I survived more than a sennight."

This was the cue for Denis to furrow his bushy black eyebrows and gesture towards his stepfather. All eyes predictably followed. Though Antoine had lived three score years, he never failed to pick up the story they had told visitors to Belisle Castle since Denis had reached an age where he took delight in mocking his own deformity.

Antoine cleared his throat. "They came armed with pitchforks and scythes—ignorant peasants."

The family made light of that terrifying time a score and five years before, but Denis recognised Antoine's enormous courage in quelling the murderous mob. He smiled and continued the story. "Struck as you are by my mother's rare beauty, you understand why Antoine fell in love with such a stunning woman."

Sybilla de Montbryce blushed to the roots of her hair, still fiery red despite her age. "You embarrass me, my son."

"Nonsense," he teased, knowing she loved his flattery. "Your marriage blessed me with membership in one of the most powerful families in Normandie."

Antoine coughed. "I might add it also protected Sybilla from execution as the widow of an enemy of William the Conqueror."

Denis took a deep breath. Next came the most difficult part of the tale to tell without his voice betraying his emotion. "Antoine raised me as his own son. Growing up in the bosom of a loving family formed me into the good-natured fellow you see before you today."

His half-brother snorted. "Not to mention the life and soul of any social gathering."

Antoine protested. "I disagree, Mathieu. It was God gave Denis his kindness and sense of humor, not I."

The guests from Caen chuckled. Some applauded politely, as he expected. Noblewomen especially enjoyed his ready wit and courtly manners. He was a curiosity, and thus no threat. They would recoil in horror if he were ever foolish enough to suggest a relationship. Women of consequence did not marry one such as he.

Truth be told, no female of his acquaintance had ever touched his heart, and no requirement existed for him to provide heirs. The risks of procreating another deformed creature were too great, and the Sancerre estate in Anjou had been confiscated by the Conqueror years ago. Antoine's eldest son, Adam, was the heir to Belisle.

Antoine puffed out his chest. "Denis is too modest. His courage and valor have only added to the military renown of this family. He's a respected warrior who has never flinched from combat alongside his brothers. His skill in a cavalry charge is well known."

Denis felt heat rise in his face. "Is there a woman here who would not wish for a husband like my stepfather?"

Antoine grinned. "And I'll wager I am the envy of every man present when they look at my beautiful wife."

Denis felt a familiar pang of loneliness and was relieved when Mathieu, seven years younger, took up the tale, recalling light-hearted stories from their youth.

Maidservants entered to offer more refreshments. Denis looked expectantly at Adam. The moment had come for him to make his usual contribution of *Indeed, we love our 'little' brother.*

The eldest of his half-brothers remained strangely silent, slumped in a chair.

A log shifted in the hearth, giving up its life to the flames with a reluctant hiss. The visitors glanced from Denis to Adam and back again.

Denis frowned. He loved all his siblings, but Adam was his best friend. A mere five years separated them. Adam the Giant and Denis the Dwarf were recognized and welcomed wherever they went.

Denis left his favorite story-telling spot before the massive stone hearth and walked to Adam's chair, reaching up to lay a hand on his shoulder. He immediately missed the warmth of the flames on his misshapen hips. "Are you ill, big brother?"

Adam raised his head slowly.

A chill of alarm surged through Denis. His brother's neck was grotesquely swollen, his eyes glazed. Drool trickled from one corner of his mouth.

Denis grasped Adam's arm and beckoned his stepfather. "Papa, *mon frère* is ill."

Antoine came to his feet with difficulty. "What ails you, my son?"

Their guests withdrew. Sudden illness tended to clear a room quickly. Sybilla de Montbryce made hasty apologies and summoned servants to light the visitors to their chambers. Then she knelt before her son, putting her hand over his. "He has a fever. Send for the physician, *vite*."

Adam pressed his fingers to his neck. "My throat," he rasped, swallowing with difficulty.

Mathieu's face showed his concern. "I recall this happening to me years ago, when Adam was away at Domfort, visiting *Oncle* Hugh."

Their mother remembered. "*Oui*, you are right, *les oreillons*. You had recovered by the time Adam returned."

Antoine took hold of his son's hand. "Let's get him to bed."

Denis chafed he did not have the stature to lift his brother and carry him to his chamber.

Mathieu cradled Adam and bore him away.

Adam could not swallow or speak. Fear gripped his innards. His neck and ears pained him greatly, but the agony between his legs was infinitely more worrisome. His throbbing *couilles* were painfully swollen. Thankfully, Mathieu had carried him, but his younger brother's voice seemed distant, muffled.

He must conceal his beleaguered male parts, keep secret that Adam de Montbryce, heir to Belisle Castle, had a problem with his testicles. "*Merci, mon frère*. I will tend to my own needs. I fear I must seek my bed. It's but a passing malady."

He thought he had spoken out loud, but the drumming in his aching ears drowned out the sound.

Mathieu placed him on the bed.

Their mother's face swam before his eyes. She was speaking, but he couldn't understand what she was saying. Oblivion released him only temporarily. Intensifying pain woke him some time later. The smell of burnt rosemary made him cough, adding to his agony. He must be in the infirmary—the only place in the castle with a fumitory. He threw the linens off his body and cupped his *couilles* to ease the discomfort. His clothes had been removed. He licked his lips. Someone gave him water that he guzzled like a man delivered from the desert. His father's face floated into his blurred vision. His hand was eased away from his groin. "*Non*, please, it helps."

His mother leaned over him, shaking her head. *Dieu*! He must cover his nakedness.

She spoke.

He squeezed his eyes shut. "What?"

Take away the pain.

His sister Bernadine should not be tending him either. She might be a married woman now, but still—

The swelling had worsened. He longed for sleep. "Where is Mathieu? Denis?" he rasped.

His father shook his head. Adam had never seen him so bereft. His brothers must have fallen ill too. He swallowed hard, pain shooting into his ears. "Am I dying?"

His mother's face reappeared, her red-rimmed eyes swollen, saying something.

His throat was a dried-up well. "*Je m'excuse, maman*—"

He reached for his groin again, groaning when a warm hand moved it away. "Leave me be," he shouted. The words echoed in his ears. "Let me die," he murmured.

Denis seethed for a sennight that he was not allowed to keep vigil over Adam. Mathieu was deemed safe from contagion because he had apparently had the same malady. Denis had suffered so many ailments as a child, no one recalled if he had been afflicted or not.

As Adam's illness worsened, Denis felt his own life slipping away. What was a Dwarf without his Giant?

Their mother was bereft, her puffy eyes red when she

returned from the infirmary. He noticed for the first time the streaks of grey at her temples. He marveled again that he was the child of such a woman, whose dignified beauty shone, despite her agony.

He hated to increase her burden but was desperate for news. He took her hand. "How does he fare?"

She inhaled deeply and sniffled. "The physician believes he will live. The swelling has improved."

Relief swept over Denis. "We must give thanks then."

His mother withdrew her hand and let out a long wail. "He is not whole."

Denis had often suffered the bitter humiliation of being looked upon as half a man. Dread coiled in his gut. His tall, handsome, well-muscled brother not whole? "What do you mean?"

Sybilla slumped into a chair, her hands clasped in her lap. "He cannot hear."

Denis was dumbfounded. "You are telling me he will not listen."

His mother shook her head. "*Non, mon fils*, he is deaf."

Denis pressed his fingertips to his forehead. His heart broke for Adam and for his parents. A castle such as Belisle demanded much of a *Seigneur* who was in possession of all his faculties.

He resolved to help Adam with this burden. "I will be his ears until he recovers his hearing."

Mathieu entered the room. His pallor and grim expression alarmed Denis.

Their mother whimpered.

Mathieu put his arm around her shoulders. "There is more, but *Maman* cannot speak of it."

Denis ground his teeth, glaring at them. "Tell me!"

Mathieu averted his eyes. "Our brother's illness has wrought havoc on other parts of his body."

Denis frowned in confusion. Was Adam blind, lame, what? "I do not understand."

Mathieu paced.

Dreadful anticipation welled up in Denis' heart. "By all the saints, tell me."

Mathieu braced his legs and folded his arms. "Adam's male parts—"

Denis lacked stature, but his shaft performed admirably whenever he romped in the hay with a willing village wench. However, Adam was not the philanderer his father had been before marrying. He had taken his role as the heir to Belisle seriously, insisting on saving himself for his bride.

If Adam had been robbed of his ability to sire children, Denis feared for his brother's sanity and worried about the implications for the succession of Belisle Castle.

IMPEDIMENTS

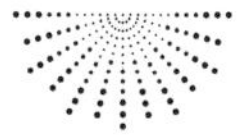

KINGSTON GORSE, SUSSEX, ENGLAND

Rosamunda Lallement had spent all of her seventeen years in captivity, hidden away as soon as her impediment became apparent.

Her imprisonment was not harsh. She enjoyed many comforts in the suite of rooms atop the manor house at Kingston Gorse. She was not alone in her captivity. Her older sister, Paulina, shared her confinement.

The doors were not barred, but leaving their chambers was forbidden. Servants made certain they did not wander into the main part of the house. Thomas and Agnès took care of their needs, and were always close at hand in their own chamber in the attic. But they were of peasant stock and never showed warmth or tenderness for their charges. Rosamunda suspected they too were not free to do as they pleased.

The only other people aware of their existence were their brothers. Lucien and Vincent visited often. Their father came infrequently. Rosamunda and Paulina had not set eyes on their mother since they were infants.

Maudine Lallement still grieved that she had birthed two deformed children, refusing to acknowledge their existence. Rosamunda suspected her mother wished her daughters had never been born.

She asked her brothers if their mother still lived.

Lucien understood and responded with sarcasm. "*Oui*, despite assuring us daily she longs for death, *Maman* yet lives."

Vincent was more forgiving of his mother. "*Maman* is unwell. We must be patient."

Rosamunda fisted her hands and scowled. The longing to leave their prison and wander to the edge of the cliff she espied from the tiny window had stolen her patience. The salty tang of the sea filled her nostrils, but she could not see it. Vincent had told them that sometimes the land of their forefathers was visible across the Narrow Sea. Their maternal grandfather, and their father, had both been born in Normandie.

Paulina, on the other hand, preferred to live away from gawking eyes. Rosamunda's affliction was invisible; her sister's was not. Even on tiptoe, the top of Paulina's head came only to the level of Rosamunda's breasts.

Paulina was a lovely doll, her skin flawless, complexion rosy. Dark, silky hair fell like an elegant drape, accentuating her high cheekbones. Her lips were pouty and full. When she was troubled, her almond eyes wide, she looked like a pensive angel. Her rare smile turned her into a madonna.

Rosamunda envied her sister's full breasts and well-proportioned figure. Despite her lack of height, Paulina was stunningly beautiful. Yet, she considered herself ugly and believed in the rightness of her imprisonment simply because she was half as tall as most people. Rosamunda raged at the injustice of it.

On the rare occasions their father visited, she dragged him by the arm to the window, pointing to the outside world. She pressed his hand to her face, tears welling in her eyes as she turned to him in supplication.

Marc Lallement always shook his head sadly. “Your *maman* will not hear of it. You must remain hidden. At least you are comfortable here at home. Many families shut their malformed daughters away in convents.”

Lucien had hinted his mother blamed her husband’s ancestry for their impediments. Perhaps, he blamed himself.

Rosamunda pondered these thoughts as restlessness gripped her this day—their brothers had failed to appear as promised. She threw her mending to the floor and stormed to the window. Trees were turning color, leaves swirled on gusty winds. Autumn was in the air. She pulled her hair out of the braids she hated, ruffling the thick blonde locks into a tangled nest.

Paulina continued to ply her needle. “I know you are bored, but there isn’t much else to do.”

Rosamunda went to sit at her sister’s feet, grabbing the half-finished embroidery sampler from her hands and flinging it to a nearby chest. She grunted impatiently. “Tell.”

Paulina sighed. “Will you never tire of hearing the stories?”

Rosamunda shook her head, smiling broadly.

“Very well. I’ll tell the story of our maternal grandfather.”

Rosamunda rubbed her hands together gleefully.

Paulina began the familiar tale. “Sir Stephen Marquand came to England and settled at Kingston Gorse before the invasion, under the protection of the Saxon king, Edward the Confessor. He passed on to his children the tales of the Conqueror’s feats. Our mother continued the tradition with Lucien and Vincent, who in turn told us the stories.”

Paulina told of battles, of heroic victories, of Saxon revolts, of the great advances in architecture the Normans brought with them. Part of Sir Stephen’s story touched on another tale, Rosamunda’s favorite. She urged Paulina to recount it next.

Her sister pouted, eying her sampler, though Rosamunda knew she loved the tale too. She assumed a pleading expression, confident it would not take much to convince Paulina.

“Oh, very well.”

Paulina shifted her weight in the chair. Entwining her fingers in the tangled strands of Rosamunda’s hair, she embarked on the story of two brothers of a noble Norman family. Antoine and Hugh de Montbryce were heroes of the Battle of Hastings. “The Conqueror granted Hugh oversight of neighboring Melton Manor, where he discovered his true love, Devona Melton.”

Rosamunda sighed and laid her head in her sister’s lap.

Paulina huffed. “You must do something with your hair. It looks like windblown straw.”

Rosamunda blew out exasperated air from between her lips. It was a familiar scolding. She sat up, swatting away her sister’s fingers. There was no-one to see her hair.

Paulina continued, a patient smirk on her face. “Antoine helped Hugh rescue Devona from an abusive

Norman who had usurped their estate. Grandfather assisted them with the loan of a rowboat."

Rosamunda had never known Sir Stephen, but it pleased her he had been willing to aid in the rescue of a damsel in distress. He would not have locked away his granddaughters. She loved the story of the intrepid Montbryces navigating caves and secret passages. She imagined herself in the stead of Devona Melton. But who would be her hero, her champion? No man wanted to marry a woman with her impediment. Vincent sang *chansons courtoises*, songs of courtly love, but it was unlikely a tall, dark knight would ride to their rescue.

She grunted the question. "Melton?"

Paulina reached to retrieve her embroidery.

Rosamunda tore it once more from her grasp. Now it was Paulina's turn to snort, but she carried on the tale, only too aware of Rosamunda's stubborn nature. "Lucien says the Montbryces still come from time to time from their castle in Normandie to visit Devona's childhood home. He and Vincent have befriended Hugh's two sons, Melton and Izzy de Montbryce, but they speak only in passing of their sister, Antoinette."

Rosamunda and Paulina had both laughed upon first hearing the name Izzy, even after Lucien explained it was a nickname for Isembart.

"Our brothers are also acquainted with Adam and Mathieu de Montbryce. They come frequently from Normandie to East Preston, an estate granted to their father, one of your heroes, Antoine. Adam and Mathieu have a half-brother, who has never accompanied them to England, and two sisters. Lucien and Vincent hardly mention them."

Rosamunda understood why their brothers perhaps had difficulty socializing with their friends' sisters. She often daydreamed about these friends her brothers boasted of, and wondered if any of them ever visited Kingston Gorse.

Paulina had long ago become resigned to a life cloistered in the upstairs chambers of her parents' home, but shuddered at the lonely existence it might have been if her sister had not been incarcerated with her. She thanked God daily for denying Rosamunda the gift of speech.

It riddled her with guilt. Her beautiful sister suffered confinement because she was mute. Their parents had failed to recognise her many talents. Rosamunda had a keen, inquiring mind. Her green eyes sparkled with laughter and her elfin smile lit up a room. Despite their situation, Rosamunda loved to laugh. She had no voice, yet Paulina understood everything she *said*, or did not say.

BIRTHRIGHT RENOUNCED

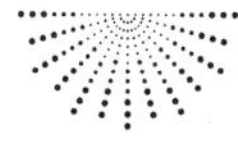

"He will never sire children."

Denis recognised Mathieu might be right, but it angered him that their younger brother was adamant in his insistence Adam could no longer be the heir to Belisle.

They had argued back and forth for a sennight while Adam convalesced. Denis fisted his hands at his side. "You cannot be sure of that. His hearing has improved a little. The physicians agree the disease has apparently changed the size and appearance of his—"

He glanced at his mother, not sure if this was appropriate conversation for a woman. He soldiered on. "But they also see no reason for his present inability to—"

He had never felt so uncomfortable. His mother's tear-filled eyes told him she understood his torment. He searched for alternative words to *shaft*, *erection*, *arousal*, but his mind went blank.

Damned if he could recall the Latin words he and his

brothers had bandied about with great hilarity in their youth. Latin would have sounded more dignified somehow.

"Let's not mince words here," Mathieu interjected. "I am as distraught as anyone at my brother's distress, but if it is permanent, Belisle will fall to me or my children anyway."

Denis strode to stand nose to hip with the brother he had never felt close to. "Unless you die first."

Mathieu braced his legs and looked down his nose scornfully. "You think Papa will give Belisle to you?"

Denis shook with rage, but he regretted threatening Mathieu. He had been driven by an instinctive need to defend Adam, not a desire for control of Belisle. How had their amiable relationship come to this?

Antoine came between them, his voice tired. "We cannot allow this curse to tear us apart as a family. Mathieu, you know Denis has no designs on Belisle, as Denis knows you want only to secure the succession. What has happened is God's will. We must all bend to it, including Adam."

The next day, Antoine de Montbryce blinked away tears, praying that when he opened his mouth to speak, sorrow would not choke off his words. He had never imagined he would be forced to ask his eldest son to renounce his birthright.

He gripped his wife's trembling hand.

Bernardine and Florymonde clung to each other,

sobbing quietly. Mathieu and Denis flanked their sisters, one holding his head high, jaw clenched, the other with stunned disbelief evident on his swarthy face.

Adam stood by the hearth in the gallery where they had shared many happy family gatherings. He shifted his weight nervously, mayhap suspecting what was about to befall him. As if his torment not great enough. He turned to the fire as his father approached.

Antoine swallowed the lump in his throat and put a hand on his son's shoulder, turning him so they were face to face. "Look at me, *mon fils*."

Antoine saw despair in the beloved blue eyes. He prayed for strength and hoped his words would penetrate the deafness.

Adam stared at Mathieu, then at Denis. He held up his hand. "I know what you intend to say, Papa, and I agree I am no longer suited to the role of heir."

Mathieu took a step forward, but Antoine waved him off. This had to be done, but he would do it. Adam's gaze seemed fixed on his father's mouth. Was he hoping to read there words of reassurance that Belisle had not been taken from him? It broke Antoine's heart he could utter no such denial. He resisted the temptation to raise his voice. "You are a courageous man, Adam. You must trust that what has happened to you will not be forever. You may recover your hearing, and your—"

He kept his gaze fixed on Adam's face. "Perhaps both maladies are temporary. But the succession must be secured."

Adam squared his shoulders, clenched his jaw, and fisted his hands at his side. "*Mon père*, I accede to your wishes. It is evident I will never sire children. Belisle needs heirs, and I am now only half a man."

Denis flinched, his brow furrowed.

Adam strode over to Mathieu and offered his hand. "You will make a fine *Seigneur* for Belisle, brother. In these troubled times a warrior needs all his abilities. Belisle deserves better. It deserves you."

Mathieu accepted the handclasp, but seemed at a loss for words. Bernadine and Florymonde sobbed louder as Adam hugged each of them in turn before returning to his father. Raking his hands through his hair, he rasped, "I have decided to leave Belisle, make a new life, and learn to live with my deafness."

Sybilla came to him and cradled her son's face in her hands. "But why must you leave us? Why not stay here, regain your health with the help of those who love you?"

Adam's eyes filled with tears. "I am aware you love me, but your faces are full of pity. I must go."

Antoine recognized his son's determination. He gritted his teeth and clasped Adam's hand, speaking slowly. "Where will you go?"

"To inspect your estates in England, with your permission. I thought to use East Preston as a base."

Denis stepped forward. "I will come with you and be your ears until you heal." He chuckled, hoping to lighten the mood with a jest. "Perhaps two half men will make a whole."

Sybilla de Montbryce's throat tightened. Long ago, after Denis' birth, despair for his future had threatened to destroy her. As she lay on the floor in a stupor after unsuccessfully trying to prevent the midwives from racing off with him, a part of her had perhaps hoped their murderous intent might come to fruition. The despicable old man her father had sold her to was dead. She was a prisoner of the hated Normans and didn't have the wherewithal to care for a deformed child.

But the intervention of her maidservant, aided by Antoine, had given Denis a chance at life. Antoine's love had saved her from madness and her son from a lifetime of rejection and degradation. Her firstborn's life had not been easy, but he had become a source of pride.

She hugged that truth to her heart now as he insisted on accompanying his brother. Adam had lost much. With Denis' help, he might survive the catastrophe that had befallen him. A spark of hope flickered in her breast.

A maelstrom of emotions swirled in Adam's heart. He and Denis had long been friends, the Giant and the Dwarf. But the giant had been brought low, and no longer cared about the future.

Denis' devastation at his half-brother's illness was obvious, but his eyes had never held pity, rather compassion. Denis despised those who pitied him.

"I will not be a good traveling companion," Adam rasped.

Denis put his fingers at the corners of his mouth and forced a wide grin, wagging his head from side to side. "Whereas I am well-regarded as a jocular fellow with whom people love to travel." He linked his arm with

Adam's. "We will make a perfect pair, as we always have, *mon frère*."

Adam clenched his jaw, trying to break the link. "I am not the same. Things are different now."

Denis braced his legs, poking Adam in the belly. "You are still my brother. With or without your agreement, I will follow you to East Preston."

The determined jut of Denis' chin convinced Adam there was no point arguing further. "Very well. We depart on the morrow."

The next day, Denis breathed a sigh of relief as Adam took his leave of their grieving parents and sisters in the windswept bailey of the castle. Mathieu had rasped his *adieu* in the Great Hall after the family had broken its fast in uncomfortable silence.

The autumn wind carried a hint of the coming winter. Denis hoped for better weather for their crossing of the Narrow Sea.

He had expected his half-brother to fight harder. Denis had tasted the bitterness of despair and rejection. He had learned to rise above it, to be the best man he could be, despite his stunted stature. He'd been born a dwarf, whereas Adam was a strapping warrior ladies swooned over. His illness had seemingly robbed him of his potency as a male and his hearing. He looked pale and dispirited.

The physician remained puzzled by Adam's impotency, and his brother refused to discuss it further. Denis prayed it was a temporary malady. Whenever he felt low, he usually found a good romp in the hay with a willing wench the perfect cure. Obviously, that was not a solution for Adam in the present circumstances.

His brother had never treated him as half a man. Denis resolved not to allow self pity to destroy his beleaguered giant.

A TROUBLED HOUSEHOLD

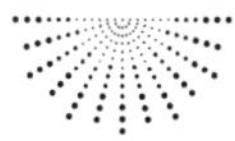

Agnès tapped at the door of her mistress's chamber, expecting no reply from the lady of Kingston Gorse. Clenching her jaw, she entered.

As usual, Maudine Lallement lay curled with her knees to her chest in the small bed, bemoaning that she had awakened at all.

"Another day of grinding misery, Agnès. Death would be preferable to the burdensome guilt I carry daily."

Agnès knew all about guilt. She muttered gentle admonitions to the woman she had served, but never liked, for more than twenty years. "Come along, milady. I'll brush your hair. It always makes you feel better."

With a deep sigh, her mistress stirred to perch on the side of the bed. Agnès took up the brush and waited for the litany to begin.

"After two boys, the birth of a daughter was a source of great joy. I had more than satisfied the need to provide an heir."

Agnès knew the girl in question only too well, having

been her reluctant guardian for many a year. She put her hand on top of her mistress's head and stroked the brush through the lank strands of dull grey hair.

Maudine shivered. "You're the only one I can confide in now. My husband turned away from me long ago. Agnès, you are my witness. For a year, I doted on my daughter, often to the detriment of my sons. If Paulina seemed not to be growing as fast as my boys had, I did not remark on it. Boys were boys. Girls grew more slowly."

Agnès nodded as she brushed. She knew her part well. "I remember that time. 'Twas as you say."

"By the time Paulina was two, my heart told me something was amiss. I saw it in my husband's eyes."

Agnès held her tongue. If she showed her true feelings, her horror at what was to come next, her mistress would cast her out. Maudine Lallement had never been an understanding or patient woman.

A tear trickled down the wrinkled cheek. "I prayed daily. I fasted for long periods of time, hoping my penance would bring God's mercy. I fashioned a knotted belt which I wore around my waist, pulling it tighter each day."

Agnès sniffled appropriately. "We feared for you then, milady. 'Twas a bad time."

Maudine nodded furiously. "I was afraid of birthing another cursed child, and refused to lie with my husband, until the fateful day he tore the clothes from my body and discovered the knots had eaten into my flesh." She shuddered. "I will long recall the agony as he carefully peeled the cord from my body, tears streaming down his face."

Agnès took a deep breath. She had tried to no avail to forget the sound of those screams. "We heard you in the servants' quarters. Sir Marc fled to the garden after, and retched till we thought he might choke. But he never said a word of what had caused your pain."

True enough, though Agnès had been summoned to tend her mistress's ghastly wounds. Bile rose in her throat even now at the memory.

Maudine fidgeted nervously as Agnès put down the brush and fingered the hair into three parts for braiding.

"We discussed our daughter's slow growth. I had to atone in order to lift the curse on her."

Agnès recognised her cue and paused in her plaiting. "What did he say?"

Maudine shrugged. "He shook his head. Paulina was small, but he insisted she would grow. She needed love, as did our sons." Anger twisted her thin face. "I snarled at him and told him I could not love a creation of the devil. His sons would be shunned when people learned they had a deformed sister.

"He lost his temper, and forbade me to carry on with my penance. I told him I would not lie with him again until our daughter was shut away.

"He argued and cajoled, but from that day forth I have shunned my daughter. He installed her in the suite in the attic. You and her nursemaid went with her. I capitulated and allowed him into my bed. Nine months later, Rosamunda was born."

Agnès doubted Maudine Lallement realized she told this tale every day, so she bore it. She and Thomas had lived for years with the shame and regret of not having fled the cursed house then. She supposed her mistress needed someone to confirm the righteousness of what she had done, even if it was a lowly servant who had witnessed the long ago events.

For Agnès, the daily diatribe was a penance she deserved for the part she had played in the unjust imprisonment of two young women. She prayed for God's mercy on her soul as she coaxed her mistress to dress.

Rosamunda threw her arms around her brother's neck, then pummeled his chest with her fists.

"She's annoyed because you promised to come two days ago," Paulina explained.

Lucien suffered the blows with good humor. He shielded his chest, laughing. "Ouch! What a warrior my sister is."

Rosamunda pushed him away, aware her face had flushed to the roots of her tangled hair. "Why did you not come?" she mouthed, trying to see what he had behind his back. "Rosemary?"

Lucien produced the sprigs, waving them under her nose. "You and your rosemary baths. Little did I know the first time I brought it, you would insist on a regular supply."

Rosamunda grabbed the herb, rubbing a sprig or two between her thumb and forefinger. She rolled her eyes as she inhaled the aroma.

Paulina explained. "She likes the way it perfumes the bath water and the scent it leaves in her hair. Thomas will only haul hot water up here once a sennight."

Lucien picked up Rosamunda, tickling her ribs as he twirled. She giggled breathlessly, then insisted he put her down and tickle her sister. Paulina would never ask, but

Rosamunda knew she loved her brothers' good-natured teasing.

It rankled that Paulina believed she had no place in the world, no right to a voice because she was tiny. Her sister squirmed in Lucien's arms, pretending not to be enjoying the fun.

Lucien bent to plant a kiss atop Paulina's head. "Vincent and I have been away, renewing our acquaintance with Melton de Montbryce."

"What of his brother, Izzy?" Paulina asked.

Rosamunda bit into her knuckles. The mention of the name brought on the urge to laugh.

Lucien shrugged as Vincent entered the chamber with a fistful of roses. "Izzy stayed home in Normandie. He still suffers greatly from *l'arthrite* in his hands."

Vincent twisted one hand grotesquely, sticking out his tongue as he presented his bouquet of roses to Paulina. "I managed to filch these from the garden without *Maman* knowing of it. She'd have my head."

Paulina beamed. Roses were guaranteed to draw out her beautiful smile. Ironically, it was Rosamunda who had been named for the prickly shrub.

She clasped her hands together, the edges of her mouth turned down in a gesture of sympathy for this unknown warrior with the painful affliction.

Paulina savored the roses' perfume and voiced her sister's thoughts, as often happened between them. "How does he hold a sword?"

Lucien frowned. "With great difficulty, I think. His hands were gnarled the last I saw him and Melton says it is getting worse."

Rosamunda took each brother by the hand and drew them to the comfortable upholstered chairs by the hearth. It was a ritual they understood. She wanted to hear about their travels.

"Melton is well," Vincent began.

Rosamunda put a hand on his arm and touched her face and hair, arching her brows.

Lucien chuckled. "Melton? He's a handsome fellow. All the Montbryces are. He's tall, strong looking, and has long dark hair."

Rosamunda pointed to her eyes.

Vincent shrugged. "Not sure. Blue, perhaps. What say you, brother?"

"No idea," Lucien replied. "I don't pay attention to such things."

Rosamunda sighed with exasperation. Eye color revealed a lot. Resignation darkened her sister's warm, brown eyes. When her brothers told of their adventures, their blue eyes lit up a room like the summer sky.

The green of her own eyes deepened when she peered into the looking glass and ran her hands over her breasts.

Lately, she had been troubled with wanton urges to touch intimate places on her body. Her thoughts and dreams wandered to images of handsome young knights, all bearing the face she had conjured many years ago from what she'd been told of the heroic Montbryce brothers.

She averted her gaze to hide the tears welling in her eyes. She desperately wanted to escape, but was certain few noblemen wanted a wife who was mute.

Lucien crooked his finger under her chin. "Don't cry, *ma soeur*. Your imprisonment is cruel and unjust. As soon as we are able, Vincent and I will free you both. But for the moment, it is *Maman* who rules the house."

Paulina backed away from the hearth, clutching the roses. "*Non*," she shouted. "I am content to remain here."

Rosamunda grasped her sister's arm, thumping her own chest, shaking her head vehemently.

Paulina broke free. "I am a freak. Do you think I want to be gawked at and ridiculed?"

Vincent came to his feet. "You are not a freak. Neither of you are. You must not allow *Maman's* despair to destroy you."

Paulina choked back a sob. "If a mother cannot love a child—"

Rosamunda touched her heart, gripping her sister's hand. "I love you," she mouthed.

"So do we," both men echoed.

The four children of Marc and Maudine Lallement clung to each other in silent sorrow for long moments.

It was Lucien who finally cleared his throat and sniffed loudly. "Anyway, there is other news from Melton. His cousin, Adam, is en route to East Preston, with his half-brother, Denis de Sancerre."

Rosamunda opened her mouth but Vincent held up his hand. "Before you ask, Adam looks exactly like Melton. But I've never met Denis, therefore I cannot describe him to you."

Paulina pouted. "What does it matter, Rosamunda? Why do you care about these men? You and I will never meet them. If we did, they would turn away in horror when they discovered our impediments."

Lucien shook his head. "The Montbryces are chivalrous noblemen. They would never slight a woman."

Paulina scowled.

Lucien hesitated, casting a glance at his brother.

Rosamunda sensed there was more. Frowning, she punched Lucien's shoulder.

"I'm not sure," he replied hesitantly. "There is something wrong, but Melton did not divulge what it is."

"Wrong?" Paulina asked.

Vincent grimaced. "*Oui,* with Adam de Montbryce. I sensed it too. They will be at East Preston after the morrow. We'll ride over in a few days to bid them welcome."

Lucien and Vincent took their leave when Agnès arrived with the midday meal. Rosamunda bade her brothers farewell, letting them know she eagerly awaited news as soon as they returned.

Lucien and Vincent Lallement did not exchange a word until they reached Vincent's chamber. It was the pattern they followed whenever they left their incarcerated sisters. The injustice of the imprisonment had grated on them more and more as they had grown to manhood.

Lucien slammed the door and leaned back against it. "It's intolerable, brother."

Vincent sat on the edge of his bed and slumped forward, his head in his hands. "I agree, but what can we do? If we expose the truth now, *Maman* will never forgive us. She will cast the girls out, maybe us too. The Lallement family will be shunned. Papa would never be invited to attend court functions again."

Lucien paced. "Not to mention people might wonder why we had done nothing before. We might be judged complicit in the crime."

Vincent looked up. "We could spirit them away to a convent."

Lucien snorted. "We may as well condemn Rosamunda to death, and Paulina would become more convinced she should remain hidden."

Vincent came slowly to his feet. "You're right. We'd better hasten to the dining hall. *Maman* will nag if we are late."

Lucien stopped pacing. "In some ways, our parents are the true prisoners."

Vincent put a hand on his brother's shoulder. "You and I are thoroughly caught in their web of lies. It becomes increasingly difficult not to blurt out something Paulina or Rosamunda has said or done. They are beautiful young women any man would be proud to have as sisters, yet we cannot acknowledge their existence."

Lucien clenched his jaw. "For now we must remain silent."

Marc Lallement sat next to his wife in the dining hall and watched her distress grow. The midday meal was ready, but Lucien and Vincent were not yet seated in their places. Maudine would not give the signal to the servants waiting to serve the food. They coughed nervously, shifting their feet, which he knew only intensified her rage. He was surprised she had not already dispatched one of them in search of her sons. They had passed the five-minute mark.

He raised his goblet to his lips, but hastily put it down when his wife glared at him.

He was bone weary of the conflict. Guilt tore at his

heart. His sweet Maudine had become a shrew, and he worried about her sanity, especially after the episode with the knotted belt. The birth of a second daughter who was mute had overwhelmed her wits. He had racked his brain for ways to rid her of her torment. The terrifying possibility that ending her life was one of them plagued him more and more frequently.

It had been madness to agree to their incarceration in the first place. He had been so besotted he had allowed not one, but two of his children to be imprisoned in their own home. Coward that he was, he had feared losing the dowry estate of Kingston Gorse if his wife repudiated him.

Rosamunda and Paulina were beautiful young women. If Maudine visited them, she would see, but she refused to discuss it. As far as she was concerned, her daughters were dead.

He worried for his sons, increasingly aware of their censure and discomfort. He thanked God at least two of his children had been born whole. When the boys were infants, it was less likely they might accidentally reveal the truth. Now they were young knights who travelled throughout Sussex. They visited sons of neighboring Norman families, often practicing swordplay and other tactics. Many of their friends had sisters.

Maudine thrust out her chin when their sons arrived.

Lucien bowed to his mother. "*Maman*, I'm sorry—"

Maudine held up her hand, her mouth puckered into a tight line. "Sorry is not good enough. You are both aware of my expectations. What are we supposed to do, sit here and wait, not knowing when you plan to arrive?"

The servants examined the oaken beams, or the

planked floor, or their feet as their mistress's voice became more and more shrill.

Vincent and Lucien stood with heads bowed. Marc's heart broke for them.

Finally, she ceased her tirade and beckoned to the cook.

Their sons took their places in silence.

Rabbit stew was hastily heaped onto the trenchers.

The servants stepped back.

Maudine glared at them, inhaled the aroma of the dish before her, then nodded.

They retreated.

She turned to look at the men of her family. "You may start now."

Marc's gut was in knots. His appetite fled as he watched the juices of the stew trickle into the stale bread of his trencher, but if he did not eat he would never hear the end of it. He tore off the edge of the trencher and bit into it, tasting the bitter gall of his own cowardice.

EAST PRESTON

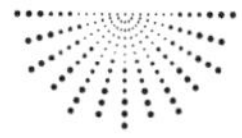

EAST PRESTON, SUSSEX, ENGLAND

After the journey from Normandie, Adam hoped to ease his weariness with a long soak in the big wooden tub. Denis had tried hard to keep up his spirits on the way, but it had been an effort to concentrate on what he was saying.

Adam had dreaded the reaction of the servants at East Preston when they became aware of his deafness. They meant well and were devastated at his affliction, but he hastily took his leave of them after ordering the tub.

If they followed the example of the servants at Belisle, they would now walk round on tiptoe, averting their eyes whenever they came into his presence. Or they would bellow at him in the belief it made a difference.

Thank God his other physical torment was not visible. His previous determination to remain chaste until his marriage did not mean he had lacked male urges. Far from it. As a youth he'd been in a seemingly permanent state of arousal. His cock had always stood ready to demonstrate its interest in an attractive female. He had never plunged his manhood into a woman's sheath, but had enjoyed the ministrations of many eager to use their mouths on him. They had taught him how to please them without penetration.

His shaft failed to stir at the memory.

As he hauled his body out of the tub he looked down at the water running off the flesh between his legs. Everything looked normal, but his shaft seemed incapable of rousing itself.

Hopelessness washed over him. Denis had assured him constantly it was likely a temporary problem, but he might as well be a monk for the interest his manhood had shown in any female he had encountered.

Perhaps encouragement might help matters. He cringed as he cupped his *couilles* with one hand and grasped his flaccid member with the other. That had usually caused things to stir, but now—nothing.

Sweat broke out on his brow as he strained to pump life into his shaft. Bile rose in his throat. Despair gripped him. He thrust back his head, willing the familiar urges to surge into his body.

Without warning, the door creaked open.

A red-faced maidservant squealed her shock, eyes bulging, hands clamped over her mouth. A heap of drying linens lay at her feet. "I knocked, *milord*, but—"

The sweat on his body turned to ice as he splayed his hands over his groin. "Get out," he bellowed. "*Vite*! Stupid wench!"

The girl fled, bumping into Denis who stooped quickly to pick up a drying cloth and thrust it at Adam. "Cover yourself."

Adam threw the linen back at him, his heart thudding

in his ears. He stretched his arms wide. "Take a good look. It will be on everyone's lips that *milord's* testicles aren't what they should be."

Denis handed the linen back and pointed to his own eyes, shaking his head. "She barely had time to see anything. And she spoke the truth when she told you she knocked." He pointed to the door. "I was down the hall."

Adam cinched the linen at his waist and slumped onto the bed. "I am a useless eunuch, a shadow of a man."

Denis stood, hands on his hips. "I am not the person to whine to. I will aid you in any way I can." He wagged a finger. "But I will not listen to your self-pity."

Adam slouched on the bed, yet Denis had to reach up to put his hands over his brother's ears. "Life has dealt you a double blow, brother." He struck his chest with a fisted hand. "But you are a warrior."

Adam hung his head. "I no longer have a warrior's heart." His words were a distant echo in his ears, but he heard the self-pity and hated himself for it.

Denis retrieved more linens. "Now, dry yourself." He lifted his hand to his mouth. "Get ready to dine in the hall."

Fatigue swept over Adam. "I cannot. I will eat in my chamber."

Denis went to the armoire where servants had stored Adam's clothing. He brought out a shirt, doublet and leggings, which he threw on the bed. He poked his brother in the ribs. "You are our father's representative in this manor. You will eat with the rest of the household. I will send a servant to help you dress."

Adam leapt to his feet. "*Non*! I will dress myself."

Denis smiled. "As you wish." He pressed his palm to

his chest and made a mock bow. "Or, as we have done for each other innumerable times before, I can be your valet."

It was true. He and Denis had often acted as each other's valet when away from home. His brother's lack of stature had not been an issue. It seemed unreasonable now to be bothered by the notion.

Denis had made it clear Adam's deafness and impotency had no bearing on his feelings of brotherly love. If it were Denis who had been stricken, Adam wouldn't love him any less.

He raked his fingers through wet hair. "I am a coward."

Fearing he might lose heart at the sight of his brother's dejection, Denis grabbed a drying cloth and vigorously rubbed Adam's thighs with it. "Listen." He chopped his hand across his arm. "When Isembart Jubert lost his arm to an enemy sword, did he immediately get to his feet and carry on his life as it was before?"

Adam inhaled deeply.

Denis hoped mention of Izzy's namesake would stir him. He rushed on. "*Non*, of course not." He touched his arm, then his heart. "The body and the soul need time to heal. He was no longer capable of being a warrior, but Isembart became the only one-armed rat-catcher I have ever heard of, acknowledged as the best in all of Normandie. It was his courage and tenacity that saved *oncle* Hugh's life."

Adam seemed to understand the gist of what he was saying. "And *tante* Devona's."

He shrugged into the doublet Denis handed to him, and

went down on one knee. Denis did up the fastenings. How often he had wished for his brother's height, though he did not envy him his present predicament.

Their eyes met. Denis determined to ignore the desolation that darkened Adam's gaze. "Not that I seek pity for myself, but life has not been easy for me. There have been times when despair has threatened to overwhelm me, but I resolved long ago to be the best man I could be. Stature has nothing to do with courage, or honesty or valor."

Adam came to his feet, resting a hand on Denis' shoulder as he stepped into his braies and then his leggings. Denis reached to fasten the points.

"*Merci*, Denis," Adam rasped. "Not only for helping me dress."

Denis slapped him on the thigh. "You're welcome. Let's go."

To his surprise, the maidservant who had seen him with his hands on his shaft winked at Adam as she served his food.

Denis leaned over. "She probably thinks you were doing what many men do to ease their needs."

Adam felt relieved, though he had not grasped everything Denis had said. His deafness was readily apparent, but the fewer who knew of his other problem, the better.

The food in England was never as good as in Normandie, but tonight's venison was excellent. It was on the tip of his tongue to ask his steward if he had employed a new cook, but he hesitated, aware he would be unable to hear Alain Cormant's reply.

He had always enjoyed a good conversation, but now—

Perhaps if he watched Cormant's mouth, he might discern what the man was saying. It was beginning to be thus with Denis, but he had known his brother all his life, recognized his mannerisms and mode of speech. Strangers would be more difficult.

However, he had to try. He did not want to be alone in his silent world. Marriage was out of the question, but his impairment did not mean he could not enjoy friends, family. Homesickness washed over him.

His departure had made things more difficult for his father and mother, but he feared his resentment at Mathieu's actions might erupt and cause irreparable damage. Thank God Denis had insisted on sticking with him. He might have gone mad otherwise.

Taking a deep breath, he turned to his left to look Cormant in the face. "The meat is tasty, Alain. Do we have a new cook?"

His steward was the son of Barat who had come from Normandie long ago to assist in the oversight of the Sussex manors the Montbryce brothers had been granted by William the Conqueror.

Barat, and his brother Théobald, had played an important role in the rescue of Adam's *tante* Devona. They had also helped in the rebuilding of East Preston, left derelict for many years after the Conquest.

Alain had been born there and taken over as steward of all the Sussex properties when his father and uncle retired to Normandie. He was a trusted servant.

Alain smiled, licking his lips. He did not raise his voice

in reply, but spoke slowly and clearly. "Indeed. Friselle came to us on the recommendation of the Lallements."

Adam frowned. "From Kingston Gorse?"

"*Oui.*"

By rights, *noblesse* obliged they ride to Kingston Gorse to thank their neighbors, but the prospect filled Adam with trepidation.

Denis tapped him on the shoulder.

Adam turned to his brother, suspecting what the persistent little devil would say.

"We should ride over there tomorrow to thank them. I have never met the Lallements." He winked. "Do they have daughters?"

Adam cringed, thankful to reply in the negative. "*Non.* Two sons. Lucien and Vincent. Good men."

Denis shrugged. "Too bad. From the stories, I thought the family at Kingston Gorse were Marquands."

Cormant nodded. "Originally they were. Sir Stephen Marquand gave the estate to his daughter as her dowry when she married Marc Lallement."

Denis came to his feet. "Then we should ride there on the morrow to thank Sir Marc and his good lady."

Adam wrinkled his nose. "I doubt if either Sir Marc or Lady Maudine were responsible for the new cook."

Denis regained his seat, his brow furrowed.

Alain Cormant interrupted. "*Milord* Adam is correct. Lucien Lallement directed Friselle to us."

The corners of Denis' mouth turned down. "The Lallement parents are not sociable?"

Adam laughed out loud, suddenly aware it was the first time since his illness. "That's putting it mildly. Lady

Maudine Lallement is downright unfriendly, and Sir Marc behaves as if he is shielding some deep, dark secret."

Denis laughed too. "We won't concern ourselves with the parents, if the sons are good company. I am anxious to become acquainted with people in these parts." He spread his arms wide and winked at Adam. "I wager they have never met anyone like me before."

Adam could not help but smile. "You are no doubt right on that score."

"We ride on the morrow then."

Adam met the challenge in his brother's eyes. "*Oui*, on the morrow."

Relief washed over Denis. Much depended on forcing Adam to face his impairment. It pained him to see his good natured, outgoing brother sink into despondent isolation. Heartened by Adam's willingness to engage Cormant in conversation, he had gambled that a gentle push would persuade him to travel to Kingston Gorse.

He worried about what he had learned of the lord and lady, but if the sons were gentlemen, there was no harm.

Denis enjoyed meeting new people, though invariably their first reaction upon seeing him was one of shock and embarrassment. They never knew where to look. He had learned to expect that. He relished their further surprise when it quickly became apparent he was not a mad freak, but an articulate and cultured man.

If only there existed a woman somewhere who might overlook his dwarfism and love him for the man he was. He had come across a few female dwarfs in his travels, mostly itinerant entertainers, part of a troupe. Their crude, bawdy humor amused him, but they did nothing to arouse his male interest.

He was destined to live a bachelor life. Now Adam had been condemned to the same fate. Was it God's will? The Giant and the Dwarf, boon companions to the end. A pang of guilt stabbed him—perhaps, deep within his heart, he was glad Adam had been rendered impotent.

One thing was for certain. He would never desert his troubled brother.

NEVER SEEN A DWARF BEFORE?

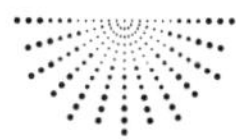

Lucien and Vincent Lallement rode out of the courtyard, bound for East Preston. At the outer gate, they reined their horses to a halt and looked back at the ivy-covered walls of their home. Their gaze inevitably travelled from the lower floor to the half-timbered sections of the second and attic stories. It had become a ritual whenever they left the house.

Lucien clenched his jaw. "She can't see this side of the house, but Rosamunda's face will be pressed against the glass of their window."

Vincent tightened his grip on the reins. "She longs to be free, to explore the outside world. She'll miss us."

They exchanged a glance, then quickly averted their eyes. Lucien's gut roiled. The injustice had become intolerable. He recognized the torment in his brother's eyes. "This situation must end," he exclaimed.

Vincent pressed his fingertips to his forehead. "You are right, brother, but I have no solution to offer."

Exasperated, Lucien urged his horse to a gallop. Vincent followed. They rode hard for half a mile along the southern coast of England. The brisk breeze and the smell of the sea filled Lucien's nostrils. He loved the white cliffs, the endless beaches and inspiring coastal vistas of his native Sussex. He half-closed his eyes, wishing he might somehow stumble on a way to free his sisters without disobeying and disgracing his parents.

Turning inland to East Preston, he crested a rise, wondering if his brother still rode close behind. He glanced over his shoulder, peering through the swirling sand stirred up by his horse's hooves. As a result, he didn't see riders coming the other way and almost careened into them. Four steeds snorted and bucked as their riders reined them in.

"By the saints," Vincent exclaimed, struggling to control his frenzied horse.

"*Merde*!" one of the unknown riders shouted.

The cloud of dust from the sandy terrain gradually settled, revealing four indignant horsemen glaring at each other, blinking away the grit, hands on the hilts of their swords.

Lucien's mouth fell open in astonishment; one of the other riders was a dwarf. He blurted out words without thinking. "Who the hell are you?"

The dwarf rose in the stirrups, drawing his sword. "I am Denis de Sancerre, who the *fyke* are you?"

A loud cough caught Lucien's attention. He immediately recognized Adam de Montbryce. The Norman looked thinner than the last time he had seen him, but there was no mistaking the black hair and noble bearing.

"*Milord* de Montbryce," he exclaimed. "We were on our way to see you."

Adam frowned as he peered through the settling dust. "Lucien! We are coming to visit you. Put up your sword, Denis."

The dwarf scowled, but did as Montbryce bade him.

Lucien's eyes were fixed on the miniature knight.

Adam nudged his horse alongside the dwarf's, putting a hand on his shoulder. "May I properly introduce my brother, Denis de Sancerre. Denis, my friends and neighbors, Lucien and Vincent Lallement."

Denis had long ago become inured to the rude stares of others when they first set eyes on him, but the way the Lallement brothers gaped was unnerving. They seemed struck dumb.

"Never seen a dwarf before?" he goaded.

They exchanged a quick glance, and swallowed hard. "A thousand apologies, *milord* Denis," Lucien stammered, his face reddening. "It's just that—er—" He looked again to his brother, as if seeking help.

Denis curled his lip in disgust. "Didn't you say these were gentlemen?" he asked Adam, though it was unlikely his brother would hear his aside.

Adam nudged his horse forward. "It is a coincidence we chose the same day to call one on the other. I estimate we are closer to Kingston Gorse. We could return there with you."

To Denis' further disgust, the Lallements hesitated, evidently afraid he might taint their home. "Your friends seem hesitant," he declared loudly. "Perhaps we should invite them to East Preston instead."

"Again, my apologies, *mes seigneurs*," Vincent offered, dismounting and bowing to both Normans. "We would be honored to escort you to Kingston Gorse. We are distracted because our mother is—not well. But that is no reason not to extend our hospitality to you."

When Adam frowned, Denis knew he had not heard Vincent Lallement's explanation. Not wanting to make his brother's impediment obvious, he looked him full in the face. "If Madame Lallement is indisposed, we should return with your friends to East Preston."

Adam had previously mentioned Lady Lallement's temperament. If she was as rude as her sons, he had no wish to ever go to Kingston Gorse.

"Please, we insist," Vincent reiterated.

Denis evidently did not scowl hard enough at Adam. With a shrug, his brother agreed to accompany the Lallements to Kingston Gorse.

As they neared his home, Vincent's guts were in knots. Lucien's face betrayed the same worry. A dwarf! Their mother would faint dead away.

He pondered a thousand ways to smuggle Paulina down from the hidden chambers to meet this miniature knight, though she might be repulsed by his features. Denis de Sancerre was the right height for his tiny sister, but he was not a handsome man, though his bearing was dignified and noble. He certainly looked strong, for all he lacked stature.

And something ailed Adam de Montbryce. He seemed detached, ignoring most of the idle chatter Vincent and Lucien directed his way. It was irritating that the dwarf kept repeating everything they said.

Montbryce had always been an outgoing fellow. Now he appeared lost in thought, morose, as if someone dear to him died.

"Are you well, Adam?" Vincent ventured.

Montbryce glanced up at him sharply, then at Sancerre. "Forgive me, Vincent. I have been ill. My malady affected my hearing. I am slowly learning how to discern what people say by watching their mouths, but I am not yet proficient in the skill."

"Forgive me. I will try to speak more clearly. My father often complains I mumble."

He is deaf.

Vincent's heart leapt into his throat. A man who was deaf might not care if his wife was mute.

But it would be difficult to arrange for Montbryce and Rosamunda to meet. Persuading their mother to allow a dwarf to remain under her roof loomed like an insurmountable obstacle. A thousand possibilities swirled in his mind. Lucien too seemed lost in thought. If only they'd had some foreknowledge of these incredible events.

A groom took the reins of the four horses in the courtyard of Kingston Gorse. He seemed unable to take his eyes off Denis de Sancerre. Lucien glared at him as he motioned the visitors to the entryway of the manor.

Adam had removed his gloves and was swatting the dust from his boots. "I hope your mother is sufficiently recovered. I wish to thank her for sending us our new cook."

Vincent's heart fell. If his mother learned he and Lucien had finagled to get Friselle away from the oppressive kitchens of Kingston Gorse, there would be hell to pay.

Lucien cleared his throat loudly as Maudine Lallement's voice echoed off the stone floor of the entryway. "Lucien? Vincent? Why are you home already? I thought—"

Adam and Denis both bowed as she came into view. The color drained from her face when she saw Denis.

Lucien rushed to take her hand as she swayed. "*Maman*, you remember Adam de Montbryce from East Preston. And may I introduce—"

Maudine Lallement stood mere inches from Adam de Montbryce. If he had not already been deaf, the strident shriek that emerged from her throat would have rendered him so. The screeching went on and on as she pointed a quivering finger at Denis.

Vincent had lived with his mother's eccentricities his whole life, but shame washed over him as the depth of her madness dawned on him. He strode to help his brother restrain her as she tried to sweep Denis from the house. "Get that evil goblin out of my home."

Their father appeared. "What is going on?" His mouth fell open when he espied Denis and he seemed rooted to the spot.

Sweat trickled down Vincent's spine as he and his brother struggled with his demented parent. "*Maman* is unwell. Please summon her maid to her chamber."

They strong-armed her up the stairs, still shrieking. Vincent looked down at the entryway. His father had disappeared, leaving Adam de Montbryce and Denis de Sancerre to gape at the scene on the stairway.

Vincent opened his mouth, but quickly shut it. His mother's madness would now become known far and wide. And he was sure Adam and Denis would leave immediately, never to set foot in Kingston Gorse again.

THE CHECKERED FIELD

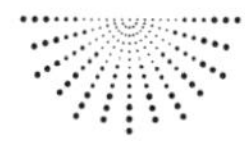

Rosamunda and Paulina clung to each other in their aerie atop the house. Even here they heard frightful shrieks. What was going on? Was the house under attack? Surely, the Saxon brigands Lucien had mentioned were wreaking havoc further north.

Rosamunda saw no evidence of invading forces through their tiny window. Seagulls soared on the breeze, but there was no sign of human life.

The screams became more muffled, then stopped entirely. Foreboding washed over Rosamunda. Had their mother died? Would her death mean their freedom?

Guilt and hope warred in her heart.

She had heard Lucien's voice amid the screaming and shouting, but didn't understand how that could be. Her brothers had gone off to East Preston.

She rang the hand bell several times to call Agnès or Thomas, to no avail. They never divulged anything in any event. Rosamunda suspected they lived in fear of their mistress. Lucien and Vincent were careful to do her bidding and their father was completely under his wife's control.

Perhaps Thomas had been summoned to assist with whatever crisis had arisen. It was an opportunity to sneak to the landing to see what was going on.

She pressed her ear to the door.

Nothing.

"What are you doing?" Paulina murmured.

Rosamunda pressed her forefinger to her lips, pointing to the door.

Paulina grasped her hand. "*Non*! I am afraid."

Rosamunda put an arm around her sister's shoulders, her other hand fluttering over her heart. "I am afraid too." She shook her head, gesturing to the chamber. "This is not a life."

Paulina averted her eyes. "I am content here with you."

Rosamunda wanted to hug her sister, to reassure her she and Vincent and Lucien would protect her in the world outside, if they were freed. It was fear of ridicule that held the tiny woman in its thrall. But time was of the essence.

Paulina gasped and squeezed her eyes shut as Rosamunda opened the door. Neither had noticed before how loudly the hinges squeaked. Rosamunda took her first step over the threshold in seventeen years, deafened by her heartbeat.

The planked floor creaked underfoot despite her efforts to tread softly. Sweat trickled between her breasts. She held out her arms at her sides, as if walking the high parapets she glimpsed daily from her window.

She inched her way to the wooden railing at the top of the stairs. Her legs felt like lead weights as she summoned the courage to look over. Their chambers were three stories up. Would she see to the bottom if she peeked over the precipice? She had been born in her parents' chamber on the second floor, but had no memory of it. The ground floor was a complete unknown.

Holding her breath, she gripped the railing and peered over.

It was the first time she had seen the elaborate checkered floor below. The design drew her. She stared until she became dizzy, remembering what her brothers had told her of its history.

When she was eight, she had listened with rapt attention to the ongoing account of a grand project taking place in the lower reaches of the house. Upon her return from the consecration of Winchester Cathedral, Maudine Lallement had insisted upon the installation of a stone slab floor in the entryway of her home, like the one in the church's north aisle. Nothing would dissuade her from the idea. At great expense, marble was hauled ninety miles from Purbeck, and a sort of light grey and dark brown pattern emerged as a result.

Their father had complained when his wife wanted white marble interspersed with the dark. She urged him to bring it from Carrara in Italy, but he balked at this. Undeterred, she ordered some of the slabs lime-washed regularly to lighten them.

As Rosamunda gazed at the floor she'd been so curious about, someone walked into the patterned space. A man. Black hair, tall. Speaking Norman French. His deep, commanding voice reached even her high perch. "I say we stay."

She saw only the top of his head and broad shoulders, but a strange warmth flooded her body. Winged creatures fluttered in her belly. "Yes, stay," she mouthed, gripping the railing more tightly, swaying in a trance. "Please stay."

She crumpled to the floor before she succumbed to the urge to rush down the stairs and into the stranger's arms.

As she lay panting, slumped against the rails, another voice reached her. Indignant, yet respectful. "You are not the one being treated like a freak."

Alarm surged through her, but she had to look. She hauled herself to her feet. Another black-haired man. He looked shorter, yet still broad-shouldered.

Vincent and Lucien had shown off their skill at a popular new game of strategy. Father had bought them a handsome set of carved game pieces. The men below postured like two knights playing *esches*, tension evident in their stance, even from a distance.

Her sister's voice echoed. "Psst. Come back."

The smaller knight looked up.

Rosamunda crouched quickly, but not before catching a glimpse of a high forehead and enormous eyes.

She sat rooted to the spot, sweating, until she heard Lucien's voice. Plucking up her courage, she stood slowly and looked over the railing again. Now there were four knights on the *esches* field. Vincent and Lucien were home, the latter apparently apologising profusely to the shorter man.

Rosamunda deduced at once that the visitors were Adam de Montbryce and his half-brother. Denis, was it? But why had they come? And why was *maman* screeching? What had gone wrong?

The men left the entryway in silence, walking stiffly, evidently bound for some other ground floor chamber, perhaps the dining hall of which Vincent and Lucien had often spoken. Echoes of their boot-heels striking stone reached her.

Rosamunda crept back to Paulina who was clinging nervously to the door frame. She held up two fingers. "Men, visitors."

Paulina dragged her back into the room and shoved the door closed. "If she catches you—"

Rosamunda shook her head, disentangling her arm from Paulina's grasp. She put her hands together and put them to the side of her head. "*Maman* is abed, I think."

"Was it she screaming?"

Rosamunda nodded.

"She has lost her wits," Paulina whispered. A tear rolled down her cheek, but she wiped it away with the back of her hand.

Rosamunda made a face, sticking out her tongue and pointing to her head. "Long ago."

Paulina sobbed.

Rosamunda handed her a kerchief, then crooked a finger under her sister's chin and lifted her face, filled with an urge to share what she had seen. "Adam de Montbryce and his brother."

Paulina frowned. "How can you be sure?"

Rosamunda raised her hand high above her head. "Tall." She touched her hair. "Black."

Paulina pouted. "Everyone is tall in my world."

Rosamunda remembered the other man she had seen. She lowered her hand. "Brother not so tall."

THEY ARE HIDING SOMETHING

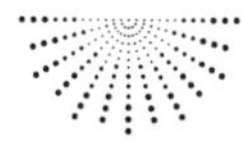

Adam did not truly understand why he had insisted they remain at Kingston Gorse. He was outraged by Lady Lallement's behavior towards his brother. But he felt badly for Lucien and Vincent, who were obviously equally mortified.

They were allotted a comfortable chamber on the ground floor. Adam was relieved they would not be on the same floor as Maudine Lallement. Vincent assured them his mother had been persuaded to take her evening meal in her chamber.

The four young men sat down to dine with Marc Lallement. Adam and Denis exchanged a glance. The lady of the household obviously exacted high standards. White linen covered the table, set with engraved goblets of fine quality. The food was plentiful and tasty, the wine full-bodied and smooth, but the atmosphere was strained, despite the tantalizing aroma of roasted goose. Denis sulked, obviously not his usual talkative self. Adam hesitated to embark on anything more than the simplest conversation.

Marc Lallement pushed carrots and leeks around his trencher with his eating dagger, his eyes downcast, occasionally scowling at his sons who talked without surcease, their mouths full of the food they ate with surprising relish.

Only the servants, to a man impeccably dressed in green tabards and yellow tunics, seemed at ease.

Denis suddenly spoke to Lucien.

The color drained from their friend's face.

Adam thought he heard the word *sisters*.

Marc Lallement dropped his eating dagger.

Lucien looked at his father nervously, then at Denis. "*Non*. Why do you ask?"

From his first meeting with the Lallement brothers, Adam had believed that they were honest men. A chill crept up his spine when he looked at Vincent's face. This family was hiding something, and Lucien was a poor liar.

Denis had sensed it too. He turned to face Adam, pointing up. "I saw a young woman earlier, peering over the railing high up in the house."

Lucien's mouth fell open.

Marc Lallement leapt to his feet. "A young woman?" he parroted.

Jaw clenched, Vincent put a restraining hand on his father's arm. The fear in his eyes betrayed him. "It's all right, father, probably one of the servants."

Whoever the woman was, the Lallements wanted her kept secret. Adam was nonplussed. He remembered his parents mentioning that the family at Kingston Gorse had lost two girls years ago, one in infancy, the other in childbirth. “I am intrigued. I recall my mother telling me you had a sister who died. Three was she?”

Lucien cleared his throat, his face reddening further. “*Oui*, Paulina.” He held up four fingers. “I was four years old.” He added his thumb to the gesture. “Vincent five.”

His brother nodded, too vigorously, his face ashen. “We barely remember her.”

Adam glanced at Denis whose furrowed brow and steepled hands showed his disbelief. “What caused her death?”

“Black measles,” Marc Lallement declared.

Lucien chewed his nails.

Vincent rubbed his forehead.

It was evident the three were lying. Adam thought he must have misheard. *Black measles?* He smelled their fear and had to continue. “I believe another daughter died in childbirth a year or two later?”

“*Oui*, Rosamunda,” Lucien murmured. “*Maman* changed after Paulina.”

Marc squared his shoulders. “The deaths of our daughters devastated my wife. She has not been well since. I apologise again for her rude behavior earlier, *milord* Denis.”

Denis bowed slightly in acknowledgement. “The loss of a child is a strenuous burden to bear.”

Marc swallowed hard. “Indeed,” he rasped.

The color drained from Vincent’s face and he looked close to tears—for a child he barely remembered. There was more going on in this household than met the eye.

Denis resolved to discuss it with his brother when they retired.

He decided to try a new ploy. Coming to his feet, he adopted his usual story-telling stance. “Let me tell you my tale. The midwife who brought me into the world believed it her duty to murder me.”

Adam must have sensed from his posture what he was doing. His grimace betrayed his feeling that this was an inappropriate time to tell the story, but Denis persisted.

As the details emerged, the Lallement brothers slid further and further down in their seats, as if willing the floorboards to swallow them up. Marc Lallement suddenly stood and left without a word.

Denis winked at Adam who was now watching their hosts intently.

He too knows they are hiding something—or someone. Why shut a daughter away?

SEND HIM TO HELL

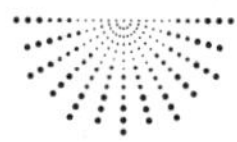

Satisfied their guests had been safely lighted to their chamber and were out of earshot, Vincent strode over to the hearth. He was not worried Adam might overhear, but suspected Denis de Sancerre did not miss much.

He put both hands on the mantel, gazing at the dying embers of the fire. "They sense we are lying."

His brother pulled up a chair and sat with his forearms on his thighs, hands clasped. "You're right."

Vincent grimaced. "Black measles?"

Lucien shrugged. "Papa feels as guilty as we do, probably more so since he is culpable for the crime in the first place."

Vincent turned to face his brother. "I will speak to father on the morrow. I intend to tell him we can no longer continue this farce. Rosamunda and Paulina deserve better."

Lucien remained silent for a long while. Vincent suspected they both had the same thing on their mind.

When the silence became unbearable, he asked, “What’s your opinion of the dwarf?”

“You read my thoughts, brother. He is a gentleman, a true knight, despite his stature.”

“He would make someone a fine husband.”

Lucien glanced up at him sharply. “No doubt, but we must tread carefully here. Paulina is not yet free, and Denis de Sancerre may have no interest in taking a wife. She might judge him repulsive. He is not a handsome man. His deformity is not the same as hers.”

Vincent stirred the embers with the poker. “You’re right. We could make a bad situation worse if we meddle. Rosamunda longs for a mate, but Paulina?”

Lucien put a hand on his shoulder. “She does not recognise her own beauty. Fear hides it from her.”

Vincent took a long breath. “We should go up and see them.”

Lucien sighed. “But what to say? Let’s wait until we have spoken to father.”

“Till the morrow then.”

Denis lay awake, listening to the unfamiliar creaks and groans of the house. Judging by the tossing and turning going on at the other side of the huge bed they shared, Adam was not asleep either.

They had talked for a long while before retiring, in agreement that the Lallements probably had a hidden daughter. They settled upon madness as the reason a parent would lock away a child.

Still something niggled at Denis. The woman he had

glimpsed for a mere second had not looked demented, though her hair was disheveled. Her beauty had struck him immediately.

In addition, the ages did not add up. The face he had seen was that of a girl of less than twenty years. According to Lucien and Vincent, Paulina would be a few years older.

He tapped his brother on the shoulder and Adam turned to face him. "Mayhap we are wrong and the girl was a servant," he said loudly.

Adam yawned. "*Non.* I might concur had they not stumbled over each other to conceal the truth. Somewhere in this house, there is a woman who has been locked away for many a year."

Denis propped his head on his hand. "But how did they perceive that a child of three was mad? She must have been a raving lunatic. Unless there was some other reason."

Adam kicked off the linens. "We've been over this already. What other reason could there be?"

Denis snorted. "You're asking me? The man who came close to being murdered at birth."

Adam chewed his lip. "Perhaps she's a dwarf."

Denis lay back against the bolster. That was an interesting notion. "She did not look like a dwarf. Besides, why wait until she was three? It is obvious at birth when one is born with my qualities."

They lay looking up at the ceiling, each preoccupied with his own thoughts.

Suddenly, Adam gripped his arm. "Do you smell that?"

Denis sat up and sniffed the air.

He jumped out of bed, reaching for his boots. "Something's burning."

Maudine Lallement gripped the railing at the bottom of the stairway that led to the third floor. Vertigo swept over her and she dropped the torch she had used to set afire the banners that hung from the rafters.

"Send him to hell," she shrieked, kicking away the fallen torch as flames licked at the hem of her nightshift. "I'll not have a troll under my roof."

She watched as the hangings were quickly consumed with a whoosh, and the fire crept towards the upper chambers. "The Devil take them," she screamed, panic taking hold as the fire scorched her legs. "*Non! Help! Au secours!*"

"Maudine!"

Marc Lallement's heart leapt into his throat at the sight of his wife frantically swatting the burning nightshift. Scorched fragments of fabric from the banners drifted in the air. He looked up at the fire taking hold in the upper reaches of the roof timbers. Finally, he acknowledged the depth of the madness that held her in its thrall. "My little girls," he rasped.

Tendrils of smoke crept down the stairway, teasing the floor on which they stood. Thank God his sons' chambers were on the lower floor.

Anger surged through him as he rushed to the screeching human torch. Her demented eyes burned into his soul. He lunged for her, consumed with a desire to end her agony and his own. "You have murdered our beautiful children," he shouted.

Screaming maniacally, she collapsed against him. He locked his arms around her, his heart at peace with what he suddenly recognised as his duty. The flames seared his flesh, but they would never burn away his sin. He embraced the agony, shoved her up against the railing and pushed with all his might, sending them both careening into nothingness.

"Devil's spawn," Maudine screamed with her last breath.

"May God forgive me," Marc Lallement prayed as his body broke on the checkered flooring he loathed.

WE WILL DIE TOGETHER

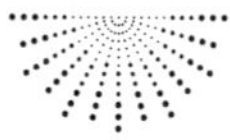

Adam, Denis and the Lallement brothers rushed into the smoke-filled entryway.

"*Mon Dieu*!" Vincent fell to his knees and made the sign of the crucifix as he stared at the smoldering, broken bodies of his parents, locked together in a fatal embrace.

"*Que diable*?" Denis shouted.

Lucien retched.

Adam shuddered, coughing as smoke constricted his throat. The scene unfolding around him seemed more horrific because he couldn't make out what was being said.

Servants ran hither and thither, some obviously frantic, others apparently in command. A human chain formed and buckets of water were quickly passed from hand to hand. Adam took his place in the line, relieved to be doing something useful.

He glanced up. The rafters were alight, the thatch beginning to smolder. Water would be a waste of time. Kingston Gorse was doomed.

Lucien seemed rooted to the spot as he stared at his

dead parents, then he looked up into the burning rafters. “My sisters,” he wailed.

Denis’ gut clenched. He hurried to Adam, holding up two fingers as he pointed to the upper floors. “We were right, and wrong. There may be two women up there. Come on. I’ll be damned if I’ll allow them to burn to death.”

He tore off the shirt he had donned hastily moments before, ripped off a length of it, soaked it in one of the buckets, and tied it around his face.

Adam followed his example.

Vincent put a hand on Adam’s arm. “It’s too dangerous. It’s our responsibility, mine and Lucien’s.”

Denis shoved him, his blood boiling. Two women might die, perhaps because they were afflicted with some sort of deformity. It was too close to his heart. “You should have thought of that before you allowed them to be kept up there.”

Denis and Adam hastened to the lower flight of stairs, Adam taking them two at a time. Burning thatch fell here and there, but the planked floor of the second story was still mostly intact.

Denis heard a choked scream and the sound of a door banging. “They are still alive,” he yelled.

It was not the smell of smoke that awoke Paulina, but the demented screams of her mother. She pulled the linens up to her chin, biting her quivering lip.

For the second time in a day voices were raised in anger and confusion. Her father was shouting foul murder.

The glow of embers in the grate illuminated Rosamunda as she stirred, then sat up. She frowned, pinching her nostrils.

Paulina sniffed. Smoke. And not from the grate. "Fire!" she exclaimed, leaping from the bed, gooseflesh crawling over her skin. She hurried to the door, thrusting it open. The landing was filled with smoke. The banners she had glimpsed briefly when she had yanked Rosamunda back into the chamber were now floating bits of scorched fabric. Flames licked at the rafters. Fear wound its tendrils into her belly. She screamed, slamming the door shut.

Hastily, she dragged a *bliaut* over her nightshift and threw one to Rosamunda. "The house is on fire. Put on your slippers, quickly. We must leave or we could be trapped."

Rosamunda's eyes widened in fear. She stumbled from her bed and ran to the door, clumsily pulling the *bliaut* over her nightshift. Paulina blocked her way. "Too much smoke."

They both looked to the window. Paulina might squeeze through it, but they were three floors up.

Smoke seeped under the door; breathing became more difficult.

Paulina covered her mouth and nose with the wide sleeve of the *bliaut*. She took Rosamunda's hand and rasped, "The *garderobe*."

Rosamunda frowned, but allowed Paulina to drag her to the privy. Their grandfather had apparently boasted proudly of the modern addition he had made to Kingston Gorse. Imprisoned as they were, both girls had been grateful that the house had a privy shaft. It made life more civilized.

Paulina had no idea where the end of the shaft came out, but braving that unpleasant unknown was preferable to burning to death.

She shoved aside the heavy curtain separating the *garderobe* from the main chamber. "Help me," she insisted, straining to push off the wooden planking that covered the hole.

They peered down into blackness. Rosamunda grimaced and held her nose. Paulina's throat was raw, her eyes watering. She hoped she did not look as deathly pale as her sister.

"Afraid," Rosamunda mouthed, stark fear in her eyes.

Paulina shook her head, gagging on the smoke. "A rope—with the linens."

She staggered to regain the chamber, but the smoke was too thick and she was forced to retreat into the *garderobe*. Rosamunda lay slumped against the privy, gasping for breath through the sleeve mask, her eyes glazed.

Hopelessness flooded Paulina. She swallowed the lump in her throat, resigned to the inevitable. Sobbing, she lay down beside her beloved sister, stroking Rosamunda's hair, praying for deliverance to heaven.

"At least we will die together."

THE PAIN OF REJECTION

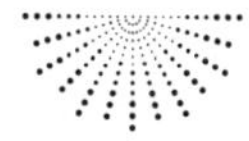

Burning thatch showered down around Adam and Denis as they made their way up the smoke-filled staircase to the upper chambers. The hungry flames were greedily consuming the house. Timbers hissed and popped. Denis glanced down to see the Lallement brothers thundering up the stairs behind them.

It angered him, but was also a relief. If there were two women trapped upstairs, it was unlikely he could carry either to safety.

Adam put his shoulder to a door. He stumbled into the chamber as it gave way easily. Denis followed. Vincent staggered in behind them, hacking breathlessly.

They peered into the smoke.

Lucien arrived. "The *garderobe*," he rasped.

Denis dropped to all fours and crawled in the direction Lucien had pointed. He bumped head first into a heavy curtain. He thrust it aside and shouted, "Here." The rag around his mouth muffled his shout.

Two women lay slumped against the privy, or perhaps a woman and a child.

A child?

He scrambled to her side, dragging her into his arms. He put his ear to her mouth. Still breathing. He could carry a child. The others would have to save the woman.

He hugged the girl to his bare chest, preparing to hoist her over his shoulder. The soft breasts pressed against him did not belong to a child. His shaft chose that inappropriate moment to stand to attention.

Perhaps a dwarf after all.

A fierce determination to save the life of what now appeared to be a tiny woman surged through him. He lifted her over his shoulder and came to his feet.

Vincent jostled him. "Let me take her."

Denis snarled. "*Non*!"

He turned to leave the chamber, vaguely aware of his brother beside him, the other woman cradled in his arms.

As Adam made his way quickly down the burning stairway, he glanced at the face of the woman he carried. Despite the smoke smudges, the tangled hair, and her pallor, she was beautiful. His heart hammered in his chest as her eyes fluttered open and she spoke.

He gasped for air. "Don't worry. I will keep you safe."

She frowned and it dawned on him his mask had muffled his voice.

She replied, but again he could not hear.

He reached the lower floor, where the bucket brigade seemed to have the fire under control. He stumbled out into the courtyard. Willing hands reached to take the woman from him, but he strode on past piles of furniture, tapestries, paintings, and the like, until they were safely away from the house. He knelt to lay her down carefully on the damp grass then tore off his mask, gulping in air.

The woman reeked of smoke and she coughed uncontrollably. He helped her sit up. She spoke again. He had never been as frustrated by his deafness. She likely judged him an imbecile too dimwitted to reply.

Lucien dropped to his knees beside them, showering kisses on the woman's face, stroking back her hair. "Rosamunda, sweet sister," he sobbed.

Jealousy ripped through Adam. He put a hand on Lucien's shoulder, seized by an inexplicable urge to shove him away. He wanted to be sure of her name, uncertain whether he had heard it correctly at dinner. "She is Rosa?"

Lucien turned a tear-streaked face to him. "Rosamunda. Thank you, Adam. You saved her life."

Adam was tempted to pound his fists into the man. Instead, he looked into the woman's eyes, seeing the glow of the burning roof reflected there, and rasped, "Rosamunda, I am Adam de Montbryce."

She smiled and replied. She might have said *I know*, but she couldn't know who he was. Impatient rage tore at his heart.

Lucien touched his arm. "She is mute."

Adam suddenly understood why this young woman had been shut away. Emotions warred within him. If he had been born deaf, would his parents have shunned him? He had only to look at Denis for the answer. But doubtless Rosamunda was not the only child who had suffered neglect because of an impairment.

For reasons unknown to him, he leaned over to brush a kiss on her lips. Her eyes widened and she returned the kiss, curling her arms around his neck.

Lucien scowled.

Adam drew back. This was foolhardy. He had nothing to offer this young woman. He wanted to run his hands over her lovely breasts and shapely hips, evident despite her wretched garb. She was a woman born to bear children.

After what she had suffered, she deserved a man who could give her children, a whole man. If only he had met her before his illness. He came to his feet. "I must find Denis. I leave you in the capable hands of your brother."

Rosamunda's heart raced. In minutes she had gone from terror to elation to despair. Choking in the *garderobe*, she'd been certain death was imminent. Inexplicably, she had opened her eyes to find herself in the arms of a man she knew in her heart was Adam de Montbryce. His nose and mouth were covered, but his ice-blue eyes had burned into her soul. Cradled against his bare chest, she had felt safe, despite the dangerous descent from the attic rooms.

What a sight she must be, yet he had kissed her. The brush of his lips against hers sent strange new sensations tingling through her body. She longed for a voice to properly thank him for saving her life.

But then Lucien's disclosure of her muteness had dawned on him fully and he had withdrawn, leaving her bereft. Perhaps Paulina had the right of it. Rejection was painful.

Lucien smoothed her hair off her face, his eyes filled with tears. “I’m sorry, Rosamunda. Forgive me my weakness.”

She pressed his hand to her cheek. “Paulina?”

Lucien peered into the darkness. “She is safe. The dwarf saved her.”

She frowned. “Dwarf?”

“It’s a long story, *ma soeur*. But I cannot tell it yet. *Maman* and Papa are both dead.”

Rosamunda closed her eyes as tears flowed unbidden. She could not cry for her mother, but she had loved her father, despite his weakness.

She and Lucien clung to each other, one in their grief.

AN ANCIENT GARGOYLE

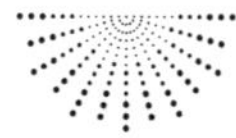

Agony gnawed at every bone in his misshapen back and hips, but Denis was determined not to lay his burden down until they were safely away from the house. He fell to his knees in the grass, thankful of Vincent's help supporting his sister as she slumped forward off Denis' shoulder.

On his knees, Vincent cradled her, sobbing.

Denis tore the mask from his face, thumping his chest with his fist as fits of coughing racked his body. Panting heavily, trying to control the tremor that had taken hold, he looked through bleary eyes at the woman whose life he had saved. At least he hoped he had saved her. She had not opened her eyes, despite Vincent's heartfelt entreaties.

He blinked rapidly, sure he must be imagining things. Paulina, for so Vincent had called her, was a beautifully formed woman—but she was his height. He shivered again, but for a different reason. This was no child. His fingertips tingled. Paulina's breasts would fit perfectly in his big hands.

This woman had been made for him.

Her eyelashes fluttered and she moaned.

It came to him what a fearsome sight he must be. His features were ugly at the best of times. If she saw his smoke-blackened face and body—

She will believe she has gone straight to hell and been greeted by an ancient gargoyle.

He scrambled to rise before she opened her eyes, but it was too late. She lifted heavy lids and stared at him. Without blinking, she took several deep breaths.

Over the years, he had become indifferent to whether people liked him or not, but his gut roiled at the possibility this woman might be repelled. As he knelt, gazing into her warm, brown eyes, aware of the rise and fall of her breasts, Denis was speechless for the first time in his life.

He wanted to tell her she was beautiful, that he would willingly spend his life making amends for the wrongs done to her. But all that came to his lips was, "I am Denis de Sancerre."

She frowned, looked up at her brother, then back at Denis.

His heart thudded in his ears. He had never felt so vulnerable, and he didn't like it. Revulsion had obviously struck her dumb.

One minute Paulina was gasping for breath in the *garderobe*, the next she was staring into the gaze of a strange little man with a barrel chest and huge forehead. She heard Vincent murmuring her name over and over, begging forgiveness.

It seemed she had not died. She had a vague memory of being carried over someone's shoulder. Had this miniature man saved her?

She had believed she was the only person of her height, but evidently such was not the case. Her savior was not handsome, but the longing in his green eyes touched her heart.

Life could not have been easy for this man whose head was too big for his body and whose shoulders seemed permanently hunched. Yet, he was an impressive presence. His name confirmed his nobility. He was Adam de Montbryce's half-brother.

A thousand questions swarmed through her head. Beside her knelt a man of stunted stature who had lived in the world. What was it like? Had he been persecuted? Would she be shunned by people? But his gaze held her in its thrall and she could not get the words out of her mouth.

It came to her suddenly that she had not given a thought to her sister. "Rosamunda?"

Vincent hugged her to his chest. "Rosamunda and Lucien are safe, but *maman* and papa are dead."

She shivered, but felt no grief for the parents who had incarcerated her. She looked again at the strange man still kneeling beside her. "Did you save me, Vincent?"

"*Non*, it was Denis who carried you out."

Paulina looked back at the house where she had spent her life, the top half now a smoldering ruin, gaunt against the night sky. She was tiny, but it must have taken enormous courage and strength to carry her from the third floor. She wondered if it was appropriate to touch his face in thanks. She had no experience of men besides her brothers.

Sancerre unexpectedly took her hand and brushed a kiss on her knuckles. His big hand swamped hers. She had a strange urge to press its warmth to her tingling breast, to touch the hand he had kissed to her own lips. The fire must have addled her wits, or made her ill.

He rolled to his side and came to his feet. For the first time she noticed his misshapen spine and hips. They shared a lack of stature, but his deformities were more severe than hers. Yet, he had apparently made his way in the world. Did she have the courage to do the same? Fear shuddered through her. Heat soared into her face when she realized she had been staring at him. "I thank you, Denis de Sancerre," was all she could manage.

He bowed stiffly and walked away.

Denis clenched his fists. He knew better than to expose his heart. How foolish to imagine that because Paulina was small she would instantly fall in love with him. He was a monster. Sometimes he forgot, but her shudder at the sight of him had reminded him of it sharply.

He felt cold and very exposed without his shirt. No wonder she had been repulsed. The night air was chilly and the Lallement household had no roof over their heads. He hastened off to locate Adam. They had to get everyone to East Preston as soon as possible.

FREE AT LAST

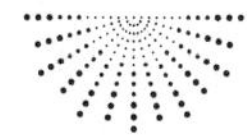

Paulina and Rosamunda found each other and clung together in silence for long minutes, Paulina's head resting on her sister's breast. Finally, the tears fell.

Vincent brought blankets, then left quickly. They huddled together, watching Adam and Denis help their brothers organize the servants in preparation for departure to East Preston at first light.

Denis de Sancerre's head came only to his brother's waist, and his gait was an ungainly stride, but he was as commanding a presence as the taller men.

The servants obeyed his orders without question. Many gaped more at the two women, obviously amazed they had lived in the chambers above them without their knowledge, one of them an obvious freak. This was how life would be now they were free.

Paulina was relieved no one else had died, though several had to have burns salved, and some of the younger female servants stood together, whimpering. She suspected

Denis and Adam had suffered burns, but neither had complained.

The stables had mercifully been spared. Horses were available for their journey. Neither she nor her sister had ever ridden.

The visitors had retrieved their belongings from the lower chambers which had suffered only smoke damage. Denis de Sancerre looked like a miniature knight, a sword that must have been specially made for him bouncing on his hip. He had donned a clean shirt and doublet, and somehow managed to wash his face and tie back his thick curly black hair with a leather thong.

Paulina sniffed her *bliaut*. "I stink, but our clothing is lost."

Rosamunda rubbed her arms and face. "I want to wash." She held her nose. "Dirty."

Paulina pouted. "The servants have ignored us. I suppose they are wondering who we are, and Thomas and Agnès are avoiding us."

Unexpectedly, Denis was beside them. He set down a bucket of water and put linen rags in their laps. "This will have to suffice, I'm afraid, until we reach East Preston. There you can luxuriate in a hot tub and wash away the smoke."

Exhausted, Paulina inhaled deeply and conjured a vision of lying naked in a tub of hot water, Denis de Sancerre washing her hair, dripping water from a sponge over her breasts, trailing his thick fingers—

As if he'd read her thoughts, he smiled, transforming his face into a thing of beauty. She breathed a sigh of relief that the darkness hid her embarrassment. "We thank you, Sir Denis," she murmured.

He went down on one knee. “Please, not so formal. Simply Denis. I wish I could do more. You have lost a great deal tonight, but at least you are free.”

Rosamunda squealed her delight.

Paulina kept silent. It remained to be seen if freedom brought what Rosamunda expected.

The linen still lay in her lap. Denis took it, dipped it in the water, and carefully cleansed her face. It was the first act of simple kindness anyone other than her siblings had ever done for her. She wanted to cry like a baby and rain kisses on his full lips.

He dipped the cloth again and moved closer to Rosamunda. Paulina reached up to take the cloth from him. For some reason she did not want him to wash her sister’s face. Their fingers touched. A strange tingling raced up the back of her thighs. “Thank you, Denis. I will take care of my sister.”

He came to his feet and shrugged. “As you wish.”

She trailed the wet cloth down her neck as she watched him walk away. Despite the chill of the night air, she suddenly felt very warm.

Denis strode away, willing his insistent erection to subside. Someone was sure to notice the bulge in his leggings. Thank goodness it was dark. He should never have touched Paulina. It had not been his intention, but desire swept over him when her eyelashes fluttered closed. The vision of her perfect little body lying in a tub of soapy water had him hot and bothered. The brief touch of her fingers was his complete undoing.

He was angry. He had realized years ago that he was destined to be a lifelong bachelor. Besides, Adam needed him now. His brother could never marry. This sudden infatuation with Paulina had to stop. He was taken with her because she matched him in height. Ridiculous! He was deformed, she was tiny. There was no reason on earth why she should have feelings for him.

And what of her sister? Why was Paulina protective of her? As far as Denis could see she had no deformity. Why had she been incarcerated? He had mentioned it briefly to Adam while they were hastily retrieving their belongings, but his brother had shrugged off the question and stalked out of the chamber.

Rosamunda chafed whenever she lost sight of Adam de Montbryce. The story of the rescue of Devona Melton had formed an image of the heroic Montbryces in her mind. Adam was its living embodiment.

She admired his immediate offer of shelter at East Preston. It was a relief they would not be exposed to the elements for more than one night. She was at once filled with elation and apprehension—she was going to his home, or at least to the place he lived when he was in England. He was a true Norman. His father had apparently fought in the Battle of Hastings, but had returned to Normandie after the conquest of England.

Rosamunda and her siblings belonged to the second generation of her family born in England. But she was a descendant of Normans, proud of the oft-told tales of the Conqueror and his people who had brought fine architecture, good government, culture and refinement to the Saxon people of England.

But she had never visited Normandie, only gazed out her window, longing to see its distant shores. Her brothers had been allowed to travel to their ancestral homeland and she and her sister had enjoyed the tales of their journeys.

As if conjured by her thoughts, Vincent touched her arm. “Let’s get you and Paulina into the stables.”

Exhausted, they made their way to an empty horse stall, where they curled up together in the straw. Vincent covered them with blankets.

Rosamunda dozed fitfully, dreaming of listening to Adam de Montbryce’s deep voice as they rode together through the green fields and forests of Normandie.

She was free at last.

NOX

The next morning, Paulina pouted, feeling like a petulant child. "You can't stay here, Vincent. You must accompany us. We are unused to people and at East Preston we will be among strangers."

Her brother hunkered down to embrace her. "Lucien and I must see to the burial of our parents and make plans for rebuilding. Adam and Denis are honorable men. They will treat you as their sisters. We will join you in a few days."

She had an urge to blurt out that she did not want to be treated as Denis de Sancerre's sister. His hungry gaze after the rescue had made her feel desirable for the first time in her life. "We should stay for the burial."

Vincent recognized this suggestion for the half-hearted ploy it was. "That's not a good idea. You would endanger your mortal soul by wishing *maman* consigned to hell."

Paulina sulked, further infuriated by Rosamunda's sly grin. She plucked straw from her sister's hair. "What is funny?"

Rosamunda rubbed her hands together gleefully, then pointed to the sun peeking over the horizon. "Sunrise."

Paulina's mouth fell open. Fear held her in its thrall, whereas her sister was already enjoying the first taste of what freedom might mean. "It's beautiful," she admitted.

Lucien came up behind the threesome gazing at the dawn's early glow. "I've made a space in one of the wagons for you."

Paulina whirled around. "A wagon? With the servants?"

Her brother took a step back. "How else will you get to East Preston?"

Paulina stamped her foot again, tears welling. She would not feel comfortable sitting in a wagon full of gawking servants. "Why can Rosamunda and I not ride?"

Vincent rolled his eyes. "How can you ride, sister? You have no horse."

Without thinking, she blurted out, "But I could ride behind Denis de Sancerre."

Rosamunda blushed.

Lucien groaned.

Vincent scratched his head. "Ladies do not ride astride, Paulina. You cannot ride behind him in a nightshift and *bliaut*."

"In front then. I can sit on his lap," she countered.

Lucien shifted his weight nervously.

Vincent coughed into his fist.

Paulina gritted her teeth. "I will not ride with the servants, and neither will Rosamunda."

~

A warm glow shivered its way from Rosamunda's core to the tips of her toes and thence up her spine to the top of her head and back by way of her breasts. If Paulina rode with Denis, Adam might allow her to ride with him.

She did not want to travel with the servants but would have complied if necessary. The possibility of being held again in Adam's arms made her heart flutter as she watched her brothers stalk off, clearly uncomfortable.

She took her sister's hand and squeezed it. "Thank you."

Paulina frowned. "For what?"

Rosamunda's body heated further when she glanced up to see Adam de Montbryce striding towards them, leading a black horse. He did not look happy. She gasped and looked quickly at her sister.

Paulina suddenly smiled. "Now I understand. If I ride with Denis, you ride with—"

Adam was beset with conflicting emotions. Rosamunda filled his thoughts despite the frenzied business of making arrangements for the move to East Preston, and helping Vincent and Lucien oversee the storage of valuables in the weaving shed.

Vincent's discomfort with the request for his sisters to ride with him and Denis was palpable. Adam's heart soared at the prospect of holding Rosamunda in his arms again. But then the memory of his body's inadequacy stabbed him in the gut.

He could not expect a beautiful young woman to commit to a man incapable of consummating a marriage.

He was thinking too far ahead in any case. She would want to enjoy her newfound freedom. He gripped the reins, gathering his resolve. "I think it best if you travel—"

He became fixated on a sliver of straw clinging to Rosamunda's disheveled hair. Her lower lip quivered and tears welled in her eyes. She gathered the blanket more tightly at her throat.

His resolve deserted him. He held out his hand. "If you are to ride with me, you must be introduced to Nox. He looks fearsome, but he's a loyal friend."

She moved forward hesitantly. Nox was big and as black as his name. It occurred to Adam she may never have seen a horse before. He put his palm under the stallion's nose, encouraging her to do the same.

Rosamunda looked uncertainly at her sister, then at the horse. Adam plucked the straw from her hair, taking her by the hand. She looked up at him sharply. The brief glint in her green eyes told him she too had felt the spark that passed between them.

She clutched his sleeve, nervously offering her free hand to the beast, snorting a giggle when Nox licked her. Her nervous amusement rippled through Adam's body. His heart skipped a beat, but nothing stirred between his legs.

He would have preferred she ride astride behind him, but her *bliaut* rendered it impossible, as well as unseemly. "I will help you mount. Don't be afraid."

Adam must not see her fear. He may change his mind. "Not afraid," she mouthed, shaking her head for emphasis.

Communicating with family members was easy. The

prospect of making herself understood to strangers was daunting. It eased her worry that Adam watched her mouth closely, considerate of her muteness.

He stood close enough she could smell the faint remnants of smoke clinging to him.

He looked at her intently. "May I touch you?"

She swayed and licked her lips, hoping the strange tautness of her nipples was not evident.

Paulina coughed.

With one arm around her, the other under her thighs, Adam lifted her effortlessly. "Put your arms around my neck. Hold on tightly."

She complied, her heart racing. She supposed it was because she was unused to men.

Before she could blink, she was sitting in the saddle, holding on for dear life, her feet dangling. The ground was a long way down. Fear coiled in her belly, but then Adam's long slender fingers steadied her waist while he grasped the pommel with his other hand.

He bent his long leg to put his booted foot in the stirrup and in one easy motion brought his body up, then swung his other leg over the horse's broad back, and eased her onto his lap.

His lithe grace took her breath away. She was tempted to ask him to do it again, but he would deem her an imbecile. Perhaps all men were accomplished in such things.

His mastery over the horse was awesome. She felt like the damsel in Lucien's stories whose knight has come to her rescue.

His thighs were solid, his arm firm around her waist. She leaned back against him as the fear lessened. With her head on his chest, she bent her knees so the *bliaut* covered her bare ankles.

Nox moved back a step or two, sending shivers of fright rushing up and down her spine once more.

Watching from the safety of the courtyard, Paulina gasped, eyes wide, hands pressed to her mouth.

Adam tightened his hold. The heat of his arms penetrated through the layers of Rosamunda's clothing, his heartbeat thudded in her ears.

She laughed, pointing to herself as she bravely touched Nox's mane. "I'm on a horse, Paulina," she mouthed.

Adam made a clicking sound with his teeth. The muscles in his thighs flexed against her *derrière*. Sweat trickled between her breasts.

"*Lentement*, Nox. We don't want to frighten Rosamunda."

The stallion nodded its head and walked slowly towards the rampart ditch that surrounded three sides of the house. The movement caused her to rock back and forth in Adam's lap. She hoped she wasn't hurting him.

They rode past Denis as he led his horse in Paulina's direction. Adam greeted him. The dwarf acknowledged the greeting, but the scowl did not leave his ugly face.

THE NARROW SEA

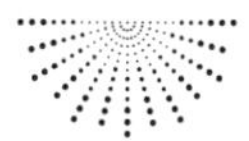

Adam understood how Denis felt. Indeed, it would be worse for him if Paulina sat on his lap. His half-brother's shaft never had a problem rising to an occasion such as this.

Rosamunda seemed to be getting used to being on Nox. He increased the horse's gait slightly. She looked up at him and smiled, letting him see she was enjoying this new adventure.

It was a relief that he did not have to hear what she said. But here he was with a stunningly beautiful and desirable woman rocking back and forth on his lap, and he felt—absolutely nothing.

That was not strictly true. He had a strong urge to cup his hand under one of Rosamunda's breasts—just to see how it felt. He glanced down. The bulky nightshift stretched her *bliaut* tight. Her breasts protested the confinement. He might not have the wherewithal to make love with his shaft, but his tongue could bring pleasure to those pouting nipples.

Adam had prized his virginity, but that did not mean he was ignorant of how to please a female. He had learned much from Denis who was never shy to boast of his prowess. Tongues and fingers could bring great pleasure.

Would a young woman be satisfied with that kind of lovemaking? Perhaps, but she would want children—an impossibility for him now.

He was drawn to this *muette*. In different circumstances, he would have pursued her.

But there was no future in it. Better to remain aloof. A man would come along who could fulfill all her needs.

Perhaps he was drawn to her because she was mute and he was deaf.

She turned to look at him again. She stuck out her bottom lip and frowned, rocking her head from side to side. "Are you angry?"

He shrugged. Angry? The word seemed inadequate. Bereft…lonely…cheated…useless. "*Non*, I'm not angry, simply concerned about you and your sister."

She touched his face. "Thank you."

His heart beat erratically. He gathered her closer to his chest. "Rest. You must be exhausted. Nox will get us to East Preston safely."

She relaxed in his arms as they reached the boundary of the Kingston Gorse estate. He paused to wait for Denis before beginning the journey along the coastal path. He thought she had fallen asleep, but then a raucous seagull caught her attention. She sat bolt upright and became agitated, pointing to the edge of the cliff, gripping his arm.

Nox pricked up his ears.

Adam patted the horse, soothing him. Her movements were making the stallion nervous. "What's amiss?"

Eyes bright with excitement, she pointed frantically to the water. "Stop! Stop! I want to see the sea."

Rosamunda held her breath as Adam edged Nox closer to the cliff's edge. At last, she was about to set eyes on the waters whose waves she had heard lapping beneath her prison all her life.

It was not what she expected. Grey, not blue. Cold, not warm. Murky, not clear. She could not see Normandie. She could barely see the wavelets breaking along the mist-shrouded shore.

Yet, it elated her. She inhaled deeply and turned to look at Adam. "The Narrow Sea."

"It's known as the Narrow Sea," he said.

It was understandable he would not know what she had intended. She was used to her sister and brothers comprehending everything she wanted to express, but it would be different with others.

She mouthed back his words.

He stared at her lips, then smiled, something he didn't do often. The unexpected gleam it brought to his usually guarded eyes took her breath away. She looked back at the water.

"On a clear day, you can see my homeland."

She took a deep breath. Homeland. The land of her ancestors. She longed to tell him of her wish to visit Normandie, but such an explanation would involve hand gestures and sounds that might make him think her demented. Paulina would have understood, but Adam de Montbryce had no experience conversing with a *muette*.

It occurred to Adam that though Rosamunda was from a Norman family, she had been born in England and because of her incarceration had probably never been to Normandie.

She leaned against him, seemingly content to gaze at the sea. He wished he could see her face instead of the top of her head. "Normandie is a beautiful place, though there is great turmoil between the factions of the newly-crowned King Henry and his brother, Robert Curthose. The Duke of Normandie thinks the throne of England should be his."

She did not turn to reply. It pained him that he was deaf, but the irony was she could make no sounds, none that he could understand anyway, without watching her lips carefully.

To his surprise, the notion appealed to him. She had a lovely mouth—kissable, seductive, the corners always tilted slightly upwards. He reined in the thought. No more kissing maidens for Adam.

He held an innocent who had been locked away, making her more vulnerable than other young women. She would need protection. Her parents were dead, her brothers tasked with the rebuilding of Kingston Gorse. He must not pursue her, but he could protect her until the right man came along. He would safeguard her at East Preston, perhaps take her to Normandie.

It was a foolish notion, yet—"Would you like to visit Normandie?"

She turned to look at him. Her radiant face outshone the rays of the sun. "*Oui*," she breathed.

His heart leaped into his throat as their eyes locked. He

had an urge to lick away the tears of obvious joy that welled in her eyes. It was the first time since his illness he had felt stirrings of desire in his heart, though his manhood remained dormant. At least his heart could love, if his body could not.

Love?

He shifted his weight in the saddle and looked away to where Denis was leading the wagons towards them. Adam was not sure who had the biggest scowl on their face, his brother or the tiny woman sitting on his lap.

A COMICAL SIGHT

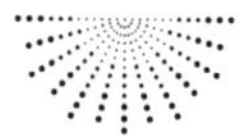

At first, the brothers rode side by side. Denis and Paulina had apparently decided not to say a word to each other, and Rosamunda deemed conversation with Adam atop Nox too difficult.

Eventually, Denis dropped back to ride behind the carts as they made their way along the cliff-top path. Though well used by horses, it was narrow.

The servants from Kingston Gorse seemed to have recovered from the shock of the fire and were chatting as the carts jostled them along the rough path. Some speculated on the cause of the fire, and the presence of two women they had known nothing about. Rosamunda recognized Thomas and Agnès. Though the couple had never treated them with any affection, she was glad there would at least be two familiar faces at East Preston. Most were people she had never met.

She felt warm now the sun had risen higher and the heat of Adam's body penetrated the early morning chill.

There was something comforting about his scent. It reminded her of her brothers. She dozed, content to be out in the air.

Strident shouts of distress jerked her awake. People were screaming. She looked back. One of the carts had lost a wheel. It teetered precariously on the cliff's edge. Denis was shouting a warning for the occupants to remain still, lest they send the cart over. Terrified women clung to each other, whimpering. Servants swarmed out of the other cart and strained to shore up the damaged one. The soft earth threatened to crumble beneath their feet.

Adam rode on.

Alarm filled her. He had he not heard the shout for help, the cries of distress. She balled her fist and thumped his chest.

He reined to a halt. "What is it?"

She put her hand on his chin and forced him to turn his head. His eyes widened as he took in the scene. Evidently, he'd been dozing when the alarm came.

He quickly turned Nox and rode back, thrusting the reins into Rosamunda's hands as he jumped from the horse. "Stay here."

Denis had dismounted, leaving Paulina atop Brevis.

The sisters stared at each other. Paulina was obviously as terrified as she was. Denis' mount was not as large as Nox, yet Paulina looked tiny in the wooden saddle.

Both horses shifted nervously as the cries for help grew more insistent.

Rosamunda looked at the ground. Her throat tightened. Determined not to end up falling, she tried to recall what Adam had done to soothe the beast. She patted the side of its neck and pulled lightly on the reins, mouthing its name.

Her touch seemed to calm him. Relieved, she turned to see how her sister was faring. Abject fear distorted Paulina's features as she clung to the mane, the reins dangling uselessly.

Rosamunda had a choice. She could do nothing, leaving her sister to the mercy of Brevis, who might throw her off.

She could somehow dismount, leave Nox to his own devices, and run over to try to calm Paulina's horse. This had the potential of alarming Denis' mount further.

Or she could coax Nox over to Brevis in the hopes his presence might have a calming effect.

In truth, she did not consider the first two choices. Digging her slippered feet into Nox's side, she urged him forward. To her astonishment, he complied.

Brevis calmed as soon as she came alongside.

She reached for the reins. "Hang on, Paulina," she mouthed, pulling the horse away from the edge of the cliff. Her sister sobbed, clutching the mane.

Adam recognised it was a grave error to leave Rosamunda alone on Nox. In the panic of the moment he had forgotten she had never ridden before. Straining to lift the broken cart away from danger, his shoulder braced hard against the unyielding wood, he feared if he looked in the direction of his horse, the stallion would have run off with her. Or she might be lying injured. He broke out in a sweat that had nothing to do with the exertion.

His racing heart calmed when he caught sight of *la muette* seemingly in control of his sometimes temperamental beast. In addition, she had apparently calmed Brevis. So much for his ambition to be the great protector.

Denis was assisting terrified servants to climb over the side of the cart to safety. Incredibly, some refused to take his hand, preferring to look away and trust their fate to the cliff.

Adam and a handful of able-bodied men succeeded in shoving the cart away from the edge. The wheel was beyond repair. They either had to leave some of the servants here and return for them, or load everyone into the remaining cart.

He sank to the ground, knees bent, breathing hard, rubbing his shoulder. Denis wandered over. He bent close to Adam's ear. "That was a close call."

Adam frowned. "I did not hear your shout. It was Rosamunda who alerted me."

Denis shrugged, raking his fingers through his dishevelled hair. "I thought as much. It isn't safe to load everyone into one cart. Many are already muttering about bad luck and curses."

Adam smiled. "Look yonder. Can you believe it?"

It was a comical sight. A young woman, grinning broadly, dressed in a soiled *bliaut* stretched over a night-shift, led both horses, Nox's reins in one hand, Brevis's in the other.

Her sister tagged behind, obviously trying to distance herself from the animals.

Denis laughed out loud. "What a relief. My only thought when I left Paulina on Brevis was to get to these ungrateful wretches. Looks like Rosamunda has saved the day in more ways than one."

Adam chuckled too. Here was a woman of great courage and resilience. She had been cruelly treated by her own parents because of an affliction. Despite her muteness, Nox had understood her. Could he do the same?

CROSSING THE THRESHOLD

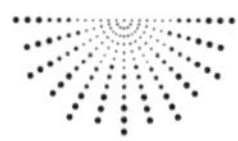

Rosamunda and her sister had listened with interest when their brothers spoke of East Preston. Derelict when granted to Adam's father, it figured in the tale of the heroic Montbryce brothers. Nigh on five and twenty years before, unable to stay in the rat and pigeon infested manor house, the brothers had camped out there on the eve of their first fateful visit to Melton Manor.

Antoine de Montbryce had decided to reclaim East Preston from its dereliction, trusting it had good fields and could be made into a productive estate. According to Vincent and Lucien, the years had proven him right.

Rosamunda expected a dark, unfriendly place. Instead, the well-appointed house seemed warm and welcoming. The Montbryce family had never leased out the estate, preferring to install a steward who took care of the place in the family's absence. It was their home away from home when they visited from Normandie.

Adam gave her over to the waiting steward, dismounted then took her back into his arms. "Rosamunda

Lallement, this is Steward Cormant. He will see to your needs while you are a guest in my home."

A thrill of contentment warmed her heart. His home. This was his home, at least when he was in England.

Cormant bowed. "Lallement? From Kingston Gorse? I thought—"

Now the questions would begin, the explanations she was ill-equipped to provide, the gasps of disbelief. Cormant would not be the last.

Adam interrupted him, evidently sensing her discomfort. "Marc and Maudine Lallement died in a fire at the house yestereve."

He gestured towards Denis, now riding in with Paulina behind the servants' cart. "We have brought their daughters here while Vincent and Lucien set about securing and rebuilding the manor. We will need several chambers prepared."

Cormant's eyes widened further, now evidently understanding their disheveled appearance. "My condolences."

Rosamunda supposed she should feel more grief for her parents, but she mouthed the word *Merci*.

Cormant furrowed his brow.

"*Demoiselle* Lallement is *muette*, Alain," Adam explained.

The man's mouth fell open. He cleared his throat, his eyes darting from Adam to Denis to Paulina, then back to Rosamunda. "The young ladies will need clothing, I assume."

His puzzlement over Paulina's size was apparent as Denis assisted her to dismount into the steward's arms. Denis scowled at him as he dismounted and relieved

Cormant of his burden. "The sooner you begin, the quicker it will be."

Cormant was about to hurry away, but Adam stopped him. "As you see, we have brought some of the servants with us who will have to be accommodated. One wagon failed. There is another contingent to pick up on the cliff path."

Cormant's eyes narrowed as he looked to the cart. The servants huddled together, evidently unsure what was to become of them. They gawked at the scene unfolding in the courtyard. Rosamunda smiled inwardly. They likely did make a peculiar sight; a giant and a dwarf each carrying a woman perfectly suited to him.

Her body warmed, but she must not assume too much. She had no experience of this new world into which she had been thrust. Adam de Montbryce might be the man of her fancies, but she had no knowledge of men.

All she knew of life beyond the attic rooms of Kingston Gorse, she had learned from her brothers. She suspected married women were not free to come and go as they pleased. She had longed for freedom.

Denis de Sancerre might appear to be the right man for Paulina, but her sister was delicate, sensitive. Her heart would break easily. Rosamunda would do her utmost to make sure that did not happen.

"You need not carry me, sir," Paulina insisted. "My stature does not preclude me walking by myself."

Sancerre's scowl deepened and she instantly regretted the hasty words. This miniature knight addled her normally agile brain. “I apologise,” she murmured as he set her on her feet. “That was a thoughtless remark.”

His glower did not lessen. “It was, but I acknowledge your apology. Since you can walk, I shall escort you into the hall.”

He put a hand to the small of her back to guide her in Montbryce’s wake. She had hugged her brothers, but this touch of thick fingers, light yet firm, was more intimate.

Not wishing to appear churlish, she allowed him to guide her. It felt good to have someone take care of her welfare.

She suspected East Preston was not as grand a house as her own, having only two stories. There were numerous sturdy outbuildings, framed with large timber uprights filled with wattle and daub. She recognised they were chinked with moss to keep out the winter cold. There was a stone building set aside from the wooden house, which she assumed was the kitchen. They had the same precaution at Kingston Gorse, and much good it had done them. She wondered if her mother had started the fire. Her father had died crying foul murder.

She looked up at the roof, which appeared to be well thatched. A shiver rippled through her at the memory of the burning thatch raining down from the roof of Kingston Gorse.

Sancerre put a hand to her elbow. “You are safe now,” he whispered.

He had sensed her fears.

She gasped as they entered the house. The interior was elaborately decorated with ornamental wood turnings, the wooden floor softened with wattle mats. Elegant tapestries adorned the walls.

Adam had set Rosamunda down in a chair before a hearty fire burning in the hearth. He beckoned Paulina. “Come, warm yourself.”

It would be an inelegant struggle to get into the massive chair he indicated, and her feet would dangle in the air. She stood by Rosamunda’s chair, holding her chilled hands to the warmth, gazing into the flames.

Fire had taken everything from her, almost robbed her of life. Yet, it had brought freedom. If the flames held the secret of what the future had in store, they did not reveal it, no matter how hard she stared.

Adam had never paid much attention to the house itself, though he shared his father’s pride in it and felt at home there. It certainly was not as grand as Belisle Castle, but it was warm and welcoming. Perhaps therein lay the reason he had chosen to come here to exorcise his demons.

Carrying Rosamunda over the threshold, he saw the house through different eyes, savoring every lime-washed panel, every stair, every chamber. Much of the old house, left derelict for five years after the conquest, had to be rebuilt from split and planed timbers, fastened together with iron nails.

Rosamunda mouthed something, but he was intent on staring at the rosy glow the fire had brought to her cheeks. He leaned closer, arching his brows, shaking his head slightly.

She looked at him curiously as he stared at her lips. “Beautiful house.”

"*Oui*, Cormant's father and uncle worked like dogs to reclaim it, not to mention the rat catcher."

She laughed. "Isembart Jubert."

"You know the story of Isembart?"

Her eyes sparkled. "Hugh and Devona and Izzy."

For some unfathomable reason he suddenly felt jealous of his cousin Izzy. "How did you learn of them?"

Paulina interrupted. "Our brothers. Rosamunda never tires of hearing the tale."

Aware Adam had not heard Paulina's explanation, Denis touched a hand to his hip. "Their brothers told them the story."

Adam smiled at Rosamunda, and she giggled.

Paulina scowled at Denis. It struck him then that of course she would not understand why he had repeated her words. But it was for Adam to speak of his affliction if he wished it known. He stood close to her, feeling the reflected heat of the fire. "Adam did not hear you," he murmured.

Paulina shrugged, folding her arms across her breasts, and took a step away from him.

Cormant entered, two maidservants in tow. Both gawked at Paulina. Denis had often been the recipient of such stares. Wanting to protect the tiny woman whose life he had saved, he moved to shield her from their view.

Fire flooded his veins that had naught to do with the flames in the grate. He itched to enfold her in his arms, but it was too soon. He had patience. He would bide his time, help her overcome her fears. He would have to stop scowling. No wonder the woman was cool towards him.

Cormant stiffened his shoulders and gestured to the servants. “Hortense and Victorine will serve your guests as ladies’ maids.”

Each girl bobbed a curtsey, then scurried off when Cormant waved them away. “Chambers have been prepared for *Mesdemoiselles* Lallement. Follow me, please.”

Smiling broadly, Denis offered his arm to Paulina. To his immense relief, she accepted and he escorted her out of the hall, leaving Adam to accompany Rosamunda.

THE HAND OF DESTINY

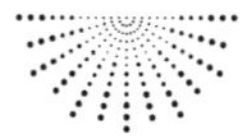

Adam chafed that he was neglecting his responsibilities to his father. He had undertaken to visit the ten manor houses in Sussex, yet seemed incapable of summoning the will to leave East Preston.

He informed Belisle of the fire at Kingston Gorse by way of the well-established pigeon relay. The message explained that no tithes could be expected from Kingston Gorse for some time to come, given the tragic circumstances of the Lallements' deaths.

No mention was made of his and Denis' presence in the house at the time of the fire; their mother would fret over it.

It was impossible to explain the existence of Rosamunda and Paulina in a short missive. He didn't know how to describe what he was beginning to feel for Rosamunda. She was full of life, determined to explore the house and grounds, asking a thousand questions about it and the other manor houses the Montbryces had been granted.

What had Antoine done to deserve such a gift? How many manors in total? Were they all two stories? All made of wood?

She rushed into the house one day, her joy evident at having discovered rosemary growing in the herb garden.

She wanted to learn how to ride. When she discovered the weaving shed, she begged to be taught how to weave.

She haunted the kitchens, never making a nuisance of herself, simply watching wide-eyed.

Adam was learning to understand her. His deafness had no bearing on their conversations. She seemed unaware of it.

She swore an oath to never take up a needle again. She wanted to hear of Antoine's bravery at Hastings over and over. Adam told her the tale of his *oncle* Hugh and *tante* Devona and she was enthralled by details her brothers had not been aware of.

She wept at the story of his father taking his mother prisoner during a siege. She shuddered when he told of Denis' birth and the mob out for his blood, making him wish he had not mentioned it. It was perhaps too akin to her family's history.

She put both hands over her heart. "Love? Your parents."

Adam chuckled. "Passionately."

A tear trickled down her cheek. "My mother—no love." She grimaced. "Only hate."

His heart went out to this young woman. He wanted to enfold her in his arms and protect her from being hurt ever again. But he was not the man to fulfill all her needs. He might bring her pleasure, but could not plant the seed of a child in her belly.

It saddened him immensely. He loved spending time with her, but keeping his hands to himself was proving increasingly difficult.

The maidservants quickly fashioned chemises, night-shifts and *bliauts* for the Lallement women to replace the borrowed raiment. Paulina was particularly grateful, having been reduced to wearing clothing of the children of servants who were not as well endowed above the waist as she.

Denis seemingly could not take his eyes off the tiny woman. "What a pair we are, brother," he remarked one day after they had been practicing swordplay in the court-yard. "God brings us two beautiful women and we have no idea what to do with them."

Leaning his hip against the wall of the well, Adam took a gulp of water from the dipper, then wiped his mouth with the sleeve of his sweat-soaked shirt. "I know what I'd love to do with Rosamunda, but that is impossible."

Denis accepted the dipper Adam had refilled from the bucket. "But think on it." He pointed to Adam's ears. "You are deaf, and we stumble into a girl who is *muette*." He touched his lips, then thumped his chest. "I am a dwarf and your *muette's* sister is the smallest woman I have ever seen. Surely the fine hand of destiny is at work somewhere here."

Adam groaned, wiping the sweat from his brow. He understood the gist of what Denis was trying to say, but—

"My inadequacies go deeper than my deafness. Rosamunda will want children."

"Have you asked her?"

Adam brought his fist down on the stone wall and threw the bucket back into the well. The windlass squealed as the rope unwound, until they heard a soft splash. "*Non*! I do not intend to reveal my problem to her. You are the only one who knows, and it must stay that way."

"She's drawn to you. Perhaps it—"

Gooseflesh marched across Adam's nape. "*Non*! She will find someone else and forget me. I will speak to her brothers. Perhaps at one of father's other manors there exists a worthy knight who would make her a good husband."

Denis looked at him sadly. "The same will not likely hold true for her sister. *Dieu!* I want that woman."

Adam put a hand on his brother's shoulder. "Then woo her."

Denis inhaled deeply, wishing he had never met Paulina Lallement. The ugliness he had striven his whole life to overcome stood in sharp contrast to her beauty. "Have you seen the way she looks at me, Adam? She may be small, but she is not an aberration like me."

"She is afraid. Rosamunda confided to me that her sister did not long for freedom as she did. She has lived with fear for a long time. She considers herself a freak of nature."

Denis raked fingers through his hair. "But she is stunningly beautiful."

"She does not see it. She sees only her size."

Denis snorted. "I know the feeling."

"She needs your strength."

Denis held his arms wide, palms towards his body.

"Look at me. Why would a beautiful woman want to bed this?"

Adam poked him in the chest. "Don't give me those excuses. You have never wallowed in self-pity. You are one of the finest men I know and have much to offer a woman."

Denis gazed into the well. "You're right, but the possibility of her rejecting me is more than I can bear. I've never risked my heart before."

Watching from windows was the habit of a lifetime for Rosamunda. Paulina at first resisted her suggestion that they watch Adam and Denis practice swordplay with their men-at-arms in the courtyard. However, curiosity won out and she brought over a stool.

Most of the combatants were stripped to the waist. Rosamunda barely noticed them, her eyes fixed on Adam's white linen shirt molded to his broad chest and shoulders. He was a capable swordsman, easily disarming any challenger. His long legs gave him a distinct advantage. She grew strangely hot at the thought of kneading her fingers into his strong thighs.

It was not the first time this idea had crossed her mind. Each day in the dining hall, she sat next to him at meal times, feeling the heat from those powerful thighs. But he was careful to leave space between them.

He apparently found her unattractive, but she had a feeling there was something else.

After their exercise, Adam cranked up the bucket from the well. The brothers shared a drink as they talked.

"Perplexed," she mouthed to Paulina.

Receiving no response, she poked her sister's shoulder, startled to see drool trickling down her chin. She traced a line from the corner of her mouth. "Drooling."

Paulina looked up at her sharply, hastily wiping her mouth. "I am not."

Rosamunda shrugged. "What are they discussing?"

Red faced, Paulina got down off the stool and left the window. "Who knows?"

Rosamunda squinted, trying to watch Adam's lips, but he was too far away. It was curious how he bent his head and stared at the dwarf when he spoke, as if the smaller man was too far away to hear.

Ridiculous! Just because he's short—

She slapped her forehead with her palm. The reality was plain to see.

Adam cannot hear.

It explained the sullen anger he often exhibited, the constant frown as he strained to understand what people said. She guessed he had not been deaf long. Her brothers had hinted at some recent change in him. An accident or a malady could render a man deaf.

Adam always watched her lips carefully, not because he liked her mouth, or was truly interested in what she had to say, but because he was deaf. Her muteness was of no consequence.

Her heart leapt into her throat.

It doesn't matter that I am mute.

Paulina was mortified. Imagine drooling at the thought of

untying the leather thong that bound Sancerre's thick curly hair, and running her fingers through it.

If only she could let go of her fear and respond to his kindness, instead of behaving like a shrew. Perhaps she was more like her mother than she wanted to admit.

He was not a handsome man, but he was strong and surprisingly agile for one with such a tortured physique. He confided in her as they sat at table that he was a better cavalryman than a foot soldier, but he had held his own in the bouts of swordplay they'd watched.

She looked forward to his conversations at meal times. He was educated, well-traveled, and honorable. He had saved her life.

But his green eyes filled with longing when he looked at her, and the intensity of his gaze stole away her wits. Her body developed tinglings in surprising places. One morning, she awoke with her hand clamped firmly where it should not have been. Her already large breasts protested against the fabric of her gown whenever Denis walked into her presence. Her throat constricted and she might have been the mute sister for all she could think to say. Perhaps the smoke had made her ill.

UNDENIABLE ATTRACTION

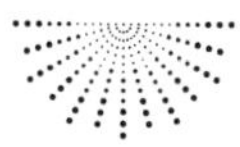

Adam decided the first official visit as his father's representative would be to the manor at Poling. The estate had changed hands several times over the years, and his father had mentioned that the current family were relatively recent occupants. Cormant had vetted them and arranged everything, but a visit from the overlord's son would not go amiss. He had delayed too long already.

He questioned his steward. "It's a Norman family, I assume?"

Cormant spread out the pertinent documents on the trestle table in the tiny Map Room. "*Oui*, Alphonse Revandel is recently retired from some prestigious position at King William Rufus' court, apparently with a generous purse from our new monarch. His references were impeccable."

Adam traced a finger over the royal seal. "Hard to fault a king, though I imagine Henry wanted to clear out many of his brother's functionaries."

Cormant chuckled. "Indeed."

"Children?"

Cormant held up three fingers. "Three, I believe. A widower with two sons and a daughter."

Adam brushed his knuckles back and forth against his cheek. "I have spoken to Vincent Lallement. He agrees we should seek a suitable husband for Rosamunda. I will ask her to accompany me. Are the Revandel sons of marriageable age?"

Cormant talked on, but Adam did not make the effort to understand, his gut churning at the thought of Rosamunda in another man's bed.

Rosamunda held the reins as she had been shown. The sweet palfrey—a gift from Adam—followed Nox out of the courtyard. Since Nox was named for the night, she deemed it clever to christen her steed Lux—light. Adam had rolled his eyes.

She loved riding. Adam declared she was a born horsewoman.

Paulina refused to leave East Preston, and Denis opted to stay with her.

Accompanying Adam to Poling was an adventure Rosamunda relished, thrilled he had asked her. She filled her lungs with fresh air, trying to put a name to the scents. There was a hint of the sea that lessened as they rode north. From time to time she caught the aroma of a certain tree, or wildflower. Denis seemed to be knowledgeable on many subjects. She would consult him regarding the names.

Then there was Adam's scent, one she recognised

every time he entered a room. Clean, wholesome, minty. She suspected that, like her brothers, he was in the habit of chewing spearmint leaves.

She was afraid she had annoyed him with endless questions about the family they were on their way to visit. Vincent and Lucien had never mentioned them. She resolved not to badger him further. It must be difficult to ride and concentrate on her lips at the same time.

They continued on for a while in silence, before Adam glanced over at her. "You are too quiet, miss."

He flushed when the inappropriateness of his words dawned on him.

She shrugged, drawing a finger across her lips.

He frowned. "Why?"

Her heart raced. Dare she reveal she had guessed his secret? She pointed one finger at him, then two to her eyes. "Watch the road."

He shifted his weight in the saddle. "It's an easy path, completely flat. The only turn we make is west at Angmering. The manor house there is one of *oncle* Hugh's."

The uncomfortable silence continued. The mention of her hero's name gave her courage. She touched Adam's arm, wanting him to look her in the face. He turned his head quickly, his eyes narrowed. She swallowed hard, pointed to him, then covered her ears, shaking her head. "You cannot hear."

She had trusted it would be a relief to him that she knew, and that it mattered not a whit, but he clenched his jaw and scowled. "You have guessed correctly. I am deaf."

He urged Nox forward to ride ahead, ending their conversation.

Adam took several deep breaths in an effort to drown out the thudding in his ears. What irony that a deaf man heard his own heartbeat.

A cruel fate had brought him Rosamunda, the one woman who cared naught that he was deaf. And for her, who better to take as husband than a man unable to hear?

It would appear they were destined to be together. She no doubt believed it. There was an undeniable attraction between them. She made no secret of her affection for him, and he loved her smile, her curiosity, her untamed hair, her body, though he was incapable of fulfilling a woman's deepest physical need.

His throat tightened as the wind carried her perfume to his nostrils, the elusive scent that was pure Rosamunda. It reminded him of something he couldn't name.

Her anger burned into his back. She probably believed her revelation had caused his rude reaction.

He toyed with the notion of returning to East Preston. The tenants had not been informed of his visit, but he dreaded the moment when the astute Rosamunda would inevitably deduce that the journey was in part to ascertain if either Revandel son might make her a suitable husband.

She would believe he disdained her. Nothing was further from the truth. The love he felt was pure, from the heart.

Rosamunda had trusted freedom would bring her nothing but joy, but now she felt slightly faint and nauseous after

Adam's rejection. Revealing what was in one's heart was evidently not the best course of action in the real world.

She had assumed he would be relieved, but he had not told her he was deaf. The thought must have occurred to him that his affliction would not lessen her regard, and might bring them closer.

She felt more alone and isolated than during her confinement. She wished she had not accompanied Adam —though he had been somewhat insistent. Better to have stayed with Paulina. Perhaps her sister had the right of it. She would have to guard her feelings more carefully.

She had fancied Adam was attracted to her—how foolish. He was from a rich and powerful family, a strikingly handsome man any woman would want, despite his deafness. She had quickly forgotten that her own mother had rejected her because of her muteness. There was no reason for Adam de Montbryce to feel any differently.

The sooner Kingston Gorse was rebuilt, the faster she and Paulina might return to the only home they had ever known. Vincent and Lucien would protect them.

INSTANT DISLIKE

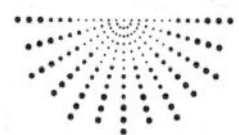

Letyce Revandel pouted as she strolled listlessly through the garden of Poling Manor with her maidservant, a kerchief guarding her sensitive nose against the ragweed pollen.

The sound of horses approaching caught her attention. Visitors at last.

Her father had buried her alive in this godforsaken place in Sussex, far from the court life she enjoyed in Westminster. He berated her endlessly about the need to marry, but she had no intention of tying herself to one man.

If her father became aware how many *beaux* pursued her, he might die of an apoplexy. And the gullible fool believed her twin brothers were saints to be emulated. He knew nothing of the money Winrod and Dareau had frittered away dicing, wenching and drinking.

Bored to death at Poling, she hurried to see who was arriving, ignoring the clucking censure of the prissy maidservant hired by her father.

Her spirits rose at the sight of a tall, dark-haired knight mounted atop an impressive black stallion, in his wake a squadron of men-at-arms.

Belatedly, she noticed a blonde woman riding alongside the knight. No competition there. The girl was tall and pretty, but certainly nothing to compare with Letyce's lush curves. And her hair! What an unruly mess. Perhaps his sister.

Letyce thrust out her breasts and fluttered her eyelashes as the knight reined his horse to a halt in front of her. He dismounted with graceful ease. She had never seen such long, powerful legs. Her heart skipped a beat as desire spiralled in her belly.

The knight bowed. "*Demoiselle* Revandel?"

She nodded demurely. "I am Letyce Revandel."

"I am Adam de Montbryce. My father, Antoine, is the overlord of Poling Manor. I have come to meet your father. Is he at home?"

He stared at her mouth, obviously already falling under her spell. "He is, my lord de Montbryce." She shoved her maidservant. "Violette will announce your arrival."

The woman sulked and glared, but went off to do her mistress's bidding.

Letyce held out her hand. "I will accompany you into the house, if you wish."

Montbryce bent to graze a kiss on her knuckles. His warm lips sent a shiver of anticipation up her thighs.

He proffered his arm. She put her hand atop it, relishing his solid strength, tempted to knead her fingers into the muscles. She smiled coyly and took a step towards the house.

But he turned to the girl standing by the palfrey she

had ridden. "Letyce Revandel, may I present Rosamunda Lallement, a neighbor of mine."

Good, the chit is not his wife.

The girl bowed her head slightly and mouthed something incoherent. Obviously an imbecile.

Montbryce offered his free arm to the blonde. "She is mute," he explained.

It took enormous effort for Letyce to suppress the snort of laughter that bubbled up in her throat.

Rosamunda took an instant dislike to the red-haired woman who greeted them. She had learned the word *harlot* from her brothers' descriptions of some women at court, and this Letyce Revandel fit the word perfectly. At first sight of Adam, she had quickly dropped the kerchief that had covered her face.

Her sneer upon learning of Rosamunda's muteness was proof enough that Paulina was right. They would encounter nothing but prejudice outside the safety of their home. She wished she had stayed at East Preston.

The harlot's eyes had popped out of her head upon espying Adam. Rosamunda saw through her thinly-veiled attempts to keep his attention.

Jealousy roared through her. She wanted to tear Letyce Revandel limb from limb. What was the other word Lucien was fond of? Ah, yes. The *hore* leaned into Adam as they walked, ignoring her completely. Rosamunda put her free hand over her ear to block out the swish of Letyce's skirts against Adam's leg.

She was older than he was. Certainly older than Rosamunda.

His voice caught her off guard. "Are you ill, Rosamunda? Does your ear pain you?"

He seemed genuinely concerned, but her wits failed her. She took her hand away from her ear, shaking her head as she gazed at the ground. He must not see the tears welling in her eyes.

Adam understood Letyce's blatant signals. There was a time his male ego, not to mention his shaft, would have risen to the challenge, but now her forward behavior left him cold. Compared to the innocent Rosamunda, this woman was a harlot.

He had managed to understand most of her constant chatter by concentrating closely on her lips. It was important he establish good relations with these new occupants.

It grieved him that Letyce Revandel had greeted Rosamunda rudely. She would probably switch off her suffocating charm when she discovered he suffered an impairment.

As they neared the main doorway, two young men appeared, twins by the look of them. Adam judged they were younger than their sister, but not by much. They had Letyce's red hair, but she had been spared the prominent nose they had evidently inherited. The feature, while not rendering them ugly, robbed them of any chance to be considered handsome.

They were town boys, tall and lanky, but lacking the muscled body of a knight. He suspected they did not spend time practicing swordplay and other military pursuits. The only weapons in evidence were daggers tucked into the belts of the identical red velvet tunics they wore.

He'd a mind to forget sizing them up as potential husband material for Rosamunda, but Denis had taught him that looks were sometimes deceiving. He would reserve judgement.

Both youths ignored him, their eyes raking over Rosamunda.

Her hand tightened on his arm as she leaned into him. He relished the swell of her breast pressed against his bicep, but he bristled at the brazen way the Revandels looked at her. Possessiveness twisted under his ribs.

Scowling, Letyce drew their attention away from Rosamunda. "*Milord* de Montbryce, may I present my brothers, Winrod and Dareau Revandel."

Both men ignored him, until Letyce remarked that he was the son of their overlord. Then they became effusive, bowing ridiculously low, as if he were King Henry. The knot in his belly tightened.

"*Milord* de Montbryce," one of them gushed. "Dareau and I are your humble servants. Had we known you were coming—"

Dareau shouldered his brother out of the way, reaching for Rosamunda's hand. "And who is this lovely lady?"

Adam gripped the hilt of his sword, bracing for another insult. "Rosamunda Lallement is from Kingston Gorse. The manor house burned and she and her sister are staying at East Preston while her home is rebuilt."

Smiling broadly, Rosamunda withdrew her hand, but to his relief said nothing.

Clever girl. The Revandel brothers would not recognize the false smile for what it was. Rosamunda was a quick study in the ways of the world. For a brief moment, he pitied whichever of these men might become her husband, but pushed the unpleasant thought away.

Letyce's fingernails dug into his arm. She huffed impatiently as she pulled him away from her brothers and into the house.

Alphonse Revandel was a portly little man, who seemed to bear no resemblance to any of his children. Adam wondered about the dead woman who had been their mother. Perhaps she had been the one with the hooked beak.

When Letyce introduced Adam to her father, Revandel's face reddened and he too bowed low. These people had supposedly taken an active part in court life, yet they seemed to have no sense of a person's rank and the appropriate level of respect to show.

"*Milord* de Montbryce! What an honor! If we had known—"

Adam unhooked Letyce's talons from his arm and raised a hand to interrupt his host. "It was a last minute decision to ride this way," he lied. "Rosamunda has seen little of the countryside, despite having lived all her life at Kingston Gorse."

As the initial pleasantries of introductions progressed it became impossible for Rosamunda to remain silent. She mouthed a greeting which Adam understood perfectly.

Revandel and his sons gaped, exchanging frowning glances.

Letyce snorted.

Adam strove to keep his temper. It was fortunate Denis and Paulina had not accompanied them. "Rosamunda is mute, but she understands everything we say. In time you will learn to understand her equally well."

Winrod swaggered forward, standing too close to Rosamunda. He fingered a strand of her hair. "Mute, eh? What a boon for your husband."

Rosamunda wanted to spit in Winrod Revandel's face. Surely this was not how young men were supposed to behave. It brought to mind a ginger cat she had seen toying with a mouse at East Preston. Adam tensed beside her, his jaw clenched. She had sensed his discomfort since the moment they arrived at Poling.

He put a hand on Winrod's chest. "Have a care. *Demoiselle* Lallement is under my protection."

Rosamunda liked the sound of that. She hoped they would not stay long with these unpleasant people.

Winrod stepped back, but the predatory glint remained in his eyes. The smile left his face when his brother elbowed him out of the way. Dareau brushed his lips over Rosamunda's knuckles before she could grab her hand away. "You must forgive Winrod. He has no notion of manners as practiced out in the country."

Manners were manners no matter where a person dwelt. She resolved never to go to King Henry's court.

HARLOT

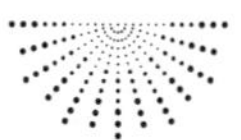

Later in the afternoon, Letyce turned her face away from her pitiful father, wishing she had refused the summons to his solar. His breath always reeked of the onions he was fond of. The whole chamber stank of the obnoxious bulb. She never understood how her mother had borne it.

"Mark my words, daughter, and heed me well. This is your opportunity. Adam de Montbryce will make a fine husband. His family is powerful here and in Normandie, and wealthy beyond imagining. God has smiled on us today."

Letyce was tempted to provoke the usual argument, but her father was right for once. Wealth and power were things she craved. Marriage to Adam would bring her both. He was certainly attractive, no doubt an excellent lover. When she tired of him, there were always discreet liaisons to be found.

She put a conspiratorial hand on her father's arm. "He

seems taken with the *muette* for some unfathomable reason."

Her father winked. "Leave her to me. She will make the ideal wife for Winrod, or Dareau."

Letyce smiled. "Or they might share her?"

Alphonse Revandel's eyes widened, his face reddening. "Share? But—"

She had gone too far. No use planting suspicions in her father's mind regarding her own proclivities. The fool might disinherit her, or worse, send her to a nunnery. "I'm jesting, Papa."

He let out a long slow breath, rubbing his hands together. "'Tis settled then. I have arranged for you to sit beside Montbryce, and the *muette* is between my two handsome sons."

Letyce rolled her eyes as she followed her father into the hall for the evening meal.

Rising panic threatened to cut off air to Rosamunda's lungs. Her belly ached. Adam was seated at the other end of the head table, the first time he had not been at her side since the rescue. To make matters worse, the terrible twosome had her hemmed in. Winrod sidled along the bench to press his thigh against hers. Dareau followed suit. She felt the heat of their bodies—it made her blood run cold.

She had not been given a trencher. Dareau stuffed a large piece of venison into his mouth, then cut more from his portion and offered it to her. Winrod did the same. She had been told men only shared a trencher with their wives, or the women they were betrothed to. The idea of marriage to either of these competitive idiots had bile rising in her throat.

She shook her head, wrinkling her nose.

Winrod elbowed her arm. "Queasy? Probably the journey."

Dareau winked, sticking out his belly. "Unless she's in the family way."

Rosamunda gasped. She did not want to embarrass Adam by jumping to her feet in protest, but—

She looked down the table, seeking his eyes. He was gazing at Letyce's lips, seemingly enthralled. The harlot pressed close to him.

Winrod touched her arm, waving the gamy venison in front of her. "You must eat something."

The room tilted. She covered her mouth and leapt to her feet, hoping to reach the outdoors before she retched.

She did not make it. The last thing she recalled was the disgusted grimace of the serving woman over whose shoes she vomited. Strong arms caught her before she swooned.

Frustration tightened Letyce's jaw as she watched Adam race from the table in time to catch the mute woman when she fainted.

Montbryce seemed fascinated with Letyce's mouth, intent on her words, yet it had been difficult to get him to respond to her advances. She had touched his arm, pressed her body close to his, even put her hand on his thigh, closer to his male parts than might be deemed proper, so there was no mistaking her intent.

All for naught.

He had pointedly leaned away, brushing her hand from his thigh as if he had been burned by a red hot coal. Perhaps, he was the sort who preferred men, though he was a far cry from the fops at court.

Some men were shy with women. She could help him overcome that.

Obviously, her brothers had failed to secure the mute's attention. She would make it clear that if they wanted help getting out of the financial morass they wallowed in before their father found out, they would have to do their part.

The Lallement girl might only be Adam's neighbor but he evidently took his protection of her seriously, though she had a feeling there was more to it.

LETYCE'S CHAMBER

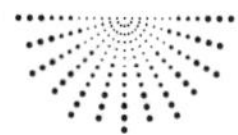

Heart racing, Adam followed a maidservant, Rosamunda cradled to his chest. He was appalled when the servant pointed to a meagre pallet in the corner of Letyce's room, far from the hearth. He placed her on the luxurious bed instead. She was pale, too pale.

"Fetch water," he instructed the servant, smoothing Rosamunda's wild hair off her face. "Wake up, Rosa."

Relief washed over him when her long eyelashes fluttered open.

She smiled and touched his cheek. "Adam."

He pressed her hand against his face. She felt clammy.

She frowned, licking her dry lips.

He put his palm against her forehead. "Are you ill, *ma chère*? You may have a fever."

The servant brought water and he helped her sip from the tumbler.

A tear trickled down her cheek. She patted a spot above her left breast.

He arched his brows. "Afraid? Why?"

She squirmed, avoiding his gaze.

He put his fingers on her chin and turned her face gently to him. "Were the Revandel brothers rude to you?"

She shook her head, but the corners of her mouth edged down.

Adam fisted his hands. This was not going well. His first impression of the twins was not positive, but if Rosamunda became better acquainted with them—

"I am sorry we were seated apart. I was hoping you might make new friends. I will not always be there to sit beside you."

A ragged breath shuddered through her. He longed to kiss away the pain flickering in her eyes. If only things were different, but it was no use pining for the unattainable. He determined to be firm with her. "I want you to try to like at least one of them. It's a good family."

Her eyes widened. "Why?"

He took her hands in his. "You are of an age to marry. We must search for a husband for you."

She tore her hands away and plunged her face into the bolster.

He put his hand on her trembling shoulder, but she refused to look at him. He did not hear Letyce enter the chamber, but, suddenly, she was at his side, a look of disdain on her pouty face.

She fluttered her eyelashes at him. "It's not seemly for you to be in my chamber," she breathed, thrusting her breasts close to his face as she leaned over the bed, her hand again on his thigh. "You must return to the hall. I will take care of the invalid. Poor thing."

He was reluctant to leave Rosamunda with this harlot, but she was right, although he sensed her chamber was exactly where she wanted him. She would experience a disappointment if he remained. But then he risked discovery of his secret, and Letyce Revandel was the last person whose suspicions he wanted to arouse.

He came to his feet and smoothed his hand over Rosamunda's hair. "*À demain*," he whispered.

Letyce kept the smile plastered on her face until she was sure Adam was well on his way back to the hall, then she grabbed Rosamunda's hair. "Get out of my bed. How dare you."

The *muette's* face contorted as she struggled to get free, but Letyce held firm, dragging the freak to the pallet. "You should be in the stables with the other dumb animals. But I suppose I will have to put up with having you here."

She shoved Rosamunda on to the pallet. "Do not move from there, and don't make a sound." She scoffed. "Oh, silly me. You're incapable of doing so anyway."

As she swept through the doorway, she turned to the maidservant lurking in the shadows. "Get clean linens and a new bolster for my bed—now!"

Rosamunda lay trembling, curled up in a tight ball as she watched the maidservant change the linens. She wished she was back in her comfortable bed, listening to Paulina's soft snoring. She ought to have stood up to the horrible Revandel woman. It galled that she had let herself be intimidated and was certain Denis de Sancerre never allowed himself to be bullied.

Better to sleep in the stables. It would be warmer, and probably a good deal safer with Nox and Lux.

As soon as the servant left, she draped the thin blanket around her shoulders and tiptoed from the chamber.

THE STABLE

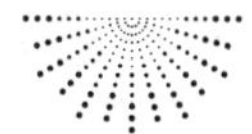

Nox snorted, waking Rosamunda from a fitful sleep in the warm hayloft. She stiffened. Something had caught the stallion's attention. A voice. Outside the stables.

Adam.

He had come to see to his horse before retiring. Her heart filled with gladness. She was about to leap up and thrust open the shutters when another voice intruded.

Letyce Revandel.

Rosamunda threw off her blanket and listened.

"I must tend my horse." Impatience edged Adam's words.

Rosamunda imagined Letyce's pout as she replied, "Can't you spend a few minutes with me? This is the first chance we have had to be alone. I fear you are ignoring me."

It was dark. Unless they stood close together and he could see her lips clearly, Adam would not have heard the *hore's* words.

Listening was not enough. Rosamunda had to see what they were doing. She crept forward on all fours, hoping she sounded like a horse rustling dry straw.

She had left the shutters of the loft open a crack in the stifling air of an unusually hot early September that had accumulated under the rafters. Holding her breath, she peeked through the narrow opening.

Adam stood in front of the stable, frowning. Letyce blocked his way, leaning against the door. Her hands were behind her arched back, her breasts thrust forward, head cocked to one side. "Please, Adam."

He folded his arms. "I am here on family matters. I prefer—"

She seized his hands and pressed them to her breasts. "Feel how much I want you."

Rosamunda's own nipples hardened as anger surged through her. How dare this *strumpet*—another of Vincent's favorite words—throw herself at her champion?

To her relief, Adam dropped his hands quickly. "*Non*, Mistress Revandel. I will not be deterred from my mission here. I am my father's representative. What you suggest is not proper."

"*Proper* does not interest me," she retorted, grasping his hips and thrusting her own towards him. "I want you."

Rosamunda gasped in shock as Letyce pressed her most intimate part to Adam's body.

He shoved her away, his face contorted in anger.

Letyce slapped him. "What kind of man are you? A eunuch? Or do men interest you more? Should I speak to my brothers, perhaps?"

Rosamunda had never heard the word *unuk*, but

doubted it was good. Why would Adam be interested in the Revandel brothers? The woman was daft.

Letyce stormed off, leaving Adam alone, staring at the moon. The look of abject hopelessness on his face brought tears to her eyes. He stood in silence for long minutes before pulling open the door to the stables.

Nox nickered as Adam approached.

"Good lad," he crooned, as the horse nuzzled him. "You're always happy to see me."

The stallion raised his head and snorted, stomping the dirt with one hoof.

"What's wrong, boy? What do you hear?"

Gooseflesh prickled Adam's nape. He was not alone in the stables. "Who's there?"

A shaft of moonlight shone on dust motes drifting down between the planked floorboards of the loft. He gripped the hilt of his sword. "Show yourself," he growled.

To his surprise, Rosamunda appeared at the edge of the loft, arms folded tightly across her breasts, straw poking out of her hair. She was studying her feet, swaying from side to side. He was tempted to laugh, but she looked bereft. It touched his heart. "What are you doing up there? Come down."

She kept her eyes averted, shaking her head.

An ugly suspicion crept into his thoughts. "Why are you not in Letyce's chamber?"

She pointed to the straw behind her.

"You cannot sleep alone in the stable."

She glanced at him briefly, then backed away into the shadows of the loft.

He peered into the dark stable, searching for a ladder. Espying one at the back of the stable, he slapped Nox's hindquarters, then strode over to it.

The climb to her hiding place resurrected a memory of pursuing a giggling wench up a rickety ladder in a similar hayloft. They had passed a pleasant afternoon pleasuring each other. His heart filled with regret—for the past, for everything he had lost. Loneliness swept over him.

Rosamunda crouched in a corner, shrouded in the blanket, eyeing him nervously as he reached the loft. Dismayed that she feared him, he held out a hand. "Come. Noblewomen do not sleep in stables. You have a bed in Letyce's chamber."

She shook her head vehemently.

"What has Letyce done? Was she cruel to you?"

Rosamunda glanced up at him sharply, the moonlight illuminating her tears. She grimaced, thrusting a clenched fist out from the blanket. "I hate her."

The determined jut of her chin convinced him that, short of wrestling her into the house, there would be no getting her back there. He would not want to spend the night in Letyce's chamber either.

He held out his hand, indicating the pile of straw. "May I?"

She wiped away a tear and shuffled to make more space for him.

He sat beside her, his back to the wooden wall, knees bent. Her heat warmed his bicep, yet she shivered. He put his arm around her shoulders, drawing her to his body. "Let me warm you," he whispered.

She remained stiff and unyielding, until he brushed a kiss on the top of her head. With a sigh, she melted into him. Holding a woman again elated him, calmed his raging heart. He could not bed her, but he could offer comfort. Being alone together was improper, though it felt right, as if she belonged in his arms.

But the planking was hard, his arse going numb. "Let's gather straw into bedding and lie down. We cannot sleep like this."

She put a hand on his chest, her eyes full of uncertainty.

He came to his feet. "*Oui*, Rosamunda, I want to stay here with you. Will you share your blanket with me?"

Rosamunda didn't need a blanket. She was on fire, perhaps because of the heat of the night, or a lingering illness. Every muscle in her body screamed to stretch, to luxuriate in the bed of straw like a queen on her couch.

"We won't require this," Adam said as he rolled the blanket into a pillow, tucking it under her head.

Rosamunda had learned to convey her feelings to her brothers and sister, despite her muteness, but couldn't explain to Adam how it felt to be enfolded in his embrace, held tight against his chest, his hips and thighs pressed to hers. They were new emotions.

Words were impossible. She nuzzled his neck and brushed a kiss in the hollow of his throat. He let out a long slow breath, playing with her hair.

"Rosamunda," he whispered.

"Adam," she mouthed, aware he could not see her lips.

She drifted into sleep, smugly content he seemed happy to lie with her, and had soundly rejected the harlot.

Adam dozed, more at peace than he had been for a long while. It felt good to hold a woman in his arms, a woman who cared for him, wanted him. It was bittersweet. As she slumbered innocently, cradled to his chest, her hips rocked against him, her body betraying a desire she would have denied or misunderstood when awake.

Rosamunda had never made any secret of her feelings for him. She was too unschooled to hide her obvious attraction, but he doubted she understood the physical aspects of her emotions. She had not had the benefit of a mother's advice and assurance. Were she to awaken at this moment, she would likely not be aware of the curious absence of hard male flesh pressed against her.

He loved the way her body nestled into him, her breath cool on his throat. He had saved her life, the life of a beautiful, intelligent young woman. She trusted him. She was his to safeguard. He rocked his hips gently, matching the slow rhythm of her movements. She licked her lips, purring as she stretched languidly against him.

She would be mortified if she knew what was happening, but he eased her away to brush the backs of his fingers over a pebbled nipple.

It was tempting to put his mouth on her, just for a moment. He bent his head to flick the tip of his tongue over the nipple. The purr became a growl, the rocking more insistent. Her body warmed as her breathing quickened.

He suckled, drawing the nipple into his mouth through the fabric. She writhed, throwing one leg over his thigh, the rocking urgent now.

He should stop. This was no way to introduce a young maiden to the ecstasy of what he had no doubt would be her first experience of arousal.

But she curled her fingers into his hair.

Was she still asleep, or had she awakened?

He glanced up at her face. Her eyes were closed, her lips open, inviting. He had an urge to thrust his tongue into the welcoming warmth of her mouth, but she firmly pressed his head back to her breast.

He suckled hard, elated as bliss carried her rigid body over the edge. He hiked up her shift, lost to the moment. He parted her legs and carefully slid a finger into her warm, wet sheath. The pulsating muscles clenched on him. He edged in another finger, his free arm cradling her to his chest. Her head fell back as her body arched again.

His pounding heart might burst. He was in love with this amazing woman. What had happened between them was the most emotionally satisfying physical encounter he had ever had.

But she would have no memory of it.

As her breathing slowed, he withdrew his fingers, savoring the scent of female arousal. He rearranged her clothing, then glanced up at her face.

Green eyes, rendered all the more startling by moonlight, stared at him.

NAMING CATS

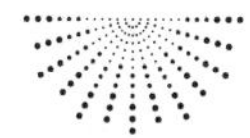

At East Preston, Denis had no doubt Paulina was avoiding him. She rarely left the bedchamber. He often caught a glimpse of her at the window, gazing out.

He racked his brain for a solution to overcoming her fears. If anyone understood the isolation of being different it was him. The woman was as much a prisoner here as at Kingston Gorse, but now she was in solitary confinement. She ate in her chamber. Seated alone at the head table in the dining hall, he played with his food, his normally robust appetite gone.

He made up a thousand excuses to pass by her window. It was within sight of the well. He adopted a routine of stopping there for a long gulp of water before glancing up. Occasionally, he caught her watching before she ducked away.

Cats abounded at East Preston, a legacy of the days when the property had been infested with rats. Denis paid them no attention. If asked, he probably would say he did not like cats, though he grudgingly admired their independence.

One hot day, a brindled kitten rubbed itself against his legs as he drank from the dipper. Chuckling, he bent to scratch its ears. "My stature matters not to you, eh *mignonne*?"

The kitten purred loudly, its little pointed tail rigid as it pressed against him. It was too skinny. "Where is your *Maman*? Is she not feeding you?"

Soulful yellow-green eyes looked up at him as a pitiful, high pitched meow emerged from its tiny pink mouth. He picked it up, likely the first time he had ever done such a thing in his life. The kitten flexed its claws, but did not struggle. It purred loudly as he held it to his chest. With gut-wrenching clarity, it dawned on him this was the runt of a litter, left to fend for itself.

He swallowed the lump in his throat and looked up at Paulina's window.

She stood open-mouthed, her gaze fixed on the kitten in his arms.

Paulina had seen several of the animals people at East Preston referred to as cats, but none as tiny as the one clinging to Denis' chest. It was small, helpless. The dwarf could probably squash it with one hand, yet the way he stroked it, nuzzling its ear, brought tears to her eyes.

Those arms offered warmth and comfort, if she gave him a chance. Her fear was perplexing. A future hiding in her chamber held no promise.

Better to be dead.

She was sure the gentle dwarf cuddling the cat had sometimes wished for death. Yet, he had made a life, one he seemed to relish, though she had noticed a recent melancholy.

He was still at the well, gazing at her window, but the cat was struggling to be free.

Struggling to be free.

She went to the door, opened it, took a deep breath, and stepped out into the hallway.

Denis took several deep breaths, hoping to calm his raging heart when he saw Paulina walking towards him, her dainty feet raising puffs of dust from the sun-baked earth of the courtyard.

The kitten squirmed, mewling loudly, but he held it firm. This scrap of fur might be his one chance.

Paulina stood in front of him, her gaze fixed on the kitten.

"Do you want to hold her?"

Her eyes darted from the kitten to him and back again. "Is it a cat?"

He lifted the animal by the scruff of the neck. It cried its indignation, its claws extended. She stepped back.

"*Oui*, but don't be afraid. It's a baby cat. A kitten. I think her mother has abandoned her."

Paulina gasped and reached out her arms. "Kitten," she whispered. "Abandoned."

"Lean back on the wall of the well, and I'll put her in

your arms. Careful, she might scratch. Tickle her ears. Kittens love that. Hold the scruff of her neck like this at first. She'll get used to you."

She held her breath as he passed the animal. The kitten quickly gave up its protests, settling into the swell of Paulina's breasts, narrowing its eyes as she stroked its head. "She's making a noise."

The innocently seductive smile that accompanied this observation sent blood rushing to Denis' groin. "It's called purring."

I'd be purring too if my head was resting on those lovely globes.

He sought inspiration to make her smile again. "You should choose a name for her."

Naming cats! His brothers would suspect lunacy.

She frowned, pursing her lips. "She's many beautiful colors, golden brown, white, black."

Suddenly, her frown intensified. "How can you tell it's a she?"

He coughed as his erection bucked. In Normandie he had never heard of a male brindled cat, but perhaps in England, things were different. "We can check."

He took the kitten from her and cupped it in his hand, lifting its tail, then parting the fur below its belly. It wriggled, clawing at the air. No little penis or *couilles*, thank God. He might have erupted in his leggings. He breathed a sigh of relief. "She does not have male parts."

Paulina looked at him curiously as he handed the kitten back to her. "Male parts?"

Dieu! How had this discussion come about? The woman had two brothers for God's sake.

He swallowed hard, feeling his face redden. "Males have male parts, whereas females have—female parts."

What an idiot!

She nodded thoughtfully, obviously interested in learning something new. But she blushed as she added, "Just as I have breasts, and you don't."

The light touch of her palm on her breast undid him. "*Ou—oui*," he stammered, running his finger over the kitten's belly. When our friend here bears kittens you will see little—"

The word stuck in his throat. Instead, he murmured, "Teats. We call them teats on cats."

"Teats," she repeated in a whisper, fluttering her eyelashes innocently. "Why will she have teats?"

Denis wished they were abed so he could lovingly stroke her breasts and discover the color of her nipples as he demonstrated how babies suckled. "A mother cat's body makes milk for her kittens. They drink it from the teats."

She looked down at her breasts. Her nipples were straining against the fabric of her *bliaut*. "Is it the same for people?"

Christ! If ever he did sire children he would make sure they were better prepared for the world than this vulnerable innocent. He took a deep breath to steady his voice. "It is."

She remained thoughtfully silent for a few minutes, watching him tickle under the kitten's chin. "She likes to be petted. I have much to learn from you, *milord* de Sancerre."

If only...

"Paulina, it would be my honor to assist you as you

make your way in a new world that can be difficult at times. But, please call me Denis. *Milord* de Sancerre was my late, unlamented father."

She kissed the kitten's head. "You did not love your father?"

He shrugged. "I never met him. I was born after his death, but my mother assures me he would have done away with me at birth."

She grimaced. "My mother wanted to do away with Rosamunda and me."

It was joy to converse with a woman and not have to crane his neck to look up. He put his fingers under her chin, gently coaxing her to turn her eyes to him. "That would have been a great loss for the world."

She blinked away tears. "I will take my kitten to the kitchen. What do they eat? She reminds me of a ring my father wore. He told me once the stone was a topaz. I will name her that. It was a beautiful ring."

"Perfect! Topaz it is," he declared, his mind full of her wistful face, not the name she had chosen. "I will accompany you, if I may."

Denis and Paulina strolled often through the herb gardens of East Preston in the ensuing days, Topaz their constant companion. Hortense brought an old satchel, sliced off the flap and padded the bottom with straw. Paulina wore the strap across her body, the kitten riding inside like one born to royalty.

"Topaz grows fatter and lazier by the day," Paulina remarked one afternoon.

"She enjoys the cool leather of her carriage. These last few days of September have brought some relief from the heat, but for a kitten, it's still hot."

Paulina turned nervously to listen to far-off voices, tightening her grip on Denis' arm. He put his hand atop hers. "No cause for alarm. Laborers are bringing in the harvest."

There was much to learn. "Har-vest?"

"The fields here are fertile. In the spring, they plant seeds that grow with the rains and summer's warmth. In the autumn, they reap the fruits of their labors. Then, here in the south where the climate is warm, they sow the seeds for the spring crop."

She had eaten apples and pears. "I like fruit."

Denis chuckled softly. "Most fruit grows on trees. Montbryce Castle in Normandie, family seat of Adam's family, boasts an apple orchard that produces the finest apple brandy in the whole duchy. The rewards here in the spring are barley, vetches, oats, peas, and beans, and in the autumn wheat and rye. Cormant sells some of the wheat and rye, and the rest is used for bread. There is also flax for linen, and I believe one of the fields yields hemp which we use to make ropes."

"And the barley?"

He laughed. "For making a thirst-quenching brew—beer."

"And the oats?"

"Brevis and Nox love their oats, as does Rosamunda's new palfrey."

She thought of her sister then, finding it odd she had not missed her for several days. Denis had filled her time and her mind. She looked forward to the hours they spent together. He was patient, kind, and understanding. Because he was her height, she did not have to crane her neck to speak to him. She did not feel beneath him. They looked into each other's eyes when they talked.

Adam had declared Rosamunda a natural horsewoman. Paulina was terrified to go near a horse, though the reason eluded her. "I hope Adam and Rosamunda are faring well at Poling. I wish I had the courage to ride. I am a coward."

Denis took her hand. "You must not believe that. You and I are small in stature. Most horses tower over us. I am not afraid because I have been riding since I was a child, but I can understand your fear."

They walked in silence for a while until they came to the edge of the fields. "Are you a farmer, Denis?"

He grimaced. "*Non, ma petite*, I am a warrior, a cavalry officer. But noblemen interested in the prosperity of their lands must understand farming."

"Like what?"

"Well, the sowing of the fields is on a three year cycle. Every field is sown for two straight years, and left fallow for the third."

"What does fallow mean?"

"Nothing is planted there. This allows the land to rest, so it can produce more next time. Also, if you plant wheat in a field one year, the next year you plant something else."

"Why?"

Denis smiled. "Land is like us. We get tired of the same old thing over and over. Do you understand?"

She snorted. "I do! Rosamunda and I grew bored and cross-eyed doing nothing but needlework."

Suddenly, she wrinkled her nose. "What a horrible smell!"

He pointed to a pile of muck. "Over there. It's manure, from the pigs and chickens. After they finish the harvest the laborers will spread it on the fields. It's good for them."

Another mystery solved. "That's what Vincent meant by muck-spreading."

Rosamunda was right, there were many interesting things to learn in the outside world. "Do they grow flowers here at East Preston? My mother grew roses."

He furrowed his brow. "I don't believe so."

It was a disappointment. "I love roses. My brothers used to filch a few for me. When they faded, I used the petals and rosehips for all kinds of things."

Denis turned to look at her. "If I had my own lands, I would plant roses for you, acres and acres of them."

"These are not your lands?"

"They belong to my stepfather, Antoine. He holds sway over many properties. Something will come to me, either when he dies—or when I marry."

Paulina's world had consisted of chambers in the attic of Kingston Gorse. It was difficult to conceive of someone owning many properties in far-flung places. She gazed around. "Would you want East Preston?"

He shook his head. "*Non*, Adam wants East Preston."

This was confusing. Vincent and Lucien had said Adam was the oldest son who would inherit Belisle Castle. "I thought Adam was heir to his father's castle?"

Denis turned away abruptly. A chill swept over her. She had said something wrong. But what? "I am mistaken. I'm sorry. I have confused the tale."

Denis turned back to her, his face bleak. "There has been a change in the succession. Adam's brother Mathieu will take over Belisle."

It was on the tip of her tongue to ask why, but he took his leave without further ado.

REVELATIONS

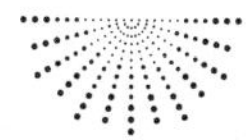

Adam stopped breathing. There was no censure in Rosamunda's startled gaze, but she had evidently awakened at some point during his pleasuring. She took a deep breath, smiled, and fell back to sleep, cuddling against him.

He dozed, strangely content, contemplating the possibility of taking her to wife. He had never felt as close to a woman, never been filled with this strong urge to protect, this overwhelming rush of possessiveness.

But he would have to be honest with her, make it clear there would never be children. He shifted uncomfortably. It was one thing to admit he was deaf, quite another to divulge his male problem. She might consider him less of a man.

Locked away her whole life, she was likely ignorant of what went on in the bedchamber between men and women. She may not know how children were created. Perhaps if he kept her ignorant, she would never become aware of what she did not have.

But then he would be imprisoning her as surely as her parents had.

He barely knew this young woman who slumbered trustingly in his arms, even after he had acted in an untrustworthy manner. He had taken advantage, but only to bring her pleasure. It had brought him immense pleasure to arouse her.

If he confided in her, she might not guard his confidences if she did not agree to marry him.

Dawn broke suddenly, its brightness heralding another warm day. Rosamunda yawned and stretched her arms above her head. She opened her eyes. His heart turned over in his chest. She would probably despise him for what he had done.

She smiled, the lazy, satisfied smile a woman might bestow on her lover. He basked in its warmth. He opened his mouth, but she touched her fingertip to his lips, then to hers. "Hush."

He sat up, drawing her on to his lap, and kissed her lips softly. She locked her arms around his neck, pressing her breasts to his chest. A need that had nothing to do with lust flooded his body. He nibbled her bottom lip, whispering her name.

Her lips parted. He put his hand behind her head and flicked his tongue into her mouth. She opened wider and sucked him. The low growl emanating from her throat echoed in his ears. She reached for his hand and put it on her breast.

He withdrew it quickly. "*Non*, Rosamunda, we must talk."

She shook her head and put his hand firmly back on her breast.

He brushed his thumb over the distended nipple. She arched her back, humming, beaming a radiant smile. He read her lips. "I like that."

He chuckled. "I know you do. I like it too. Your breasts are beautiful."

Her eyes widened. She put a fingertip on his chest. "I like you."

It was suddenly difficult to breathe. "I like you, Rosamunda, but we must talk."

Rosamunda did not want to talk, she wanted to touch, to be touched. She did not know where the wanton urges had come from, but she liked them. It did not feel wanton with Adam. It felt right.

She hoped his desire to talk meant he would profess his love, ask her to be his wife. Her dream of being wedded to a member of the noble Montbryce family might yet come true.

"You are aware I am deaf," Adam began.

She flicked her fingers in the air as if shooing a pesky fly and shrugged. She pointed to her mouth. "And I am mute. Do you care?"

Relief washed over her as he shook his head.

He stared at her for long moments, then exhaled loudly. "I have not always been deaf."

Her heart went out to him. She had been born mute, but Adam had been forced to accept an impairment.

"A few months ago I became ill—*les oreillons*."

She cupped her hands over her ears, then pointed to herself.

"You had it too. And Paulina and your brothers?"

She nodded, pressing her palm low to the floor.

"When you were small." He raked a hand through his hair, imitating her gesture with his free hand. "I was big." He raised his hand to the top of his head. "When grown men suffer this disease, they sometimes lose their hearing."

She sensed great sadness in him. But she knew he was deaf and surely he was aware by now it did not matter to her. There was something more. She took hold of his trembling hand, pressing her fingers into his palm. "Tell me."

To her surprise he lifted her to her feet, then went down on one knee.

Oh, God.

He looked into her eyes. "Rosamunda, I care for you deeply. I want you to be my wife."

She gasped, her heart soaring.

He averted his gaze. "But I cannot ask it of you."

Something happened to her knees. She swooned towards him as the rafters crashed in on her. Adam put his arms around her hips and buried his forehead in the aching place between her legs. He growled out something incoherent, his words muffled by sobs racking his body.

She gripped his shoulders, willing the loft to stop spinning.

Her head throbbed, but it came to her in the midst of her pain that he was suffering. He had something dire to tell her. She cradled his face between her hands and forced him to look at her. Despair darkened his gaze.

"Tell me."

He put his hands over hers and squeezed his eyes tight shut. "I am not a whole man, Rosamunda."

A maelstrom of thoughts whirled through her head. What did he mean? If Denis had said the same thing she would have understood. Apart from his deafness, he looked hale.

She tried to withdraw her hands from his to make him look at her again, but he held firm. Her belly roiled as she gasped for breath. She bent to kiss the top of his head.

A sigh shuddered through him as he looked up at her. “I am impotent.”

Silence hung in the air as Rosamunda desperately revisited conversations with her brothers, but *impotent* was not a word she remembered. She blinked away tears. She couldn’t help him if she did not understand his problem.

He must have sensed her confusion. He opened his eyes. “You don’t understand, do you?” he said wearily.

She shook her head, afraid to mouth the word *no*.

He came to his feet to stand with his body touching hers. He swallowed hard. “Has anyone told you what happens between a man and woman in the bedchamber?”

The heat rose in her face as she shyly touched her breasts and then the intimate place he had pleasured.

He smiled, but it was not a happy smile. “*Oui*, that is part of it, but there is much more. When I stand near you like this, what happens to your body?”

Rosamunda and her sister had never discussed their bodies, and certainly the topic would have been unthinkable with her brothers. But she had felt the need for a man’s touch as her body developed. The man of her dreams was asking to share her most intimate secrets. She cupped her breasts. “Ache.”

He brushed his knuckles against her mons. “And here?”

Fire consumed her now. She pounded her fist into her palm. "Hot, wet."

He enfolded her in his arms. "Do you know why?"

She frowned. "Because I like you?"

She was too innocent. Adam cursed the mother who had abandoned her daughter to ignorance. "*Oui*, again that's part of it. But when a man and woman wed, they join their bodies. The woman becomes warm and wet to welcome her husband's male parts."

She had brothers. Surely she knew they were made differently? But they had not grown up together in the normal way of siblings.

Her eyes widened as she glanced at his groin. He was in too deep to withdraw now. He took her hand and pressed it against his shaft. "I have a male part, Rosamunda, as you can feel."

Inquisitive as ever, she flexed her fingers over him, exploring. She smiled, obviously having no inkling his manhood had not responded as it should at her touch.

"A man's body makes seed. From that seed children grow in the woman's womb when the man and woman join."

She blushed again, patting her belly.

His head and his heart were pounding, his throat dry. He should stop now, walk away, tell her he did not love her. He was about to break her heart anyway. Better to keep his secret.

But he did love her. She was his one chance at happiness, and she needed him, for all his problems.

"*Les oreillons* stole that from me, Rosamunda. I can never sire children."

He held his breath, staring at her breasts. A bee buzzed somewhere in the loft. The roof had not fallen in, nor the floor collapsed beneath his feet. There had been no clap of thunder, no bolt of lightning. Yet the world had changed profoundly.

AN INVITATION

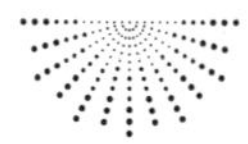

Rosamunda held her breath, her innards churning. She would have to seek the *garderobe* soon or disgrace herself. Nox snorted below them, no doubt sensing his master nearby. Lux whinnied in reply.

In the courtyard people were stirring, beginning the business of the day, a day like any other. Except it wasn't.

To say she had longed for children would be untrue. She had felt cheated of the chance to bear sons and daughters. But the longing had been for a man who loved her. In her fantasies she had assumed marriage to such a man would bring children.

Adam de Montbryce was that man. Her heart bled for him that he suffered this torment. He stood before her like a lost child, unable to hide the pleading in his eyes.

She knew nothing of real life, of men and women, of what it meant to live with other people, least of all a man. But she loved Adam. The idea of not joining her life with his weighed on her like lead. She put her hands on his shoulders and pushed him down to his knees. “Ask again.”

He glanced up at her sharply, hope flickering in his blue eyes. “You understand what I am telling you?”

She nodded, then put one hand over her heart, the other on his chest.

He exhaled loudly, rubbing his face with his hands. He laughed nervously, swallowing hard. She held out her hand. He cradled it in his warm palms. “Will you wed with me, Rosamunda Lallement?”

She launched at him and they collapsed in a tangled heap in the straw.

Yes, yes, a thousand times yes.

He folded her in his arms. “I’ll take that as a *yes* then.”

The urgency to get Rosamunda back to East Preston consumed Adam. He did not divulge the betrothal to the Revandel family. Denis and Paulina must be the first to share the news.

Denis would understand, despite that a marriage would end the partnership of the Giant and the Dwarf. Denis loved him and would rejoice in his happiness.

Paulina would be devastated. She and Denis should marry. It was evident they were made for each other.

He ought to have given Rosamunda more time to consider her response. He dreaded she might change her mind. He would free her of the betrothal if she did. If they could be married quickly, he would pleasure her silly and she would never want to leave him.

She was beautiful. Their children would have been

angels. It grieved him he would never see her belly round with his child.

She agreed to keep their promise secret, grimacing at the notion of Letyce Revandel and her rude brothers finding out.

Adam informed his hosts of their intention to depart that afternoon, much to Alphonse Revandel's spluttered disappointment, Letyce's disgusted sneer, and the twins' crestfallen sulk.

~

Letyce Revandel fumed that a handsome knight such as Adam de Montbryce preferred the company of a mute nobody. She had used all her wiles to snare him, but had not succeeded in arousing his male interest.

Something ailed him. She had guessed early on that he did not hear well. But there was more. He avoided physical contact, especially when she attempted to press her body against his manhood. There was nothing—no hard male length saluting in honor. Any man became aroused when a young woman pressed her attentions on him, unless—

He clung to the *muette* as if to a lifeline. Letyce was glad they were leaving today and wished heartily protocol did not demand she be present in the courtyard to bid them adieu. She suspected Adam had spent the night with her rival in the stables.

Her father bowed and scraped, his fat face red. His toadying sickened her.

She suppressed a giggle when Winrod and Dareau lavished completely inappropriate farewell kisses on the mute, flustering her, until Adam stepped between them to spoil the fun, a scowl on his face.

Her brothers' actions emboldened her. There was no harm in one last try. When Adam bowed his *adieu*, she flung her arms around his neck and kissed him on the mouth, grinding her mons against him. He stumbled backwards in an effort to evade her, but in the brief moment their bodies touched, her suspicions were confirmed. The man was either a eunuch, or he was impotent.

That could explain his evasive answers when her father had brought up the topic of Belisle Castle. He had mumbled something about his brother inheriting. Her father's disappointment was palpable as his dreams of wedding his daughter to a wealthy Norman heir dissipated.

She didn't care. Let the eunuch dote on his *muette*. There were plenty of other fish in the sea. She watched them ride away, plotting how to escape Poling, and her father's constant supervision.

As the departing visitors neared the gate, another group of horsemen appeared. She narrowed her eyes, her spirits lifting when she saw they wore the king's livery.

Montbryce exchanged greetings with the royal messengers. He accepted what looked like a document from them, then continued his journey home without a backward glance.

The king's men rode into the courtyard. Her father repeated his bowing and scraping as the leader dismounted and came forward.

"I am Sir Bertrand de Poitou, herald of His Majesty, Henry, King of England. I bear a message from our Sire concerning his sojourn at Arundel Castle. You are Sir Alphonse Revandel?"

Her father smiled broadly. "Did I not tell you the king would remember me," he whispered to Letyce as Sir Bertrand handed him a parchment.

She rolled her eyes. The size of the satchel stuffed with documents that Sir Bertrand's squire bore across his body seemed to indicate every Thomas, Richard and Henry in Sussex had received the missive. Still, excitement bubbled within her. Arundel was less than an hour away, and the king would be there, with his courtiers. She was certain a few of her more wicked bed partners wouldn't miss the opportunity to participate in the All Hallows' Eve frolics.

Sir Bertrand stepped back. "I await the favor of a reply."

"*Oui, oui,* of course we will do his majesty's bidding. Whatever it is."

The herald folded his arms across his broad chest. "You have not yet read the missive."

Letyce peeked over her father's shoulder as he unfurled the document.

He laboriously intoned the message for the benefit of his sons. Her eyes skipped through the meaningless preamble: *Year of Our Lord...Glorious Reign...Majesty*....yes, here was the crux of the message:

...His Illustrious Majesty commands your presence at Arundel Castle for the celebrations of the Triduum of Hallowmas.

At last, a chance to escape this dreary manor and have some fun. Granted the second two days of Hallowmas were solemn occasions, but All Hallows' Eve promised to be entertaining.

"The Revandels will be there," she gushed, to Sir Bertrand's evident surprise.

For the first half hour of their journey to East Preston, the angry scowl did not leave Adam's face. His jaw remained clenched, his thoughts obviously far away. Rosamunda deemed it wise not to open a conversation. She too had been repelled and disgusted by the behavior of the Revandel twins towards her, and Letyce's brazen conduct with Adam. She was upset for him, but secretly elated he obviously had no affection for the *hore*.

He had accepted the document from the royal herald at Poling, but had not read it, nor given any indication of what it might contain. She was agog. A message from the king. She would have ripped it open immediately.

It had not escaped her attention that the impressive herald had shown great deference to Adam when he identified himself.

When they turned south at Angmering, he called a halt for the men in the escort to water their horses in the Arun River. His anger seemed to leave him as he helped her dismount. She relished his big hands at her waist as he lifted her safely to the ground. She held on to his shoulders, drawing on the strength she felt there.

"I apologise for my demeanor, Rosamunda," he said. "I am disappointed for my father that such a family lives in one of his manors. No gentleman would behave thus towards you."

Nor any lady towards you.

Impatience seethed. She pointed to the document tucked in his belt. He looked down and seemed surprised. "I forgot about it."

He tucked his hand under her elbow and guided her to

a fallen log by the river. "Let's see what his Illustrious Majesty wants."

For a family that had rubbed shoulders with kings since William the Conqueror, a royal missive might not seem important.

Adam unfurled the parchment, read the message, then rolled it up again.

She gripped his arm, shaking it. "Well?"

"We are invited, nay, commanded to Arundel Castle for the Hallowmas observance."

She had heard of Arundel from her brothers. "The Earl of Arundel?" she mouthed.

"You are right that the castle used to be the *demesne* of the Earl of Arundel, Roger Montgomery, but after his death it passed to the Crown. Henry loves Arundel, and I can understand his wish to celebrate the first Hallowmas of his reign there. It is a magnificent castle."

She pointed to herself, shaking her head.

"You have no choice, Rosamunda. When the king commands a household to attend, everyone of consequence goes."

He brushed a kiss on her knuckles, sending shivers up and down her spine. "I will be proud to take you as my betrothed."

She liked the sound of that. She would be safe with Adam to protect her.

"Paulina will be expected to go also."

A problem. "She will refuse."

I HAVE TOLD HER

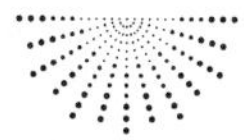

"Absolutely not," Paulina shouted. "I will not accompany you to Arundel."

Denis was worried. Paulina had made great strides in a short time. She had asked him many questions about his deformity and how he had coped with the censure. He'd willingly admitted to fears and resentments he'd never shared with anyone before. She seemed to relax as the days passed and they strolled together around the estate. He felt she was coming to trust him.

Now the fear was back.

Adam rolled his eyes. "You risk angering the king if he gets wind of your refusal. Your brothers will be there, as will Rosamunda. Your existence will come to light. We cannot lie about it. That has gone on too long. Henry will be angry enough with Vincent and Lucien without your compounding the problem."

Paulina turned away, her attention seemingly on the kitten in the satchel she bore across her body. "Rosamunda need not go. She can stay with me."

Rosamunda stamped her foot. "I want to go."

She shot a strange glance at Adam, her face reddening.

Denis wondered what was going on.

Adam put his arm around Rosamunda's shoulder and cleared his throat. "This was not the way we wanted to tell you both, but, we are betrothed."

For a moment, Denis thought he had misheard, but one look at his brother's face quickly disabused him of the notion. His Giant had fallen in love. He was not surprised, having recognised Adam's immediate attraction to Rosamunda. A deaf man and a *muette.* A perfect union. His heart overflowed for his brother's happiness.

But it was unlikely he had he recovered in the short time he had been away, unless Rosamunda had worked some miracle.

In a few weeks the young mute had seemingly won Adam's trust. That should not irritate him as much as it did.

Paulina swayed beside Denis, staring at her sister. How bereft she must feel at this moment. He wanted to fall to his knees and promise to treasure her forever.

A chill washed over him. If Paulina rejected him, the Dwarf would face a future alone. But he did not want her to come to him to escape loneliness, or out of fear.

He wanted her to love him, as the blushing and smiling Rosamunda so obviously loved Adam. His fledgling hopes had risen during the past few days.

He had known the insidiousness of jealousy before, having envied everyone who was not a dwarf. But he had overcome that. Now, he was ashamed because he begrudged the love his dearest brother had found.

Adam laughed nervously. “Won’t you congratulate me, brother?”

It jolted Denis from his reverie. He was truly happy for Adam. It was the miracle he had prayed for. He pushed aside his melancholy, as he had many times. He winked. “You’re a sly devil.”

The brothers embraced, the Giant lifting the Dwarf as Denis’ arms strained to thump him on the back.

Paulina’s worst fear had come true. She had never seen a snake, only knew of them from her brothers, but now she held her breath, waiting for the lethal bite of the adder coiled around her heart.

She wished she had died in the fire.

She wished she had never been born.

She was happy for her sister, but the words stuck in her throat.

If only Denis would cradle her in his arms and assure her of his love.

Rosamunda’s warm hand grasped hers. Paulina looked at the face of the courageous person she loved most in the world who now knelt before her. It was a face full of hope and happiness. She inhaled deeply and threw her arms around her sister’s neck. “Your dream has come true. Your Montbryce hero has come for you.”

Topaz mewled her displeasure at being squashed between them as they hugged.

“I have told her,” Adam whispered in Denis’ ear as they broke apart and the Giant set him back on his feet. “She knows everything.”

Denis was reassured. He looked over at the Lallement women locked in a tearful embrace.

Only he could offer Paulina a way out of her loneliness and fear. Her wretched parents were dead. Rosamunda and Adam had pledged to each other. Vincent and Lucien would marry and have families of their own.

Denis should walk away, keep his heart safe.

But he had always stood for what was right, no matter the challenges.

He waited until the women broke apart.

Rosamunda came to her feet.

Adam put his arm around her.

Paulina wiped her tears with the sleeve of her *bliaut*, gasping in exasperation as Topaz crawled out of the satchel and scampered off.

Denis took her damp hand, and went down on one knee. “Shall we make it a double wedding, my lady?”

INDECISION

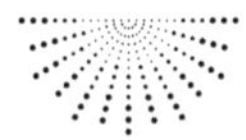

Paulina's captivity had denied her the necessity to make decisions. She might ponder how much water to add when steeping faded rose petals, or which of her three *bliauts* to wear, or whether to braid her hair or let in hang in the style Rosamunda loved. The first major decision of her life was the name chosen for a cat.

Marriage was something she had never considered. Even if she had been free, no man would want a wife half his height.

Before her knelt a man asking for her hand. He wasn't attractive, but he was brave and honest and strong. He knew what it was to be ridiculed, but had triumphed over his deformity, and could help her do the same. She had no doubt he would protect her with his life if necessary.

He had asked out of pity, knowing how bereft she would be without her sister. He seemed to enjoy spending time with her, but it was because she was his height. He sought companionship, and probably didn't feel the same stirrings in his heart she felt whenever she was near him.

Her mind went blank. If she said yes, she would never be lonely. She would have a champion, a friend, a bedmate. He would see her naked. She was too small. A man could never love a body such as hers.

If she said no, he would believe she had refused him because of his deformity, when she was in reality drawn to his strength, drawn to him.

He was such an honorable man that if she denied him, she trusted he would not abandon her. Perhaps, it would be better if they remained just friends.

Denis watched indecision plague Paulina. It was the longest minute of his life. He had never felt uglier or more inadequate. How grotesque he must appear, wobbling on bended knee, his hips aching like the devil.

He had to push her into a decision, or they might be there all day. Adam and Rosamunda stood nearby, clearly embarrassed, not knowing what to say. However, both had expectant looks on their faces. Rosamunda's hopeful smile in particular emboldened him. If anyone knew Paulina well, it was her sister.

He had to hope the woman he believed was his destiny saw the sincerity in his eyes. "I beg you to say yes, Paulina."

She drew in a long shuddering breath, her arms rigid at her sides, fists clenched. Tears trickled down her cheeks.

She shook her head. "Yes, I will wed with you."

Adam feared Denis might not get off his knees. He need not have worried. His brother sprang up like a frog, raining kisses on Paulina's hands, talking so quickly Adam deciphered only a few words. *Champion—protector—safe.*

Paulina swayed like a sapling in a gale, her face expressionless.

Tell her you love her.

It was brave advice, yet he had not said those words to his own betrothed.

Rosamunda turned her radiant face to him. "So happy!"

Adam was happy too. Denis had found the impossible. They both had. Hope had replaced hopelessness.

He suspected Denis would also want a quick wedding, but they would need the king's permission to marry. It was fortuitous they were going to Arundel.

He twirled a lock of Rosamunda's hair around his finger. "I am anxious for our marriage, but can I ask that we wait until we can go to Belisle after Hallowmas? Denis will want to wed there. Our parents—"

She stood on tiptoe to kiss his nose. "Of course."

Normandie!

Not only was Rosamunda going to Normandie, she would be married there. She basked in warm contentment.

Her betrothed had trusted her with a confidence she would carry to her grave rather than betray him. She vowed to pray for a miracle, but she would love him despite his male difficulties.

Her sister had found her soul mate, though she seemed

intent on denying it. Life would not be easy for Paulina and her dwarf, but Denis was strong, and she believed he loved Paulina.

Not long ago the prospects for the future seemed dire. Now life was full of promise.

A DIFFICULT RIDE

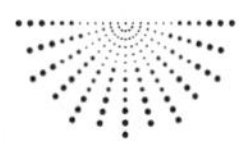

Adam and Rosamunda rode Nox and Lux as they made their way to Arundel Castle. Denis rode Brevis, Paulina on his lap.

Lucien and Vincent had ridden to East Preston and now journeyed with them.

Rosamunda had lost patience with her sister in the last few days before their departure. Arundel was not a great distance away, a mere two hour ride over flat terrain, but Paulina refused to ride a horse of her own, despite Denis bringing a docile mount he had found. Her brothers' assurances counted for naught.

When Adam warned that King Henry hated cats, and insisted Topaz remain at home, she threw a tantrum, refusing to accompany them. No amount of coddling on Denis' part or Rosamunda's eye-rolling soothed her. Adam flung up his hands in frustrated capitulation, and so Topaz also rode Brevis, perched atop the wide pommel like a lion rampant.

Curiously, Nox had taken to the kitten, much to

Adam's annoyance. From time to time, the stallion sniffed the feline, snorting his approval when he seemed assured she was still atop her precarious perch. In return Topaz swatted his nose.

At least this amusing partnership brought the occasional smile to Paulina's lips. If only her sister would admit her feelings for Denis and relax with him, enjoy his attentions, acknowledge he loved her.

Rosamunda resolved not dwell on it. She had her own life to lead with a man she sensed needed all her love. Impotency must be a heavy burden for a once virile man to bear, despite her reassurances she was happy to forgo the bearing of children. How isolated he must feel in his deafness. She had known isolation. It destroyed hope, led to self doubt.

It was ironic her reluctant sister's joining with Denis might result in children as deformed as he was. She tamped down a twinge of jealousy, wondering if Adam felt envious of his dwarf brother.

Her mind wandered as Lux kept up to the steady pace set by Nox. She glanced at Denis. Perhaps he too had difficulties with his male parts. He was not properly formed. Was that why he and Adam were good friends? Did Denis know about Adam's impotency?

Her impression was they shared an unbreakable bond, but she would never ask him, for that would breach her oath to Adam.

Denis unsuccessfully willed his rock hard arousal to abate as Paulina's sweet *derrière* pressed rhythmically on his shaft with the horse's movements. Her attention seemed fixed on the benighted cat. It would not take much to swat it off its arrogant perch and send it flying like a pesky gnat.

She had to be aware of his arousal pressed against her. He must remember she was an innocent, though warmth welled up in his chest when he recalled their conversation about male and female parts. His heart was aglow and his body had been doing strange things ever since he'd set eyes on this miniature woman. Lust he had known before, and often, but now his emotions were in knots.

He was in full agreement with Adam that they must wait to wed in Belisle. Paulina had promised to marry him, but he dreaded she might yet change her mind. It was evident she had not wanted the marriage. Fear had pushed her into it, not love.

He told himself he did not care, squelching the ache in his heart at the prospect such a beautiful woman could never love a man like him.

Had she not been such a coward, Paulina would not now be trying desperately to ignore the wanton feelings surging through her when her *derrière* pressed against Denis' male part. She had no doubt after their talk that's what she felt. She closed her eyes, conjuring a vision of the surprisingly hard and substantial flesh beneath her.

She had shifted her position several times, but doing so seemed to increase his discomfort. Denis' body betrayed his desire to join with her, the undesirable, unloved, unwanted Paulina.

Thank goodness she had brought Topaz. The kitten

was at least a distraction from the heat emanating from Denis.

A leaden lump of dread lay in the pit of her belly as Arundel Castle loomed ahead. She had never imagined the existence of such a large edifice. A king and his court waited there; sophisticated men and women of the world who had probably never set eyes on one such as her, though Denis had said many dwarfs were entertainers in royal courts. Would she be expected to entertain?

What a spectacle she and Denis would make. Her heart raced. She had to get off the horse, escape, flee back to East Preston. If she appealed to Vincent and Lucien, surely they would take her home.

Denis' arm tightened around her waist. He leaned forward to nibble her ear, his warm breath sending sparks of fire into her breasts. "I am here," he whispered. "I will not allow anything to happen to you. Be brave."

Her heart calmed. She found strength in his words and his embrace and the husky timbre of his voice.

He chuckled. "Besides, what a disappointment for Topaz not to meet the king who hates cats."

ARUNDEL

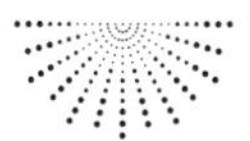

They halted a short distance from the castle, several groups ahead of them queuing to enter the gate. Rosamunda opened her arms high and wide, her eyes bulging.

Adam too was awed by the splendor of Arundel. "You are right. It is huge. I've heard about it, but it's my first visit."

Rosamunda frowned.

Adam shrugged. "The Montbryces and the Montgomerys were never friends. My uncle, the Earl of Ellesmere, considered the late Roger de Montgomery a cruel beast of a man. He treated him with the respect due a fellow earl, but avoided him whenever possible."

He glanced at Paulina. Her rigid spine and clenched jaw betrayed her fear. Adam was apprehensive too. He had often seen smirks and taunts directed at Denis. There were no doubt people like Maudine Lallement and Letyce Revandel at Arundel. His gut clenched at the prospect of meeting the *whore* again.

Denis appeared relaxed as he helped Paulina stuff Topaz into her satchel under the watchful eye of Nox, but Adam had seen that icy calm before. His brother was preparing for the battle ahead.

Adam must prepare too. There was not only Rosamunda to protect. Some would mock his deafness. And if they ever discovered his other secret—

He dismissed the fear as unlikely. Only Rosamunda and Denis knew, apart from his family in Normandie. He was confident they would not betray him.

To calm everyone's nervousness, he recited the history of the castle. "As you see, it commands the landscape. It was founded on Christmas Day in the year of our Lord One Thousand and Sixty-Seven."

Paulina gasped. "Only a year to the day after the Conqueror was crowned at Westminster."

Denis chuckled. "You know your history, *ma petite*."

Lucien chimed in. "Paulina has always been rapt with attention whenever we have talked about the years of the conquest. Of course, it took years after the founding to complete the castle."

Paulina blushed. It gladdened Adam's heart. Denis was making progress with his reluctant bride to be.

He decided to continue. Henry might be impressed if his unusual guests knew something of the castle he loved. "*Oui*, the Conqueror granted Montgomery large tracts of land and the earldom, on condition he build a castle near the mouth of the River Arun, to protect coastal Sussex from attack. It's also the closest to Normandie so reinforcements could be brought quickly in the event of a Saxon revolt, a distinct possibility in the early days of Norman rule."

Denis took up the account. "With typical arrogance, Montgomery believed he should have all of Sussex. He was furious when Ram de Montbryce was granted eighty six manors there. *Oncle* Ram in turn deeded several of them to his brothers, Antoine and Hugh. That's how my stepfather gained control of East Preston, Poling and the remainder. The Conqueror was careful not to give anyone too much power."

Adam snorted. Mention of Montgomery invariably set a Montbryce on edge. "Besides, the man did not fight at Hastings, whereas my father and his brothers played an important role in the Norman victory. Roger stayed in Normandie to keep the peace for William, who was his cousin, by the way."

Vincent joined the conversation. "Henry is expanding the castle. When we pass through the gate, you'll see they are adding a vault for a portcullis."

Adam winked at Rosamunda. "Montgomery is probably turning over in his tomb."

She grinned, pointing to the Keep towering over the gatehouse, tracing its crenelated shape in the air with an outstretched hand.

It dawned on Adam neither of the women had seen a castle before. "It is high. Mottes are always raised so the Keep atop it has a commanding view, but Montgomery outdid himself here. As you can see this earthwork is at least a hundred feet high. It has two baileys, one to the north, and the other to the east. It's impressive."

Rosamunda touched his arm, shading her eyes with her free hand. "Normandie?"

Her bright anticipation elated him. "*Oui*, I am sure you can see Normandie from up there. We'll find out."

Rosamunda grinned, clenching her fists in glee, her shoulders hunched, bursting with excitement. Her thirst to experience sights and sounds she had been denied brought home to him how blasé he had become. He resolved to look at things in the future as if it was the first time he was seeing them. He could no longer depend on his ears. It was time he used his eyes to the fullest.

"My sister is full of life," Paulina murmured wistfully.

Why can I not be like her?

She felt the strength in Denis' arm. The tension that had rippled through him as they journeyed was gone. He had grown strangely calm. She stole a glance at his face. There was a glint in his eye, as if he relished the coming fray. Their eyes met. He smiled, sending winged creatures fluttering through her veins.

"Are you ready, my lady?"

Strangely, she was.

A rapid pulse in his throat made it hard for Denis to swallow. He had faced taunts and ridicule before and invariably walked away unscathed. Now he had more to protect—the honor and happiness of his betrothed. What happened to her in Arundel would affect their future forever. Her wistful remark betrayed her longing to be more like her sister, to be free of her fear. He worried he might kill anyone who looked at her the wrong way.

He had learned over the years that allowing his

emotions to control him was the best way to lose a confrontation. Paulina had tied his heart in knots. He inhaled deeply, bracing for the test ahead as Adam signaled the party to move forward through the impressive vaulted stone gateway of Arundel Castle.

KING HENRY

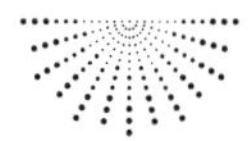

Vincent and Lucien flanked the others as they made their way to the bailey. Most of the gawks and stares were directed at Denis, but few let their gaze linger in the face of stony glares from four knights.

Rosamunda glanced over to her sister. Some of the fear had left her face as they proceeded without being molested or challenged.

Adam dismounted, then helped her down from Lux. "Only a few paid any attention to Paulina," he whispered. "They perhaps took her for a child."

Rosamunda was relieved yet saddened. It was an unhappy truth that wherever Paulina went she would be stared at and mayhap taunted.

Indeed, once Paulina was on her feet, people turned to stare and nudge each other. Denis gallantly proffered his arm to his betrothed. "The secret, my lady, is to pretend they do not exist. Or, if you feel in need of amusement, imagine them naked."

Paulina giggled.

Rosamunda did not recall a time she had ever heard her sister giggle. It brought joy to her heart as the warmth of Adam's hand seeped into the small of her back.

The liveried squire assigned to them at the gate led the way to the northern bailey. Rosamunda's mouth fell open. As they descended the terraced steps, she gazed at the colorful round pavilions crowding together in a large circle around the perimeter. At the far end of the ward, one large pavilion stood alone, its white walls emblazoned with an elaborate device she supposed was the king's. His pennant fluttered from the peak of the roof above an onion-shaped finial. The decoratively fringed roof was square, but the base was octagonal. A large canopy shaded the entry. At intervals along the walls of the tent, three thin ropes emerged like tridents to form one, which was then staked to the ground. Men with mallets patrolled, occasionally stooping to pound a stake into the earth.

The king may be within at this very moment.

The attic at Kingston Gorse suddenly seemed a long time ago and a long way away. Another lifetime.

The centre of the ward had been left open, she assumed for festivities. Around the perimeter, trestle tables sagged with the weight of foodstuffs. People milled around, eating, conversing, laughing, watching. Strolling musicians played. Braziers glowed at intervals, chasing away the autumn chill. Groups of chattering ladies huddled around them.

It was an enchanted land. She gazed about, taking it all in.

Adam's agitated voice broke into her reverie. "Let's keep moving."

She became aware that the music had stopped. All eyes followed them as they made their way to their assigned pavilions.

"Hold your head high, Paulina," Denis reminded her. "Remember what I said."

Rosamunda breathed a sigh of relief when Paulina did exactly as instructed. She was further relieved she and her sister had been billeted next to Adam and Denis.

Adam ushered them into their own small pavilion. "I made a special request, directly to the king. Most of the unmarried knights will stay together, and the unmarried ladies are probably in those tents over there. I explained our betrothals, and, I am proud to say, the Montbryce name carries weight. Henry expects us later when we petition for his permission."

Her heart lurched. "Permission?"

He kissed the top of her head. "To wed. It's a formality. He's delighted."

Vincent and Lucien Lallement dreaded the audience with King Henry, possibly more than their tiny sister. The monarch had been informed of the goings on at Kingston Gorse and had apparently expressed angry disbelief.

When told of the betrothals of both their sisters, Lucien had dropped to his knees in prayerful thanks. Vincent had quickly joined him and the brothers had shared a tearful embrace.

Now they faced the censure of their king for the incarceration of their sisters.

Lucien paced as they waited outside the royal pavilion,

then stopped abruptly in front of his future brothers-by-marriage. "Thank God we do not have to face him alone."

Denis glared. "You are agitating your sisters with your pacing."

Paulina swayed on her feet.

Rosamunda's eyes were wide with apprehension.

Lucien was instantly contrite. "I'm sorry. I've never been summoned to answer to a king before."

Vincent scowled. "You're making me nervous, brother."

Rosamunda took Lucien's hands in hers. Paulina joined them. "We do not blame you. You were powerless in the face of mother's madness. Father was more to blame than you, but he has paid for his sins."

Adam inhaled deeply as he was ushered into the pavilion of Henry, King of England. He had some inkling now of how his father and mother had felt many years before at the trial of *oncle* Hugh and *tante* Devona before the *curia regis.* Henry's father, William the Conqueror had presided. His mother's testimony had been vital in securing the release of Hugh and Devona.

They were obliged to wait their turn behind several courtiers and local noblemen. Adam fiddled with the sleeve of his doublet, worried not only by how Henry would react to his deafness, but nervous too for the Lallements.

Rosamunda leaned into him, a comical grimace on her face.

Adam bit his lip to stifle a smile. His betrothed's impersonation was not far off the mark. Henry looked down his long nose at the latest petitioner, his coronet slightly askew on his long brown hair. He appeared chilled, though the heat from a nearby brazier had reddened his cheeks.

To Adam's dismay, the petitioners ahead of them included the Revandel family. He nudged Rosamunda, angling his head in the king's direction.

She grimaced again, snuggling closer. Contented warmth spread through him. He bent to whisper in her ear. "Pay them no heed. Keep your eyes on Henry. He can be as ruthless as his father. When his brother, King William Rufus, died in mysterious circumstances two months ago, Henry moved quickly to secure the throne. Everyone had expected the older brother, Duke Robert Curthose to become king.

"No one ever understood why William chose to grant the crown of England to his second son, William Rufus, the Duchy of Normandie to Robert Curthose, and five thousand pounds to the third son, Henry, whom everyone assumed would become a bishop.

"Henry spent his youth preparing for a role in the church, as youngest sons do. But his ascension to the throne of England has plunged this country and Normandie into further conflict between the two brothers for control of a combined kingdom."

Adam glanced over at Denis. He had apparently heard nothing of his murmurings and appeared calm. But his jaw was clenched and he had a firm grasp on Paulina's hand. His unruly hair had been tamed into a queue, his face shaved. Adam prayed under his breath the monarch would not look upon him with contempt, but as the brave and loyal knight he was.

ALL SHAPES AND SIZES

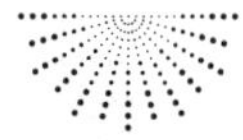

Out of the corner of his eye, Henry Beauclerc espied the motley group waiting in line for an audience.

He shifted his weight. This should prove interesting. Audiences were tedious affairs, consisting often of toadying petitioners whining about something or other. Over the years, he had heard of the exploits of the Giant and the Dwarf and the Montbryce family had proven its loyalty time and again since the early days of the conquest.

Henry had admired the way Ram de Montbryce, Earl of Ellesmere, had maneuvered to survive and prosper during the thirteen years his late brother had ruled as king.

The dark-haired knight waiting with the dwarf had a look of Ram's son. Henry's minions had informed him of the young man's unfortunate deafness. His older brother would continue the fight to take the Crown of England away from him and he would need every able-bodied loyal knight. One thing was for certain, the Montbryces were loyal, deaf or not, and one had only to look at the dwarf half-brother to know valor came in all shapes and sizes.

Henry shrugged deeper into the blue woollen cloak he had donned against the chill. Two or three servants rushed to aid him. They evidently considered him incapable of pulling on a cloak. He waved them away impatiently. "Find out where the infernal draught on the back of my neck is coming from, and get rid of the smoke before we choke."

Irritated and anxious to get to petitioners more interesting than the sniveling Revandel and his brats, he dismissed the family abruptly. Thank goodness Rufus' minion had acquiesced to the strong suggestion he retire to the country with his harlot daughter and immature sons. Henry had not been aware the Revandels had ended up at Poling. Too close to Arundel for comfort. And now the upstart wanted his wayward daughter named as lady-in-waiting to his future queen. Matilda would have his head if he bestowed such an honor on the whore.

Letyce kept the decorous smile on her face until she turned away from the hypocritical king looking down his aquiline nose at her and her family.

Her ill-humor intensified when she caught sight of Adam de Montbryce and his imbecilic neighbor standing with the next group. And a dwarf. No—two dwarfs.

She jutted out her chin, passing them with her nose in the air, a smirk on her face. She glared at Winrod and Dareau when they paused to speak to the mute. They quickly fell in line behind their pompous father.

It occurred to her as she swept out of the pavilion that there had been two other young knights with Montbryce. She should have paid them more attention.

The king leaned forward to whisper to his chamberlain. His blue cloak fell open, revealing a jewel-encrusted metal collar resting on the royal shoulders—gold no doubt. The official struck the wooden dais with a staff topped with a silver sphere, drew back his shoulders, and declared, "His Majesty wishes to speak to Vincent and Lucien Lallement."

Denis vacillated between exasperation and relief as the Lallement brothers stepped forward, amid the disgruntled murmurings of people ahead of them. He wanted this interview over with. Never one to shy away from a challenge, he preferred to remain in the background, not be on show as they were now in this circus.

Richly dressed courtiers clustered around the edges of the royal pavilion, obviously anticipating entertainment.

Vincent and Lucien bowed low until given leave to rise. Henry eyed them sternly. "Your grandfather came to these shores even before my father. Now I am told his name has been sullied by recent events at Kingston Gorse. Explain."

Denis itched to step forward, but changed his mind at a wary glance from his brother. He had advised Vincent and Lucien to be forthright. Their parents' transgressions were not their fault.

Vincent braced his legs. "Our parents are dead, killed

in a fire at our home. We believe our mother may have started the blaze."

Denis had a new respect for Vincent's courage.

Rosamunda gasped and swayed against Adam.

Paulina tightened her grip on Denis' hand.

A collective murmur of surprise soughed through the assembly.

The glowering monarch said nothing.

Lucien cleared his throat. "Our mother has been unwell for many years."

A few in the crowd snorted quietly. Evidently, they knew Maudine Lallement.

Lucien stiffened his shoulders. "The birth of two daughters with—difficulties, stole her wits."

Henry pointed a royal finger at Rosamunda and Paulina. "These are the women you speak of? Your sisters?"

Paulina's shudder shook Denis. He gripped her hand. "Courage, *ma petite*."

"Adam de Montbryce and Denis de Sancerre, escort the Lallement sisters forward."

A spark of relief flickered to life in Denis' breast. The king respected that the women would need the support of their men. He put Paulina's trembling hand atop his arm, smiled and led her forward.

Adam followed suit with Rosamunda.

Henry studied them intently. He smoothed his thumb and forefinger over his mustache. "Adam de Montbryce. We welcome you and acknowledge your lineage and the support your family has given mine. I trust your accommodations are in accordance with your wishes?"

Adam bowed his head. "They are beyond my expectations. I thank Your Majesty."

Denis was thankful the king had spoken clearly and Adam had understood, then he felt the weight of the king's gaze. Sweat beaded on his brow.

"Denis de Sancerre, your prowess as a warrior is well known, your loyalty to my person appreciated. You have proven that stature has naught to do with bravery and honor."

He glanced around the pavilion. "There are some here at Arundel who might learn much from you."

One or two in the crowd murmured their agreement, others looked away, scowling.

Denis' heart raced. Praise and honor from a king—a valiant knight could wish for no more.

Henry turned his attention to Rosamunda and Paulina. "We are aware of the difficulties imposed upon you by your parents, and we express our sorrow. We understand you now wish to marry?"

Both women nodded.

Henry chuckled. "You have chosen two fine knights to wed—and bed!"

A ripple of bawdy laughter shimmered through the pavilion.

Paulina blushed, smiling at Denis.

Rosamunda and Adam stared straight ahead.

Denis' heart lurched for his brother.

Henry held up a hand and the laughter ceased. "We give royal assent for both marriages. However, I suspect you will wish to marry in Normandie. As the duke, my brother will expect you to seek his permission."

It was not until the six were safely away from the royal pavilion that Denis and Adam swore at once, "*Merde!*"

LE MANIO

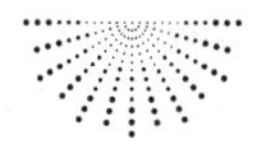

Malraux de Carnac held his palms to the brazier, welcoming its warmth. The English damp chilled his Breton bones. He rubbed his hands together then transferred the heat to his biceps.

Not of a rank to be granted entry into the royal pavilion, he had taken up a position in sight of the comings and goings of the petitioners where he might still enjoy the brazier. There was invariably some advantage to keeping an eye on people who wanted something badly enough to petition a king for it.

He rather relished the demonic look he imagined the glow of the brazier's embers gave his thin face. After all, everyone was here to celebrate Hallowmas.

He rolled his eyes, yawning away his boredom. Normans were too conservative, too much in love with form and order. The much-vaunted upcoming celebrations for All Hallows' Eve, the first day of the Triduum, paled in comparison with those planned for Carnac. Bretons knew how to organize truly spine-chilling festivities. No matter. It was not his intention to remain at Arundel for Hallowmas.

While he waited for the unusual group with the dwarfs to emerge, he ran over the details of his departure in his mind. Ride to Portsmouth, ship rigged and ready to take him to Ouistreham, horses and a pack animal waiting near Caen for the long ride across Normandie and Bretagne to his coastal home. It was a tedious journey, but All Hallows' Eve in Carnac could not be missed, especially for the patriarch of the local ruling family.

Believing the crowning of a new king might bring opportunity, he'd made the long journey to Henry's court. However, it seemed the *cleric-turned-monarch* intended to sweep clean like a new broom. Malraux had little to show for his sojourn in England except some deliciously wicked sexual encounters, and a bevy of new "friends" to blackmail, if he were so inclined. Normans looked down their noses at Bretons, though they would never have triumphed at Hastings without the fearsome Breton cavalry. However, in Carnac Malraux was respected and feared by his inferiors. As it should be.

It was taking too long for those infernal dwarfs to reappear. A tingle ran up his spine. There might be amusement with those two in Carnac.

No one knew why the ancients had erected hundreds of standing stones in his village. Some were big, others small, but only *Le Manio* towered over twenty feet high. Malraux's ancestors had refined a way to use the giant phallic symbol for the amusement of the general populace. A yearly dose of terror kept peasants in line.

A maiden was selected each year to be thrown from the top of *Le Manio* into the arms of eager men gathered below. A few did not survive the fall, though most were happy to show their gratitude to the men who saved them. Perhaps this year they might toss the female dwarf and see if her bowlegged beau could catch her.

He closed his eyes, his shaft hardening as an image of the tiny woman clinging desperately to the giant phallic monument settled in his mind. He snapped his eyes open, his attention caught by the rustle of skirts and disgruntled male voices. A scowling woman bustled out of the royal pavilion. It seemed her petition had not been granted.

Something struck a chord of memory. He narrowed his eyes. It was Letyce *what's-her-name*. His arousal turned to granite as he recalled a night of erotic passion. She was a woman who knew how to enjoy herself. He had looked forward to many nights of pleasure, but then she had disappeared from Henry's court. What was she doing here, pouting mightily?

He stroked his pointed beard, shifting his weight to ease the stiffness at his groin. Letyce would find Henry's Hallowmas celebrations tame and might be persuaded to accompany him to Bretagne.

Some of Letyce's anger dissolved when she cast eyes on Malraux. She had spent only one night with him, but he had proven to be an excellent lover who understood her need to give, and receive pain—just the right amount to make the joining memorable.

Her heart skipped a beat as he strode towards them. Perhaps these festivities might prove to be worthwhile after all. She stopped so abruptly, Winrod walked into her. "Dolt! Careful."

She turned to her father. "Papa, take my dear brothers to the groaning board over there and keep an eye on them." She tweaked Dareau's cheek. "They tend to be gluttons. We would not want them disgracing our family name."

As usual, the gullible fool took her words at face value. Thanks be to the saints she had not taken after her father, though she was not like her mother, either. Impossible to conjure a picture of her *Maman* with the likes of Malraux de Carnac. She suppressed a snort of amusement.

The Breton swept his hat from his head and showed an elegant leg, bowing ridiculously low. His hair had thinned on top, but he was still attractive in a devilish sort of way. The glint in his eye told her he remembered their night together.

"*Demoiselle* Letyce," he oozed. "*Enchanté*. I have missed you. Where did you disappear to?"

His eyes narrowed as he watched her father and brothers' progress towards the trestle tables. "Your family?"

She rolled her eyes. "Indeed."

He proffered his arm. "Delightful as it is to spend time with siblings and parents, I believe I am a much more suitable escort for you, *ma chère*."

Dizzying desire spiraled through her.

He winked, the gleam in his eye sparkling in the gathering darkness, and pinched one of her pebbled nipples—hard. She feared she might swoon if he did not bed her quickly. "Come to our pavilion," she urged, taking his arm.

He held fast. "Alas, lowly Breton that I am, I was not

assigned my own pavilion. However, your family may return and happen upon us."

She snorted. "They will not leave the tables until there is no food left to scoff, but we can probably find others willing to share our fun."

A movement at the royal pavilion caught his attention. "A moment, my dear. I am curious to watch this entourage of dwarfs."

Letyce pressed her breast to his bicep. He was not muscled, but lean and sinewy. Pliable. The memory sent shudders of anticipation through her. "Huh! It's Adam de Montbryce and his *muette*."

"A Montbryce? You know them?"

"Vaguely. They are not important. He's impotent."

Malraux chuckled. No wonder the black-haired giant was not important to Letyce if she judged him incapable of servicing her in bed. This was proving to be interesting. A member of the Montbryce family impotent. He squirreled the knowledge away. "The woman is mute? Who is she?"

Letyce clucked impatiently, reinforcing his belief she had made a play for the handsome knight and been rebuffed. "Apparently his betrothed. Wait until the poor girl gets him in bed."

Malraux tucked the knuckle of his forefinger under her chin. The chit was practically salivating for him. "Indeed, a man who fails to respond to your tempting wares must be a veritable eunuch."

She looked at him curiously. Had she gleaned the insult? He doubted it. "And what of the dwarfs?"

Letyce shrugged, pulling him away from watching the giant and the dwarf engage in some sort of heated discussion. All was not well. He would be patient and discern later what was afoot. Tossing a dwarf off *Le Manio* was suddenly within the realm of possibility.

LIMITED FACILITIES

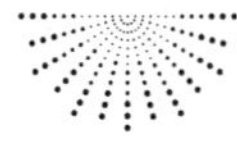

In the pavilion he shared with Adam, Denis kicked away the footstool. "Another fortnight of these so-called festivities. I will go mad."

His brother took a swig of watered ale. "Me too. I am impatient to be off to Normandie. Who knows how long it will take to get Curthose's permission to marry? He may refuse to give it, in view of our family's lack of support for him."

Denis fumed. "While I appreciate this fine marquee we've been allotted, it is too cramped even for me to pace in. We cannot go out and about. The bonfires terrify Paulina. I need to get her away from here. She refuses to leave their pavilion, convinced some evil will befall Topaz. The only time she agrees to go out is when we help ourselves to Henry's excellent fare on the trestle tables."

Adam finished off his ale, put the tankard down, and leaned forward, resting his forearms on his thighs. "She may be right. Some of these people are whipping themselves into a frenzy, overeating and imbibing too much ale and wine. They'll be out of control by the time All Hallows' Eve dawns. Why Henry wanted to spend a whole month here is beyond me. A sennight has been enough."

Denis also leaned forward, untying the thong that bound his hair, letting it cascade down over his face. He scratched his scalp vigorously, then tossed his head back. "I long for a good bath. Bathing in the Arun is all well and good, but my body tends to draw unwelcome eyes."

Adam wrinkled his nose. "Imagine how the ladies feel. There is no privacy. Most of the women douse themselves with sickly perfumes. Turns my belly."

Denis smiled. "Not like my sweet smelling Paulina, who complains she will soon run out of the rosewater she brought."

Adam arched his brows. "She'll have to borrow some of Rosa's rosemary. Fortunately, it grows wild here, so she's been able to keep a good supply. I love the scent of it on her."

Denis came to his feet. "We're a pair of lovesick fools. I'm amazed you can stand the smell of rosemary. I almost choked on it when you were sick in the infirmary."

Adam slapped his forehead. "I remember. Shows what love can do to a man. I crave the aroma now."

Denis frowned, retying his thong. "Do you love Rosa? Forgive me, but I worry sometimes that I want Paulina only because she is my height, and you want Rosamunda because she is mute."

Adam hesitated. "I have pondered the same thing, worried they feel drawn to us because you are a dwarf and I am deaf. But I trust her. She has accepted more than my deafness."

Denis threw his head back, scratching the hollow of his

throat. "I have evaded the lice, but there are many here not as fortunate. I'm constantly itchy. Another reason to stay cooped up."

Adam scratched his neck. "You're in love with Paulina, but not because she's tiny."

Denis shrugged. "You're right. We need to get out of here. Lucky for Vincent and Lucien the king allowed them to go back to Kingston Gorse."

Adam agreed. "Just as well. Even with the laborers Father sent from Belisle, they'll be hard pressed to get the house repaired and thatched before winter sets in."

Denis scratched an armpit. "I cannot stand this any longer. I'm off to the river."

Adam retrieved two linen drying cloths, tossing one at Denis. "I'll join you."

Paulina patted rosewater on her neck, sniffing her underarms. "Come away, Rosa. They will see you spying. Being cooped up in this pavilion is worse than the attic at home. At least there we could bathe. They are fortunate they can go to the river. Men do not suffer from our need for privacy."

Topaz lay asleep in her lap, purring contentedly. She stroked the tip of a twitching ear, but the kitten did not waken.

Fear for her pet lay like a lead weight in her belly. "I wish I could sleep peacefully, like my cat, unaware of the dangers. Denis has dismissed the tales of horror of All Hallows' Eve, but I have seen the malicious glint in the eyes of some queuing at the tables when they espy her in my satchel. I wish I had heeded Adam's advice and left her at East Preston."

They sat in silence, listening to the purring. Paulina fidgeted, nervous her movements would dislodge the cat, robbing her of the warmth of its little body on her thighs. "How long does Vincent say the repairs will take?"

Rosamunda shook her head.

Paulina inhaled deeply. "Sometimes I think it would be simpler to go back there, forget any of this happened."

Rosamunda fell to her knees at her sister's feet, alarming the cat, who scurried off to jump on Paulina's pallet, where she commenced licking the back of her neck, glaring. "No. You love Denis. Man for you." She pressed her palms to her breast. "Love Adam with all my heart."

Paulina took her sister's hands. "If what you say is true, why do I sense a melancholy in you? His deafness does not matter, but is there something else?"

Rosamunda shook her head vehemently, then lay it in her sister's lap. But Paulina had seen the pain in her eyes.

Malraux blinked as daylight assaulted his eyes. The sun was well up. He had got a late start on the day, but it did not worry him. There was no reason to get up, especially after another long night of wild love play. He looked around, wondering whose tent he was in, and then remembered. It was of no importance.

He shoved away the warm body snoring next to him, wincing at the deep scratches on the man's inner thighs. He looked quickly to his own body, breathing a sigh of relief that Letyce, the hell cat, had not left the same marks on him. He preferred not to draw curious eyes when he bathed in the river.

Letyce was gone. It amused him that she scooted back to her family pavilion before dawn. Surely, her father and brothers must be aware of what she got up to. Still, better safe than sorry. He did not want them suspicious of their plans to leave for Carnac.

Thrilled by Letyce's willingness to accompany him, he had delayed his departure in the hopes of formulating a plan to abscond with the dwarfs. She had been more than enthusiastic.

Now he had the means to drive a wedge between the Normans and their women. Hints concerning Montbryce's impotency had been dropped in the ears of the three dissolute men with whom he had shared Letyce. He was confident the rumor would spread quickly.

Whistling, he set off for the river, drying linens thrown jauntily over his shoulder.

BETRAYALS

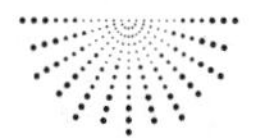

Denis had learned to ignore rude stares, taunts, elbowing, and the tittered laughter that ensued whenever he took off his clothes in public. Did grown men have nothing better to do? He concentrated on scrubbing his skin, glancing up occasionally to make sure none of the imbeciles bathing in the river had taken it into his head to come any closer.

Adam had gone off to swim in the deeper water. This had become his habit, Denis suspected, to ensure his shaft was not uncovered for long periods of time. To Denis his brother looked normal, but Adam preferred not to strut around naked.

His blood ran cold when he glanced up again to discover the gawkers were not directing their gaze at him, but at his brother emerging from the deeper part of the river, water streaming off his well-muscled body.

Nobody looking at Adam would know there was anything amiss. Few men emerged from cold water with a stiff shaft. But the onlookers somehow knew. Denis' gut roiled as he watched their lewd gestures. They thrust their hips forward, pointing to the shafts they had aroused by their own hand.

They flapped their elbows like chickens, crowing like cocks.

They know.

Adam had not looked up, had not heard the guffaws. Denis wanted to rush to his side, warn him, but he remained frozen as Adam strode on, shaking water from his hair.

He halted a few feet away and raised his head. He frowned. "What's amiss?"

How Denis wished he could spare his brother the cataclysm about to descend upon him. Illness had stolen a great deal, but he had kept the one thing that strengthens men to face of the worst of torments—his masculine pride.

Denis shook his head slightly and then cocked it to one side. "Behind me," he mouthed.

Adam looked beyond him.

Do not cover yourself.

The blood drained from Adam's face. He scowled, jaw clenched, hands fisted at his sides.

Denis breathed a sigh of relief when his brother walked on, passing him with only a nod.

Adam stooped to retrieve his drying cloth on the bank.

Denis followed suit, deliberately presenting his bare arse to the revelers as he bent over to dry his feet. Better they poke fun at him than his brother.

Adam watched, tucking the cloth around his waist, his gaze fixed on the men who were now imitating a woman pleading to be plundered by a big cock.

"Ignore them," Denis urged. "They do not know."

Adam grimaced. "They know. So much for trust."

Adam willed himself to slow his pace, to not give any hint of his desolation and anger. He had somehow managed to pull his leggings on over his damp legs, and shrugged on his shirt, despite the trembling in his hands.

Denis struggled to keep up.

Adam turned on his heel and poked him in the chest. "Did you tell them?"

The pained expression on Denis' face wrenched his gut. He knew better than to accuse his loyal brother of such a thing. But who else held the secret? Though he tried mightily to dispel the notion, it was Rosamunda who had betrayed him. "Perhaps she told her sister."

Denis scowled, panting for breath. "I doubt it, but if she did, Paulina would not divulge such a thing. Whom would she tell? My betrothed speaks to no one. It's as if she is the mute."

Adam's mind whirled. Rosamunda would not have betrayed him knowingly, but she was outgoing, anxious to fit in, and may have revealed his malady inadvertently. He slumped onto a fallen log, his head in his hands. "How can I face her now?"

Denis put a hand on his arm. "Hold. Someone calls us."

A breathless squire approached. "My lords, I have searched everywhere for you."

Denis braced his legs, coming between the squire and his brother. "You have found us. What news?"

The man steadied his breathing, a hand over his heart. “The king.”

Denis glared. “Well?”

“His Majesty wishes to see you both—now.”

“You’ve been bathing in the river,” Henry observed.

Denis touched his wet hair, doubting a more bedraggled pair had ever stood before a monarch. Adam appeared to be in a stupor beside him, and may not have heard. “We have, *Majesté*. Apologies for our appearance.”

The king chuckled, tugging at the edge of his blue cloak. “If only I could divest myself of these trappings and wade into the Arun. Hasten the day we have bathing facilities finished here at Arundel.”

Denis realized for the first time there was no one else in the pavilion.

Henry rose from his massive chair.

Adam and Denis bent the knee.

“Rise. No ceremony on this occasion. I have need of your services.”

They remained silent while the king paced. Denis worried about his brother, seemingly lost in his torment. Perhaps a loud voice might bring him back to his senses. “We live to serve you, *Majesté*.”

Henry ceased pacing, clearly surprised by the exclamation, but Adam’s eyes widened, as if waking from a deep sleep.

His Majesty declared, “Someone I trust must deliver a message to Westminster.”

Denis’ heart lifted. At last, a way out of Arundel. A

leisurely ride with Rosamunda and Paulina to Westminster. Get Adam away from taunts and insinuations. Just what they needed to get reacquainted, solve the dilemma of Rosamunda's apparent slip of the tongue.

He coughed into his fist, stifling an urge to snort with laughter. A mute with a slip of the tongue!

The king's voice pulled him back to reality. "Secret...plot...Curthose...alone."

Dread rose in Denis' throat, but he had to speak. "Your pardon, *Majesté*, but the women we are betrothed to must accompany us. They are not used to—"

Henry glared at him. "You ride alone, and in haste. They will be perfectly safe here. I will appoint a champion."

There was no arguing with a king. He bowed and approached as Henry leaned close to his ear. "The message is not to be committed to parchment."

What was whispered into his ear froze his blood; details of a plot to assassinate the king, naming familiar names, all Curthose loyalists.

"Repeat the message back to me, softly."

If he obeyed, Adam would not hear. Was he alone to be the bearer of these dire tidings? He whispered the message into the king's ear.

Henry smiled, apparently satisfied. "On the road to Westminster, you may share the details with your brother. You are to leave immediately and speak to no one else until you reach my future queen. It is to her you must deliver the news." He pulled a ring from his little finger. "Give her this. She has the authority to issue warrants. Go now. Your horses have been saddled."

ARGUMENT

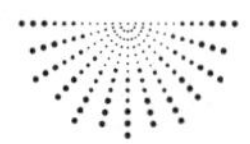

They rode as fast as the rolling terrain permitted across the South Downs, resting Nox and Brevis momentarily at Pulborough. Denis wondered idly what the consequences were for disobeying a king, not once, but twice.

Firstly, he had not waited until they were on the road to impart the message to Adam. In the privacy of their pavilion, he had explained the details as they dressed for the journey.

Once aware of the plot, Adam had insisted on leaving immediately, but Denis had sought out Paulina—his second transgression.

The fear and dread, and—dare he hope—longing, were evident in her eyes at the news. She had sobbed, clutching a squirming Topaz, as he reassured her they would be gone three days at the most. That only served to increase her upset, and she had hurried away.

"I told Paulina we had to leave."

Adam frowned. "Rosamunda knows?"

Denis feared Adam's progress had been destroyed, and he fretted that an end to his brother's relationship with Rosamunda would doom his own chances. "Paulina will have told her by now. She will be bereft you did not bid her *adieu*."

Adam clenched his jaw. "She has betrayed me."

Denis drew Brevis away from the river. "That does not make sense. Who could she have told? I cannot conceive of her having such a conversation with anyone. She did not tell Paulina."

Adam snarled. "But you did?"

Denis bristled. "I had to explain your abrupt departure. I did not break faith with you. I merely mentioned you were upset because you believed Rosamunda had given away a private secret. Her look of surprise told me she had no idea what I was referring to. They are not women of guile."

Adam said nothing as he remounted Nox and they galloped away, bound for Westminster.

The only sound in Adam's ears as they sped north across the flat fields and forests of southern England was the pounding of Nox's hooves. How foolish he had been to trust a woman with his secret. Women were gossipy creatures, as evidenced by his sister, Florymonde. He had believed Rosamunda loved him, despite his deafness and impotency. His heart ached that he had been wrong.

He was honored he had been chosen to relay the message. It pained him that his beloved Normandie had become a hotbed of intrigue. Perhaps, he would never get to take Rosamunda there.

He needed her, loved her. The admission struck him like a physical blow. He hoped Denis was right that it was not she who had betrayed him. But who else knew?

Paulina wailed. “They’re gone.”

Alarmed, Rosamunda lay aside the clump of rosemary she had picked and hunkered down beside her sister. She extricated the struggling kitten from Paulina’s grip. “Who?”

Paulina sighed with exasperation when Topaz scarpered. She raised her tear-streaked face. “Adam and Denis.”

Something cold slid unbidden under her ribs. “Gone?”

“On an errand for the king.”

Her belly calmed. Errands took only a few hours. They would be back soon. “Errand?”

Paulina sniffled, wiping her eyes with her sleeve. “They’ll be gone three days.”

Now the unwelcome creature was in her lungs. She held up three fingers, frowning. Paulina could only nod.

Three days loomed like a lifetime. Perhaps in the outside world men went off without farewell. “No goodbye?”

Paulina averted her eyes. “Denis bade me *adieu*.”

An icy chill gripped her. “Adam?”

“Denis said he was angry.”

“With His Majesty?”

Paulina shook her head, pointing to her sister.

"With me?"

They had shared only looks of longing, kisses, touches, smiles. "What did I do?"

Paulina hesitated, then brought her accusing gaze to Rosamunda's face. "You betrayed a secret."

In the years they had shared the chambers at Kingston Gorse, they had rarely argued. Paulina had never directed the anger at her that twisted her sister's face now.

She searched her memory. What secret had she given away? And to whom? She had barely spent time with anyone apart from Adam. What secret did he—

Suddenly, her body was on fire. She dropped the kitten as her hands flew to her mouth. That secret! She would rather die than divulge that secret. Had she inadvertently said something to give away the confidence Adam had shared with her?

Paulina scowled. "If Denis does not come back for me, it will be your fault." She ran out of the pavilion in search of her beloved kitten.

Rosamunda fell to her knees. Even her sister believed her capable of revealing a confidence. Adam trusted her so little he thought she had betrayed him.

Paulina could walk no further. She shivered, despite the warmth of her cloak, a gift from Denis. A special pocket for Topaz had been sewn into the lining. The glow of the braziers in the bailey seemed distant. Before her loomed a dense wood of barren trees. Where had the naughty kitten got to? She hadn't heard it mewling for a long while. Had she not been distracted over the argument with Rosamunda and her mixed feelings about Denis, she would never have wandered away from the pavilions.

She felt very alone.

A twig snapped.

She peered into the trees. “Topaz?”

Dry leaves rustled underfoot. A tall, thin man emerged from the forest, Topaz dangling from one hand by the scruff of her neck. He was one of the revellers. She smiled and held out her hands for her pet. From behind his back, he produced a sack and thrust the kitten into it. Alarm skittered up her spine, but she was knocked to the ground before she could utter a protest. A hood was pulled over her head, her hands quickly bound.

Terror stole the breath from her lungs.

“One down, one to go,” someone declared. It sounded like one of the ugly twins from Poling that Rosamunda avoided like the plague.

Her mind whirled, then everything went dark.

MISSING

Adam and Denis camped on Burgh Heath, before continuing their journey at dawn the next day. They were ferried across the River Thames and rode into Westminster Palace in the early afternoon.

They sought out the king's chamberlain, requesting an audience with the future queen. The elaborately dressed official eyed their dusty raiment skeptically, until Denis produced the ring. To their consternation, he summoned two guards. "Take them to the Tower."

Adam protested. "We have an urgent message. Every moment you delay puts this kingdom in jeopardy."

The portly official guffawed. "You wave a ring in front of me which you purport belongs to His Majesty, yet you bear no document to prove what you state."

Denis persisted. "His Majesty did not want the message committed to parchment. It concerns his brother, Curthose, and an assassination plot."

The chamberlain arched his brows, eyeing the ring

once more. "If what you say proves to be true, you will be released from the Tower."

Adam's hopes for a quick return to Arundel went up in smoke. He had thought long and hard and come to the conclusion he should not have assumed Rosamunda was the guilty one. There was no future without trust.

Denis shrugged out of the guard's grasp, straightening his doublet. "You do not need to manhandle me. I am not a criminal. We must return with haste to Arundel. King Henry awaits confirmation of our success."

Adam looked straight at the chamberlain. "It's on your head."

The man stared at him, but then averted his eyes. "Remain here."

With that he was gone.

Darkness had fallen and Paulina had not returned. There was no sign of Topaz. Rosamunda was frantic, not knowing what to do, where to turn for help. Raucous laughter and the insistent beat of a *bodhran* filled the night air. She knew no one in the encampment, save for the king and Letyce Revandel. She had no intention of seeking the *hore's* help.

She had no voice to gain admittance to the royal pavilion. It would be better to wait until daylight, but she could not lay awake all night wondering what had happened to her sister.

She cursed that they'd been left alone. Her heart ached for Adam's lack of trust in her. It was the king's fault for sending Adam and Denis on this errand, whatever it was.

If only Vincent and Lucien had not gone off to Kingston Gorse.

She paced, until a chilling truth dawned. The only thing stopping her from seeking the king's help was her muteness. If she was a woman with a voice she would be hastening across the bailey, screeching loudly.

She must draw as much attention as possible instead of hiding in the shadows. Taking a deep breath, she peeled open the flap of the pavilion and ran into the night, flailing her arms wildly in the air, screaming a silent plea for help.

Lounging on a chaise near the food-laden trestles, Henry Beauclerc held a half-eaten chicken leg in mid air, listening. The music and laughter had stopped. Unease skittered up his spine. Was some dire plot afoot, orchestrated by his brother?

He followed the gazes of several people nearby who seemed to have been struck dumb. They stared at a woman, running across the bailey, waving her arms in the air. Her mouth was open but no sound emerged.

What the devil!

She was coming straight at him. He was to be assassinated by a madwoman, not by his brother. His guards were apparently of the same mind. They encircled him, pikestaffs at the ready.

It struck him as somewhat amusing. A squadron of armed men to ward off one shrieking woman. But she wasn't shrieking. There was no sound.

No sound.

Of course, the Lallement child. “Hold. I know her. She is in distress.”

The guards moved aside. The woman fell at his feet, looking up at him with imploring eyes. “Speak, child. Oh, no, you cannot speak.”

This was frustrating. Something had upset her greatly. He had appointed Guillaume de Terrence to watch over the two women in the absence of their betrotheds. He needed the smaller woman to help him understand the *muette*. “Where is your sister?”

She shook her head, tears streaming down her face.

“Is she missing?”

She nodded so vigorously he feared her head might fall off.

“Where is Sir Guillaume?”

She frowned.

The dread returned. There was mischief here. Henry abhorred mischief, especially at his favorite castle. Surely the strapping Guillaume had not made off with the tiny woman.

He turned to the captain of his guard. “Escort this lady to my pavilion. Extend her every courtesy. Do not leave her unprotected. Then take men and search for Guillaume de Terrence and the other Lallement girl.”

He did not recall her name, and her sister could not tell him, so he added, “The dwarf.”

Denis paced in one direction, Adam in the other. Each time their paths crossed they scowled, or shook their heads, or made some other exclamation.

A strange foreboding had crept into Denis' heart. He put a hand on Adam's arm. "Something is wrong."

Adam snorted. "Henry's kingdom is at the mercy of a pompous official who—"

"I don't mean that. Something has happened. I sense Paulina and Rosamunda are in danger."

Adam frowned. "But Henry has provided a champion."

Denis scratched the stubble under his chin, longing for a shave. "You are right. Still I am concerned."

The chamber doors were thrust open abruptly and the chamberlain flounced in.

Denis rolled his eyes. "Well?"

The fool held out the ring. "I have verified this as the king's ring, and I am prepared to believe you have an important message for our future queen—"

Relief surged into Denis' heart.

"—but Her Majesty is not here."

His heart stopped. "Where is she?"

"She has gone on a pilgrimage to the shrine of Saint Alban in preparation for her forthcoming marriage to our king."

"How far is that?"

The chamberlain tapped his chin. "Half a day's ride to the north. She will return in—"

Denis grabbed the ring and turned to his brother. "Come along. Saint Alban's it is."

EARNEST PRAYERS

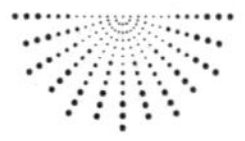

Denis and Adam rode north, following directions given them by an ostler in the royal stables. The indignant chamberlain had assigned two guards who followed close behind.

Nox and Brevis weren't fully rested from the journey to Westminster, thus preventing an all-out gallop. Even at the slower pace, conversation was difficult for Adam, and it was not until they were watering their horses in the Cyebourne at Kilburn that they had a chance to talk.

"Who is this saint whose shrine we journey to?" Denis asked.

Denis' earlier warnings of danger had unsettled Adam. A lead weight lay in the pit of his belly, and something else that made him sweat. A faint tingling he had not felt since his illness tugged at the base of his spine. It would be foolhardy to get his hopes up. It was mayhap the urgency of his mission causing the stirrings. He shrugged. "Alban. First English martyr."

"Martyr?"

Adam was hungry. He broke apart the meager loaf the ostler had given them. "Hundreds of years ago. Executed by the Romans."

Denis accepted the food. "Why would Matilda chose St. Alban's?"

Adam chewed on the stale bread. "When Alban was beheaded, a miracle was reported. Can't remember what it was. He supposedly parted the waters on his way to execution, and the executioner refused to behead him. Another man was ordered to do the deed. His eyes fell out at the moment he chopped off Alban's head. Probably superstitious nonsense.

"Anyway, rumor spread that miracles had happened there, and men and women have journeyed on pilgrimage since. A monastery was built hundreds of years ago, and now there's an abbey, begun ten years after the Conqueror's victory at Hastings."

Denis eyed the remains of his portion of the loaf with distaste. "Mayhap we should pray for a miracle while we are there."

Adam's buttocks tightened. There it was again, a faint stirring in his loins. Sweat broke out on his brow. "Mayhap we should."

King Henry was furious. Before him knelt the knight he had sent to guard the Lallement women. One eye was swollen shut, his lip split. A large goose egg on his forehead seemed to grow larger by the minute.

Rosamunda Lallement hovered nearby, twitching like a nervous cat, her hair a wild tangle.

"What have you to say for yourself?" Henry asked Guillaume de Terrence.

"I was attacked," he replied sullenly.

Henry came to his feet. "I can see that. By whom? And where is *Demoiselle* Lallement?"

Guillaume squirmed. "There were too many of them. Someone bashed me on the head while I was in—"

He glanced up nervously from studying the floor.

"Well?" Henry insisted.

"—the latrines, Sire."

A murmured titter rose from the assembled courtiers. Henry glared at them and they fell silent. "What were you doing in—never mind. Did you ever get to the pavilion occupied by the Lallement sisters?"

Sir Guillaume hung his head. "*Non, Majesté*. I was dragged into the woods and beaten. I regained my wits only a short while ago, a moment or two before the guards came upon me."

Henry pointed to Rosamunda Lallement. "This young woman's sister has been abducted. The blame lies with you, Sir Guillaume. You had better hope we find her soon. I will not have my loyal subjects kidnapped from under my nose. Do you recall nothing?"

Sir Guillaume rubbed his damaged eye, then winced. "I was strolling with Letyce Revandel. She had a cat. I excused myself to go to—"

Rosamunda lunged forward with a grunt.

Henry narrowed his eyes. "You have something to say concerning Mistress Revandel?"

The mute took a deep breath, her face red with anger, and mouthed what he was sure was the word *hore*.

Henry chuckled inwardly. The girl might be mute but

she was not dumb. "Letyce Revandel is to be sought out and brought here to me forthwith."

Blindfolded, her hands bound before her, Paulina clung to the doublet of the unknown rider with her fingertips during the terrifying ride in the dark, sure with every twist and turn of the road she was about to tumble under the hooves.

She had no notion of how long they rode, exhausted by the time she was hauled off the horse, shoved up against a tree and given a blanket. She had soiled herself for the first time in her life. Sore, ashamed, and terrified, she soon fell into oblivion.

The raucous call of a seagull woke her. She smelled the sea, and her own body. She flexed her numbed fingers and wiggled her toes.

Bread was thrust into her hands. "Eat. We depart soon."

The man's accented voice was familiar. She gathered up her courage. "Where are you taking me?"

No-one replied, though she heard movement. "My betrothed will search for me. He will come after you."

The man chuckled. "I sincerely hope so. I left enough clues."

She had heard the voice before.

"I have need of a place to bathe and see to my needs."

A woman giggled.

The cool air assaulted Paulina as the blanket was torn from her grasp. "Time enough to bathe once we reach Normandie. On your feet."

Normandie!

They were taking her across the Narrow Sea. She had never known her grandfather, but she prayed to his spirit now as she faced a perilous journey to the land of her forefathers.

Denis' heart was in turmoil as he and Adam bowed before the future queen of England in the royal chapel of Saint Alban's abbey. He felt uncomfortable under what must be the enormous weight of the soaring abbey tower they had seen on their approach. He stared at the icons of Alban holding his head in his hands and dread filled his gut. He barely recalled the details of the message he was to deliver.

Relieved when Adam began the narrative, he set his mind on Paulina, for he had no doubt she was in trouble. He felt her fear and pain keenly. He was a pot simmering on the fire.

Matilda listened carefully to Henry's message, then uttered a curt, "Thank you. I will see to the warrants. Your loyalty will be rewarded."

She eased a signet ring off her little finger, replacing it with the ring they had brought. "Take this to His Majesty."

They bowed and were dismissed.

Denis gazed at the tiny ring, but did not see it. "We need divine help, Adam. Come, let's pray to this martyred saint. Then we must return quickly. Something is wrong. I feel it in my twisted bones."

Adam knelt before the altar, wondering at the sacrifice of a man hundreds of years ago. Faith had convinced this Roman Briton to provide refuge for a Christian priest, assume his clothing, and go willingly to his death rather than denounce the fugitive from Roman justice.

Stranger still was the tale of the reluctant executioner who had also gone to his death rather than behead Alban.

And eyes popping out? People believed anything in those days.

Yet, miracles had taken place here. Discarded crutches hanging from the groin vaults bore mute testimony. Dare he hope for one? Was he worthy? Perhaps, it was the will of God he remain impotent, and deaf.

Denis rose from his knees and made hurriedly for the door. Adam looked up at the altar. "The deafness I can bear. I love Rosamunda. She would be a wonderful mother. I want to give her children. If it's your will."

He waited, aware of the impatient echo of Denis' boots on the flagstones of the entryway. He bowed his head, crossed himself and rose, his gut in knots.

MIRACLE AND CATASTROPHE

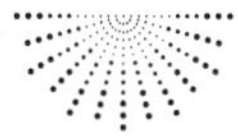

Adam and Denis rode like madmen. Nevertheless it took two days to regain Arundel. Denis' agitation over his premonitions aggravated Adam's confusion over his continuing inability to experience arousal, despite the recurrence of the occasional tingle at the base of his spine. Time and again, his hopes were dashed. He was a piglet roasting on the spit. His entreaties to Alban had been for naught.

They barely spoke during the ride, and Adam was glad of it. He could not have articulated his feelings and was relieved Denis was completely absorbed in finding out what had happened at Arundel.

They reined in hard at the castle gates, only to be urged to the royal pavilion by the guards. A shiver ran up Adam's spine. Denis' jaw tightened further. Something was definitely wrong.

They were quickly ushered into the royal presence. Stripped to the waist, Winrod and Dareau Revandel knelt before their sovereign in shackles. Their father cowered at their side, his forehead beaded with sweat.

Adam scanned the crowded space. His eyes lit on Rosamunda, leaning heavily on the arm of a knight he recognised as Guillaume de Terrence, who seemed reluctant to meet Adam's gaze. Rosamunda had perhaps turned to another because of his impotency, or on account of his suspicions.

A shiver of relief and burning jealousy surged through him. He gasped audibly as the blood rushed to his groin. His shaft stood to attention. He was on fire, his heart beating so loudly he was sure every eye would turn to him. He wanted to cry out his jubilation, rush to Rosamunda and impale her on the rushes strewn on the hard-packed ground. Then he would fall to his knees and vow his eternal devotion to Saint Alban.

No one paid him much mind, their attention riveted on the cowering twins. Only Denis turned his head, his eyes coming to rest on Adam's groin. He looked up, frowning.

His knees trembling, Adam managed a smile, then whispered, "You could tether a horse to it."

Only the knight's strong arm prevented Rosamunda from swooning when Adam strode into the pavilion. Relief buckled her knees. She wanted to run to his embrace, but doubted it would be deemed appropriate.

A grimace twisted his handsome face. Perhaps he regretted his suspicions or did he still deem her capable of betraying him? He had left without farewell and might not welcome her into his arms.

Even her sister had believed her capable of betraying him. It was an unbearable truth that anger had been between them the last time they were together.

The king's voice penetrated her confused thoughts. "The longer you hold your tongue, Revandel, the worse it will go for you. Where is your daughter?"

Alphonse Revandel's voice shook. He blinked away sweat. "*Majesté*, Letyce has ever been a wayward chit. I am ignorant of her comings and goings." He pointed a trembling finger at his sons. "These two have more knowledge of her than I."

Rosamunda felt sorry for him. Three children and he had been unable to control any of them. She and her sister had been controlled to the point of incarceration. There had to be a middle ground.

Henry turned his attention to Winrod Revandel. "You are the older twin?"

Winrod swallowed. "Yes, Sire. Two minutes."

"Then you have exactly two minutes to tell me where your sister has taken Paulina Lallement and who her accomplice is, otherwise your brother will be interrogated."

Winrod glanced at Dareau. It took him less than a few seconds to apparently decide he loved his brother more than his sister. "They have taken her to Bretagne."

Without warning, Denis de Sancerre burst from the crowd and seized Winrod by the throat. "What mischief is this that my betrothed has been abducted and taken to Bretagne?"

Hampered by his shackles, Winrod lost his balance and fell backwards. Denis leapt on top of him, his hands still locked on Revandel's throat.

A wave of shocked murmurs crested. Two guards pulled Denis off the choking man, holding him fast as he struggled to set upon Revandel once more. Dareau Revandel edged away on his knees.

"Enough," the king bellowed.

Adam strode over to Denis. "Hold, brother. If you kill him we will not uncover the truth."

Denis calmed, shrugging out of the grasp of the guards. "I apologise, *Majesté*. I am distraught at what has happened to my betrothed. She is vulnerable."

Henry drummed his fingers on the arms of his massive chair. "Where in Bretagne have they gone?"

Winrod mumbled something.

Rosamunda strained to hear.

Adam frowned.

The king's face reddened.

Denis, closest to Winrod, declared, "They have taken her to Carnac."

Henry came to his feet quickly. "Now it becomes clear who the ne'er-do-well is at the bottom of this mischief. Guards, search the grounds for Malraux de Carnac, though I doubt you will find him."

He turned to the Revandel twins. "You are a disgrace to your family name. You have aided and abetted a criminal act. In addition you have heaped calumny and rumor upon a member of an illustrious Norman family, the Montbryces."

Ice splintered in Rosamunda's veins. She looked at Adam, standing proudly by his brother's side—a magnificent man about to be shamed publicly. The king may have the best of intentions, but this would make matters worse.

Henry carried on, the corners of his mouth edging up.

"You have insinuated Adam de Montbryce is less than a man, but it seems to me he is perfectly capable of performing the functions of a lusty male."

All eyes turned to Adam. Rosamunda's mouth went dry as she stared at the bulge in his leggings that the short doublet did nothing to conceal.

Desire coiled in her belly, sweeping her off her feet as she swooned.

Pandemonium broke out.

Denis was unsure what to do first: rush to embrace his brother; help Guillaume de Terrence with Rosamunda; slice off Winrod Revandel's head with his sword, then plunge it into Dareau's heart; or fall to his knees weeping.

He did nothing. His heart had broken into a thousand pieces. Malraux de Carnac had carted off Paulina. The malicious Breton had naught good planned for her. There would be no ransom demand.

He'd always been a decisive man, but now he stood rooted to the spot, unable to act.

His Majesty demanded calm be restored. He consigned the Revandels to the Tower, thus removing them from the danger of certain death at Denis' hand.

Adam strode quickly to take Rosamunda from Guillaume's arms. Scowling at the knight, he carried her out of the pavilion to the cheers of onlookers.

The only thing left was to weep. But weeping would not help Paulina. Suddenly, he remembered Matilda's ring. He extricated it from a pouch at his waist and bent the knee before Henry, holding out the ring. "Sire, we have completed your mission. Now, I beg leave to pursue Malraux de Carnac."

Henry inhaled deeply, accepting the ring, which he clasped tightly in his hand. "I give leave, though I fear he has a head start."

A loud cough sounded behind Denis. Henry looked beyond him. "What is it Terrence?"

Guillaume de Terrence came to kneel beside Denis. "Sire, this catastrophe is my fault. Had I been more vigilant—"

Denis needed to blame someone. He glared at de Terrence.

"*Milord* de Sancerre, allow me to accompany you on your quest to save *demoiselle* Lallement."

Denis wanted to kill the man, but a knight without honor might as well be dead. Guillaume sought to regain his. "I welcome your offer. We depart on the morrow at dawn."

THE WEDDING IS OFF

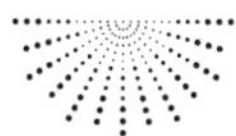

Paulina's acquaintance with gentlemen was limited, but it did not take long to ascertain that Malraux de Carnac was no gentleman. She recognized the woman as Rosamunda's nemesis, Letyce Revandel.

Malraux fawned over Letyce during the sea crossing, pawing at her inappropriately even as she retched over the side. Antoine de Montbryce's tendency to *mal de mer* had been an integral part of the heroic story of the Montbryces. She chuckled inwardly that Letyce had been thus afflicted, though she wished they had kept her blindfolded rather than witness it.

They had unbound her hands. Short of jumping into the waves, there was no escape.

Her predicament angered her. It was her own fault. She had behaved like a child, throwing a tantrum with Rosamunda, accusing her of betraying Adam, as if her sister would do such a thing. Whatever his secret was, Rosamunda would never divulge it.

By heedlessly following Topaz, Paulina had walked

straight into the trap set for her. She had no doubt Carnac had chosen her deliberately because she was a dwarf. Fear of what he planned sat like a weight in her belly, but at least he seemed to have no carnal interest in her. If he touched her inappropriately she might retch on his boots.

Tears threatened when she thought of Denis. She longed for his touch, yet had remained aloof, afraid to admit her feelings. But she determined not to cry. She would not give Carnac and the Revandel woman the satisfaction. She was a Lallement, of proud Norman stock.

"Ouistreham," came the shout.

As the village loomed out of the fog, she recalled Rosamunda's longing for a glimpse of the land of their forefathers. She resolved to remember every detail so she could relate it to her sister when next they met. She prayed her abductors would not deem the blindfold necessary once they started out on their trek across Normandie.

Rosamunda awoke in her pavilion, but she was not lying on her pallet. She snuggled into the warm chest of the man who held her on his lap.

Adam.

She struggled to sit up, but he held her fast. "Forgive me, Rosa, for my suspicions. I should have immediately thought of Letyce Revandel, and not of you."

She looked away, longing to kiss him, but still angry.

He gently turned her chin to his gaze.

She pouted, then mouthed the nagging question. "Letyce?"

He shrugged. "The woman constantly pressed her body

to mine. I suppose she is used to men becoming aroused. I didn't."

Sitting on his lap, Rosamunda felt his arousal now, hard and insistent beneath her. She flexed the muscles of her *derrière*, grinning mischievously. "What is that?"

Adam groaned into her hair, tightening his hold. "A miracle," he whispered. "I prayed to Saint Alban. He apparently paid heed to my heartfelt wish to give you children."

Children!

He chuckled. "*Oui*, I won't simply have to dream hopelessly about our bodies joining. I can look forward to the day it happens."

Gooseflesh marched across her skin. But he had hurt her. She pointed to him, then to herself. "No trust."

He inhaled deeply, then exhaled. His full lower lip pouted slightly as the air left his lungs. Her heart skipped a beat. "I was a fool, Rosa. Forgive me. I was too blinded by my masculine pride."

She brushed her thumb over the lip that held her gaze. "Still marry?"

He grinned. "More than ever, and I am no longer content to wait until Normandie. We might spend months trying to obtain Curthose's permission. We will wed before I go off with Denis to retrieve your sister."

She struggled to her feet, indignation an arrow in her heart. "Go with you."

He shook his head. "*Non*, it will be dangerous."

She thumped her breast with the flat of her hand. "My sister. I will go with Vincent and Lucien. No wedding."

~

Messengers were dispatched to Kingston Gorse advising Vincent and Lucien of their sister's abduction and instructing them to be on the Portsmouth road at dawn if they wished to assist in her rescue.

Denis paced the narrow confines of the pavilion. There would be no possibility of sleep with him this night. Adam moved from his pavilion to Rosamunda's and curled up with her on the pallet.

He stroked her hair as she sobbed, marveling that, despite everything, the scent of rosemary still clung to her. "Let me lie with you, Rosa. We will comfort each other. I will be a gentleman, much as I want to make you my wife in every way."

It was ironic. He had longed for his male potency to return, yet now it had, he was content to simply lie with her. The ache of longing he felt with her soft *derrière* pressed against him was sweet torture. He could wait.

LONG NIGHT AT SEA

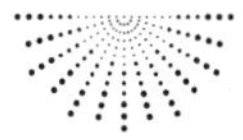

Denis, Guillaume and Adam argued back and forth from the moment word came during the early morning hours that Winrod Revandel had confessed Carnac and Letyce's plan to take ship from Portsmouth to Ouistreham.

"We should follow the same route," Adam insisted. "They evidently plan to travel west through Normandie to Bretagne, and thence to Carnac on the coast."

Guillaume considered it a sound plan.

Denis disagreed vehemently. "We will never catch up. We need to take a different route, to arrive sooner. We must seek out a ship bound for Bretagne, not Normandie."

The argument continued throughout the ride to East Preston, despite the darkness. Rosamunda grew tired of it, but they ignored her huffs of displeasure and didn't even notice her pouting. She wished she had a voice to scream her annoyance.

At East Preston, Adam took her to the pigeon cote and explained what he planned. "I'm sending birds to Robert at

Montbryce, *Oncle* Hugh at Domfort, Ronan at Alensonne and, lastly, to my father at Belisle, explaining the urgency and requesting contingents of spare men at arms be dispatched to Carnac with all possible haste."

Rosamunda watched him carefully attach the messages to the pigeons. As he was about to release the one bound for Belisle, she touched his arm, pointing to herself.

He shook his head. "*Non*, Rosa, I did not mention you, nor my miracle. Best to cross that bridge when Mathieu and I are standing at either end of it."

Steward Cormant organized provisions for the journey. They set off and the argument continued.

Rosamunda was heartily glad to see Vincent and Lucien waiting for them when they reached the Portsmouth road. She dismounted quickly to share a tearful embrace with her brothers.

Guillaume de Terrence also dismounted and knelt before Rosamunda's brothers. "Forgive me, *mes seigneurs*. Had I been more vigilant, your sister would not now be in the hands of Malraux de Carnac."

Vincent lunged, but Denis stopped him. "We have no time to waste on recriminations and accusations. We are all at fault for not protecting Paulina, none more so than I. She is to be my wife. I should have taken greater care. Mount up and let's be gone."

Vincent and Lucien gaped at each other. A spark of hope kindled in Rosamunda's breast. Denis truly loved her sister. He spoke as if he believed she would be rescued. She prayed as she remounted Lux, then rolled her eyes as the argument about their route was taken up again, this time with two more male opinions loudly expressed.

In the event, no boat was available to take them to Ouistreham, but a Breton captain from Rosko agreed to transport them and their horses on his return trip home. He apparently did not share the opinion of many that a dwarf was bad luck. The vessel seemed sound enough and his crew curious but honest.

Denis' mood lightened. As far as he was concerned, going by way of Ouistreham would have sounded Paulina's death knell. The Breton informed him Rosko was only two and a half days ride from Carnac. This would buy them time overland, though the sea voyage would be longer, and probably rougher.

On their first day at sea, the sailing was reasonably smooth. Denis determined to find out as much as possible about Carnac from the captain. Why had they taken Paulina there? Traveling such a great distance with a hostage was fraught with difficulties. Why had they undertaken such a scheme?

The seaman spoke mainly Breton, but they managed to communicate. What Denis learned chilled his blood, and he hurried to impart his news to Adam, passing Guillaume en route.

The knight averted his eyes as they passed each other on deck.

Denis located his brother wrapped in blankets, under the canvas shelter, his body shielding a sleeping Rosamunda from the wind. A pang of despair jolted Denis. Would he ever hold Paulina in his arms, or were they already too late?

Adam moved over to make room. "What does he say?"

Rosamunda woke as Denis wrapped a blanket around his shoulders. "He knows Carnac well, the place and the lord. He has naught good to say about Malraux de Carnac. He is the sort of *Seigneur* who rules by fear.

"Carnac itself is distinguished by hundreds of standing stones. No one knows how they got there, or why they were placed in the formations they were. One legend tells of Merlin turning a Roman legion to stone.

"Most of the stones are small, no taller than me, apparently, and cover a wide area."

Rosamunda frowned. "Why take her there?"

A nasty suspicion had risen in Denis' mind. "There is one stone much taller than the rest. Standing twenty feet high, it's shaped—forgive me, Rosamunda—like a man's shaft. They call it *Le Manio*."

Rosamunda blushed, averting her eyes.

Adam looked at him intently. "You have a suspicion about this stone, am I right?"

If Denis gave voice to the horror he imagined, it would make it seem possible. But he had no choice. He shouted over the wind. "Every year, on All Hallows' Eve, Malraux chooses a virgin from the village. She is hauled to the top of *Le Manio*, then tossed to the ground.

"Local youths try to catch her, and whoever does can have her. It usually takes more than one to break her fall. There is much drinking and carousing beforehand. At the very least there is the danger of injury, to the men and the girl. Some have died."

Rosamunda clasped her hands over her mouth, burying her face in the blanket.

Adam tightened his embrace. "You believe he intends to toss Paulina off the stone?"

Denis raked his hair back. "Such a fall will kill her. She is too small. And who will want to catch her?"

Rosamunda dozed fitfully during the long night at sea, her sleep disturbed by fits of sobbing. Adam cradled her to his body, giving what little comfort he could. He thanked God that, though the circumstances were far from ideal, the woman he loved was at his side. They were together.

In Denis' place he would have become a screaming lunatic, imagining the horror they believed was planned at Carnac. His brother had comforted him in his distress, but now there were no words. In any case, Denis had refused to listen to admonitions about the advisability of sleep and instead paced the decks, muttering loudly.

Dawn brought rougher seas. Denis smirked when Guillaume became violently ill.

The horses grew restless and most of the daylight hours were spent calming them and making sure the tethers did not loosen. Rosamunda stayed with Lux, providing reassurance.

By nightfall everyone was exhausted as they pulled into shore. Adam curled up with Rosamunda and did not wake until dawn. They set off again and by midday sighted an island, with a harbor beyond.

"*Enez Vaz*," the captain declared.

"Batz Island," Denis explained to the others. "It guards Rosko harbor. We have arrived. There is plenty of daylight left. Let's get the horses off as soon as we make landfall."

DESPERATE FLIGHT

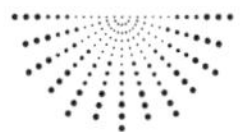

Paulina was awed by the size of the town as Malraux led them into Caen. Her hands were bound and she was wedged between two small iron chests, clinging to the strap that secured them to the donkey. Letyce sulked, seemingly slow to recover from *mal de mer*. Her sneering smile had flickered only once when she espied the animal Paulina was to ride.

Ignoring Letyce's pouting glare, Paulina gazed at the soaring towers of the two *Abbayes* built by William the Conqueror, one for men, the other for women. She had secretly dreamed of a day she might visit the tomb of the Conqueror's wife, marked by a black slab under the choir of the *Abbaye aux Dames*. Now, there was no hope of venturing inside.

As they rode on through the cobbled streets, a shiver snaked up her spine at the forbidding sight of Caen Castle, citadel of Robert Curthose, Duke of Normandie.

Here was the seat of a power that threatened peace in England and Normandie. Vincent and Lucien had explained to her the political struggle between Curthose and King Henry.

Denis had told her of the Montbryces' support for Henry and Curthose's anger over what he perceived as a betrayal. Little had she known she would be passing within a stone's throw of Curthose's gates.

They lodged in the home of a kinsman of Malraux's. He led the donkey into the stable and plucked her from between the chests. "You'll sleep here," he said gruffly.

Anger flared. "I am not an animal to sleep in a stable. You promised a bath."

He chuckled. "Fiery little gnat, aren't you? There's water in yon horse trough. Goodnight."

He swaggered off, his arm wrapped possessively around Letyce's shoulders. They were confident there was no escape in this hostile town, but they were mistaken if they thought they had cowed her. She determined to watch and wait for the right moment. They had taken away her newly-found freedom, but she would not go meekly to whatever fate they had planned.

A curious stable lad unburdened the donkey and led it into a stall. When he gawked at her, she put her hands on her hips. "Leave me be."

To her surprise, he scarpered. She gritted her teeth, found a bucket, and dipped it in the frigid water. The donkey raised its head from the feed bag and fixed its large brown eye on her as she huddled in the corner of its stall, washing as best she could. She stayed as far away from the animal as possible, though sooner or later she would need its warmth or she might freeze to death. Carnac had left her no blanket to ward off the autumn chill.

She knew nothing about making friends, especially

with an animal, but fancied knowing a name might help. "I am Paulina," she whispered to the curious beast. "What is your name?"

She covered her ears, hunching her shoulders as the donkey brayed a loud response, its belly heaving, nostrils flaring.

Determined not to show fear, Paulina responded, "I see. Your name is Soufflette, because you sound like the bellows Agnès pumped mightily to get the fire going in our grate."

She doused a spark of nostalgia for the cozy chambers at Kingston Gorse and set about arranging a bed in the straw.

The next day, they travelled south from Caen through the flat fields and plains of Normandie. Paulina was not permitted to control the donkey, but her fear of the animal lessened. It seemed that once the beast had a name, it was less intimidating. She was relieved not to be riding a horse, such as Letyce's palfrey. At least a fall from a donkey would not be from as great a height.

Letyce's only interaction with Paulina consisted of sneers and snide remarks about being afraid of horses. Paulina did her best to conceal her growing level of comfort with the donkey.

Let her think what she will.

Letyce's main preoccupation was with Malraux de Carnac. She flirted with him constantly, fluttering her eyelashes, and thrusting her breasts. Her behavior disgusted Paulina. Malraux's eyes held only contempt.

He fondled Letyce's breasts frequently, even on horseback. Horrified as she was, Paulina's body heated at the thought of Denis putting his hands on her breasts. She regretted treating him coldly.

She was confident Denis and Adam had already set out to rescue her, but they couldn't know where she was. They were headed for Malraux's lands, wherever that was. It would be foolhardy to rely only on Denis.

She overheard Malraux mention her betrothed more than once. The realization that he wanted Denis to follow and attempt a rescue chilled her blood. She was the bait.

She determined to watch for an opportunity to escape, though how to accomplish such a thing in unknown foreign territory on a donkey with her hands tied was daunting. But if she did not escape, death awaited, of that she was sure.

They encountered few people on the road. Malraux's snarls deterred those who gawked at Paulina. Letyce whined when informed they would be avoiding castles and villages. "I cannot sleep out of doors. Why can we not stay where there is a bed?"

Malraux shook his head. "Normandie is a land full of fear and mistrust, divided in two camps, Curthose's and Henry's. People are suspicious of strangers. They remain indoors and do not travel about. We will keep to ourselves and avoid arousing interest."

Each time they espied a castle off in the distance, Letyce sulked, asking petulantly, "And what fine *demesne* are we bypassing now?"

This had a curious effect on Malraux. Instead of ignoring her, he called a halt, announced the name of the castle, assisted her down from her mount, and then escorted her behind nearby bushes or trees.

Paulina was left atop the tethered donkey, ignored, watching the placid animal's ears twitch away flies.

When they emerged, Letyce's hair and clothing was disheveled, the pout replaced by a sultry grin.

Malraux constantly complained of their slow pace as he swaggered back to his mount, yet, every hour or two, the scene would be repeated as he and Letyce disappeared into the bushes.

They were rutting dogs, Paulina thought with disgust, but their appetites might provide her only opportunity for escape.

They had been on the road for hours. Paulina was exhausted and barely heard Letyce ask her usual question. Her heart fell as she contemplated another wait while the fools fornicated. She narrowed her eyes in the fading light and in the distance saw the outline of a large castle atop a promontory. It seemed to be flanked by trees.

Malraux dismounted, but came to her instead of Letyce. The certainty that he intended to touch her inappropriately beat a tattoo in her throat. He untied her wrists, and put his hands on her waist to lift her down. She thumped his chest with her fists.

He laughed. "What a ferocious little chit you are. Don't worry; you're too small for my tastes. We will camp here. Make yourself useful and gather wood for a fire, while Letyce and I entertain each other. It will be a delicious irony for her since yonder is the *demesne* of the mighty Montbryces."

Fear and elation swirled in Paulina's heart. They were within sight of Montbryce Castle, stronghold of Adam's cousin, Robert. Here was her opportunity, but was she courageous enough to seize it? Malraux evidently judged her too much of a coward to attempt an escape.

Rubbing her wrists, she searched for firewood, all the while watching the Breton and a simpering Letyce saunter off, his hand on her *derrière*.

She looked over to where Malraux had tethered the animals. Impatient for his tryst, he had not removed the saddles. Soufflette turned one sad brown eye to her. If she attempted to escape on the donkey the animal might obey her, or balk, sensing her fear. Soufflette's braying was enough to wake the dead and would surely bring Malraux running. In any case, the baggage would make a speedy ride impossible.

Letyce's palfrey stood next to the donkey. If she reached the stirrup and clambered onto the horse, how would she get it to go where she wanted? She closed her eyes, her knees trembling. "Rosa, if only you were here."

A vision sprang into her memory; Rosamunda, laughing confidently atop Nox the first time she had ever sat a horse. What made her sister a horsewoman?

She shows no fear.

Paulina's eyes flitted to the only other mount, Malraux's enormous gelding. Not an option. It had to be the palfrey. She took a deep breath, dropped the kindling she had gathered, and strode over to the horse, brushing dirt from her hands.

The forlorn look in Soufflette's eyes undid her. She stopped a moment to kiss the donkey's nose and rub her ears. It struck her like a thunderbolt that she was not afraid of the animal.

The realization gave her courage. Willing her hands not to shake, she untied the palfrey's tether. The beast shifted, making it difficult to get her foot in the stirrup. She prayed the donkey would not sound the alarm.

Grunts and moans drifted from the bushes. The palfrey's ears pricked up. Paulina hung on to the saddle for dear life, but the animal refused to stand still. The gelding shifted nervously. Sweat trickled down Paulina's spine. The lovebirds would soon return.

She looked the horse in the eye, pointed a rigid finger at it, and whispered through gritted teeth, "Be still."

To her surprise, the horse obeyed. Her foot slipped into the stirrup just as she feared her hipbone might break. She struggled to lie belly down on the saddle, then swung her leg over. She tightened her grip on the reins, dug in her calves, and turned the horse in the direction of the castle.

She would not later recall much of the ride, except the mind-numbing terror of it. Her feet dangled above the stirrups. The horse seemed determined to go in a direction that would take her past her goal by a mile. She dared not turn around to look behind, but there was no mistaking the sounds of a horse in hot pursuit.

Malraux.

He yelled curses and threats. She curled her body lower, clinging to the mane, willing the horse to make for the safety of the castle.

She would never know if it was someone lighting torches on the battlements to dispel the gathering darkness that caught the horse's attention, or if it sensed the presence of other animals. In any event, the palfrey changed its course, headed straight for the castle's walls.

She remembered Malraux's caution that guards would be on the watch for intruders. How to make them see she was not a threat. Screaming seemed a good idea. She took a deep breath and let out a high pitched wail. It startled the horse into galloping faster. If she fell now—

Her cloak billowed like a flapping sail, and suddenly it was gone, torn away by the cold wind that had numbed her face into a grimace.

The castle gate loomed up. It was shut. Unless the horse stopped of its own accord, she would be dashed to pieces against the thick wood.

Suddenly, the gate crashed open. Horses spilled out, riding towards her. They thought it was an attack and had come to thwart her advance. Could they not see she was a woman, a tiny one at that?

Her screams echoed in her ears as she bellowed the first thing that came into her head. “Sancerre, Sancerre, Sancerre!”

Robert de Montbryce was inspecting the guard on the battlements when he was alerted to the incoming rider. He ordered the torches lit earlier than usual. “Whoever it is approaches at great speed,” he said to his steward.

The gloom of dusk made it difficult to make out the rider. He had flattened his body to the horse, and rode as if the hounds of hell pursued him. As the rider neared, Robert gasped. “It’s a child.”

Then another horseman came into view.

Robert cupped his hands to his mouth and yelled out an order to the mounted knights waiting below. “It’s a child seeking sanctuary. Ride out to provide safe passage. Another is in pursuit.”

From his vantage point he watched the drama unfold.

His men-at-arms rode out towards the boy. The pursuer reined his horse to a halt. The boy came on at speed, shrieking something. It sounded like *Saint Cyr*. Why would the lad be—

He gripped his steward's arm. "Can it be Denis' betrothed, the kidnapped girl of the message brought by pigeon? She has saved us the trouble of rescuing her."

The pursuing rider skidded to a halt, leaned down to pick up something from the ground, then rode away at a gallop.

One of Robert's outriders grasped the reins of the incoming horse and slowed it to a trot. The woman slumped forward as her mount was led through the gate. Robert hastened down from the battlements to lift her from the snorting horse.

She was tiny! He cradled her in his arms as she sobbed. "You're safe now. I am Robert de Montbryce."

It occurred to him she was not from Normandie and might not understand his language, so he reassured her in Anglo-Norman.

The little woman seemed unable to speak as he carried her into the Keep and placed her in the *Seigneur's* chair by the fire in the hall. The warmth rallied her. A shudder tore through her body. "I was abducted. I am Paulina Lallement. I am betrothed to Denis de Sancerre."

Robert smiled. "Welcome, Paulina. We received a message and have been preparing men to ride to your rescue. Now you can rest and we will send word to Denis that you are safe."

Paulina gripped the arms of the chair. "No, my abductor plans to lure Denis to his estates. I don't know where his lands are, but we must find out. Your cousin, Adam, is probably with Denis. You resemble him."

Robert chuckled, but then frowned. "Who is your abductor?"

"Malraux de Carnac."

"Carnac is in Bretagne. Why did he kidnap you?"

Paulina combed her disheveled hair off her face. "Because I am a dwarf." She took a deep breath. "I believe he has some evil intent that has to do with All Hallows' Eve."

Robert nodded thoughtfully. A maidservant entered with tumblers filled with golden liquid. Robert offered one to Paulina. "It will chase away the chill and calm you."

Paulina accepted the tumbler. "I have never drunk wine before."

Robert smiled as he took a tumbler from the maidservant. "This is not wine. It's a special apple brandy we make here at Montbryce. Sip it slowly."

"Denis told me of your orchards. Never did I think to be sipping your brandy in the place it is made."

Robert furrowed his brow. "Did you know you were near Montbryce Castle?"

Paulina related the tale of her escape, astonished as much as Montbryce seemed to be by her courage. "It is the first time I have ridden a horse by myself," she admitted quietly. "I am afraid of them."

Robert hunkered down beside her chair. "It seems to me Denis has chosen well. You are a courageous woman. He is a lucky man."

She felt her face redden as heat surged through her. "I have been a lifelong coward, afraid of exposure to the outside world. It is Denis who has given me courage by his example, by who he is. We must ride to prevent his capture."

"First, rest from your ordeal. We will find you clean clothes. A chamber is being readied, and a bath prepared."

Paulina inhaled deeply. "I thank you. Adam and Denis have boasted of the nobility of their family, and I understand why."

Robert hesitated. "How fares Adam?"

Paulina smiled, not sure how much to reveal. "He seems well enough. He is betrothed to my sister, Rosamunda."

QUIBERON

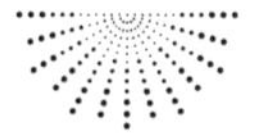

The other men had a right to their opinions, but Denis had grown increasingly weary of the argument raging now over how they should proceed to Carnac. He had made up his mind after another talk with the Breton captain. He pointed to the water. “I intend to go by sea to Carnac.”

Adam groaned.

Denis persisted. He held up three fingers. “Overland will take us three days, in unknown territory. Our captain assures me it is impossible to get lost if we hug the coast-line. He will lend us two of his men and yon sturdy skiff.”

Vincent protested. “We can’t take the horses in that.”

Denis looked sadly at Brevis. Adam would be distraught at the loss of Nox. “I propose a solution. We cannot all fit in the boat. Guillaume, Lucien, Vincent, and the men at arms will take the overland route with the horses. Adam, Rosamunda, and I will go by sea, which will save us two days. We will rendezvous in Carnac, then make our way back through Normandie to Belisle.”

Vincent shook his head. “Lucien can go with the horses. I am coming with you. Paulina is my sister.”

Recognising further argument would waste more time, Denis agreed. “Are we as one mind, then?” he asked Adam.

Adam hesitated, but shrugged when Rosamunda laid a hand on his arm. “I am loath to leave Nox, but you are right.”

Denis’ heart was heavy as the Breton sailors pushed off the boat and clambered aboard. Adam could not conceal his distress at leaving Nox behind. Denis sensed his brother might never forgive him if he and the stallion were not reunited. He hoped he had made the right decision.

Adam cuddled Rosamunda close to his heart as the Bretons rowed them past miles of rugged coastline. His gut had been in knots watching Nox stomp the ground and throw his head back in a snort of protest as they left the harbor at Rosko. Denis had said nothing about Brevis, but Adam knew his brother felt the loss of his mount keenly.

Brevis was a treasured find, a horse small enough for Denis, but with a courageous heart.

Rosamunda had been sad to leave Lux. But her tears were for Lucien.

Denis kept his face to the wind, his swarthy features twisted into a grim mask of determination.

Adam laid a hand on his brother’s rigid shoulder. “This was the right decision. Time is of the essence. All Hallows’ Eve is only two days hence.”

After several hours, the oarsmen were tiring visibly.

Adam and Vincent took their places.

Denis moved to Rosamunda's side and reached his arm around her shoulders. "Lean on me, sister, we will bring each other warmth and comfort."

She was grateful for his kindness in the midst of his grief and worry. She was feeling the loss of Adam's heat.

Her betrothed smiled at her as he rowed. His powerful arms made the exercise look easy. She became rapt in the rhythm of his movements as he pulled the oars to his broad chest then leaned forward to gather strength again, his long legs braced in the boat. As night fell, the Bretons directed them into shore.

They camped in a wood. Exhaustion soon claimed her and she fell asleep in Adam's strong arms, cradled in the security of his embrace.

She seemed to have just fallen asleep when Adam gently shook her awake. "It's dawn, we must move on."

She rubbed her eyes, gathering the blanket more tightly around her shoulders as a brisk wind buffeted her.

Denis stood on the rocky shore with the Bretons. She followed their gaze out to the choppy waves. "Not a good day to be on the water," he grunted.

Within minutes of setting out, everyone in the boat was drenched. The Bretons advised pulling further from shore in an effort to find calmer waters. Adam feared someone might get swept overboard in the rolling swells as the oarsmen struggled to make headway. He and Vincent wedged a shivering Rosamunda between them.

The gentle drizzle that had begun on shore turned into a torrential downpour. Denis untied the cord controlling the rudder from the foot of one of the oarsmen and moved to the stern of the boat, grasping the tiller.

Suddenly, after what seemed like hours of rowing in place, land loomed before them.

Denis pointed and yelled.

Adam hoped it was the Quiberon Peninsula that the Bretons had told them protected Carnac from the sea. Once around its tip they would be in more sheltered waters.

"Quiberon?" died on his lips as an enormous swell picked up the boat and overturned it, casting them into the roiling waves.

TWIST OF FATE

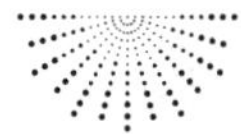

Letyce Revandel squinted into the pounding rain to make out the outline of Carnac Castle. Much as she longed to be dry and warm, she dreaded entering Malraux's *demesne*.

Since the dwarf's escape, the Breton had treated her cruelly, blaming her for the loss of his intended plaything. He had offered her no covering for warmth, save Paulina's inadequate cloak.

He had disdained her attempts to placate him with sexual advances, and threatened to toss her from *Le Manio* if no suitable replacement was found. She cursed the day she had accompanied him on this mad excursion.

It was not her fault the dwarf had escaped. Blame instead his rapacious appetite for intercourse. However, he was not a man to be reasonable when angered. She shrank from his touch, now sensing great evil in him.

If she wanted to avoid death she would have to escape, or find a replacement for Paulina. She doubted there were many dwarfs in the vicinity. The heavy rain might provide enough cover for an escape. Malraux was far enough ahead he would not notice her absence for a few minutes.

Turning the donkey, she urged it to a trot, heedless of the danger of the animal losing its footing in the muddied terrain, and having no idea where she was headed.

Malraux did not turn when he heard Letyce flee. “With any luck the whore will fall off the donkey and break her neck. Sadly, such a fate would deprive me of the pleasure of seeing her dangle from the top of *Le Manio*.”

He yawned as he rode through the gate of his estate, patting his horse. “Feels good to be home, eh boy?”

A groom rushed to take the reins as he dismounted.

His steward appeared, adjusting his half-fastened doublet, shoulders hunched against the downpour.

Malraux scowled. “Roget, my traveling companion appears to have become lost. Send out a search party for her on the morrow, if the weather improves. Is everything in readiness for All Hallows’ Eve?”

Roget flinched. “Not quite everything, *milord*.”

Malraux braced his legs, hands on hips. “At least assure me the scaffolding has been erected.”

“Most of it,” Roget stammered.

Only a day left to complete preparations. Heads would roll if everything was not ready in time. “Forget the search party for the woman. Too much to do. We will need all hands.”

Roget bowed low.

Letyce screamed when the donkey shied, almost throwing her off. Trembling, she dismounted, trying to calm the braying beast. As the first gray light of dawn streaked the sky, her knees buckled as she gingerly peered over the edge of a cliff overlooking the sea.

Another few moments and she would have been dashed to pieces on the rocks below. The pounding surf drew her gaze as her belly twisted beneath her ribs.

Her eyes fixed on an object on one of the rocks. It looked like a person. Indeed, it was a person—a woman. Perhaps from a shipwreck.

Indecision plagued her. Let the woman fend for herself. Letyce feared injury clambering down to aid her. If she was badly hurt, there was no way to bring her up from the shore.

The donkey stopped braying and turned one soulful eye to her.

Letyce glanced about, looking for a path to the beach. "You want me to rescue her, don't you, dumb beast?"

Now she was talking to a donkey. Madness wasn't far behind. But one of her words stuck in her head.

Dumb.

She looked down again at the body on the rocks. Unlikely as it seemed, she felt a connection with the woman below.

She remounted, directing the animal along the cliff top. "Find me a path, donkey."

She was soon praying hard as the sure-footed animal picked its way down a rocky path that twisted and turned many times before she was delivered to the beach, panting and sweating despite the chill of her rain-soaked clothing.

She dismounted on shaky legs and hurried to the body

lying face down on the rock, frustrated by her shoes bogging down in the wet sand.

She strained to turn the woman over. Her face was bruised and there was a bloody gash over one eye. But there could be no mistaking the hair. Even plastered to her head, Rosamunda's untidy locks betrayed who she was. "The mute," Letyce gasped, a flicker of hope sparking in her breast.

A maelstrom of conflicting thoughts assailed her. She wanted to laugh in the girl's face and ask her if she knew she was marrying a eunuch.

She had a notion to bash her head against the rock and finish her off, then Adam de Montbryce would have no one. Serve him right.

But there was still the problem of Malraux. No doubt he would come after her as his sacrificial offering for All Hallows' Eve. Here was a perfect substitute, handed to her by the saints. Not a dwarf, but the dwarf's sister, and a *muette* to boot.

Her heart lurched. Pray God the woman was still alive.

She shook her shoulders. "Wake up, wake up, Rosamunda."

La *muette* coughed, flailing her arms, but did not open her eyes.

Letyce took hold of her hands. "Be still. You are safe now. I will take you to your sister."

Rosamunda opened one eye, frowning as she grunted. Letyce was not sure what she was trying to say, so she shoved the ends of Paulina's cloak into Rosamunda's hands. "See, Paulina's cloak. We escaped from Malraux. He's evil. She is safe. I will take you to her."

Rosamunda fingered the fabric, bringing it close to her

face. Another unintelligible grunt. How did this woman survive without the gift of speech? Such creatures had no place in Letyce's world. Better she provide sport for Malraux. At least, better her than Letyce.

She helped Rosamunda to her feet. The blond swayed against her, holding a hand to her head, but seemed to have no broken bones.

Weighed down by wet clothing, the two exhausted women staggered like drunken serfs to the donkey. Letyce tilted her head to lick a few drops of rain from the air to soothe her parched throat. "Hold on to the saddle."

Rosamunda clung to the pommel, resting her head on the saddle.

Letyce strained to put her shoulder under the mute's *derrière*. "Climb up," she wheezed.

It took several attempts to get Rosamunda atop the donkey. Letyce feared the dazed woman might yet fall off as they ascended the steep path. "Hold tight," she urged, pressing her hands atop Rosamunda's.

As she led the donkey up the path, it occurred to her this was a lot of effort to save a life that would be sacrificed to Malraux's evil. She fell to all fours at the top of the path, breathless and aching. This was about saving her own life, but she was exhausted. "I'll have to leave you here. We will never make it together. I will come back, with Paulina."

She dragged Rosamunda from the donkey, helped her to the shelter of a rocky overhang, tucked Paulina's cloak around her, remounted, and rode off to retrace the path to Malraux's estate.

EVIL INTENT

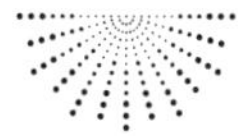

Adam broke the surface, gasping for breath. He raked his hair off his face, rubbing the salt from his eyes. Rosamunda was nowhere to be seen. Panic gripped his vitals.

Denis popped to the surface not far away, coughing and spluttering, his thick hair covering his face.

Adam swam over to him, feeling the tug of the current. The one thing Denis feared was deep water. He had never learned to swim. Adam threw an arm around his brother's chest. "Don't struggle," he rasped. "Lean back into me."

Denis obeyed.

Adam scanned the water frantically, looking for any sign of Rosamunda. There was none. If he let go of Denis to dive down and look for her, his brother might drown. But he had to try. "I have to let you go." He took a deep breath. "A moment only." He eased his arm away from Denis. "Kick like hell."

He dove beneath the surface, searching the clear water for any sign of his beloved. Only when his lungs were ready to burst did he resurface. Denis was still afloat, but his drawn face betrayed his belief he was about to die. “Rosamunda?”

Adam shook his head, again clamping his arm around his brother. “Current—too strong.”

He kicked out for the shore, which did not appear to be far away. Exhaustion numbed his limbs as he dragged Denis with him. It occurred to him swimming would be easier without his sword, but he determined not to discard it if possible.

Once in shallow water, they crawled to the beach on hands and knees, coughing up sea water, then collapsed on the sand, breathing hard.

Denis rolled to sit up, his knees bent. “*Merci, mon frère* for my life. That was a close call. I have to learn to swim.”

Adam too sat up, his head in his hands. “The current was strong. You may not have made it anyway. It probably carried Rosamunda further down the coast. We must search for her.”

Denis came to his feet. “But Paulina.”

Adam looked up sharply into the green eyes of the brother he loved. Denis feared for Paulina as Adam feared for Rosamunda. Time was of the essence. If they spent time searching for Rosamunda, they might be too late to save Paulina from Malraux’s evil intent.

If they abandoned Rosamunda, she would likely die, cast up on some lonely shore, if she hadn’t drowned already.

And where was Vincent Lallement?

As if conjured by the thought, Vincent staggered from the water and collapsed next to Adam, looking up at the sky, his chest heaving.

Adam shoved his shoulder. "Turn over before you choke."

Vincent heeded the warning. "Where is my sister?"

Denis studied his feet. "We don't know."

Vincent sat up abruptly. "You mean she drowned?"

Denis shook his head. "We don't know."

Vincent lunged at Denis, grabbing the front of his tunic. "It's your fault, insisting we come by sea."

Denis made no effort to fend him off, but Adam wrenched him away. "I am as desolate about Rosamunda as you are, but it is not Denis' fault. We were aware of the dangers. Now we must decide the next step. We have no horse, and no idea where we are."

Vincent relented, wiping the back of his hand across his mouth, looking out to sea. "The second problem might be remedied if that's our crew struggling to shore yonder."

Adam's heart lifted. The men were Bretons who might be familiar with the area. He and Vincent strode out to help the sailors.

As the men recovered their breath, Adam pondered their next move. He itched to strike out on foot to find Rosamunda, but night would draw in soon, and everyone was already shivering in wet clothing. "We must get dry before we do anything else. Scavenge for driftwood and kindling. Call out Rosamunda's name as you go. She may be nearby."

He turned to the older Breton. "Do you know the area?"

"I do, *milord*."

"Is there adequate shelter in the trees?"

The man rubbed the stubble of his dark beard. "There is, but if memory serves, there's a cave around the cliff."

"Is the tide coming in or going out?"

"Going out, *milord*."

"Very well. We'll search for the cave and build a fire there."

As the other men set off in search of wood, Denis remained with Adam, his face a mask of pain. "It is my fault we are in this situation. Now we have both lost the women we love. Can you forgive me?"

Adam clenched his jaw, his gut filled with a dread that Rosamunda might not survive a cold, wet night alone. Refusing to believe she had drowned, he offered Denis his hand. "There is nothing to forgive. Come, help me locate the cave."

Malraux de Carnac was warming his backside by the hearty fire, when a servant came to him with a surprising message. He had lost patience with Roget's inefficiency and spent hours working on the scaffolding that would be used to haul the chosen virgin to the top of *Le Manio*. It was heavy work, lifting sturdy wooden poles in chilly temperatures. It had numbed him to the bone and filled his fingers with irritating splinters.

He would either have to select a girl from the village, or go in search of Letyce, who surely could not have gone far on a donkey.

Now, a woman had turned up at his door, seeking entry. He resisted the urge to smirk when a bedraggled Letyce was shown into the hall. Despite her rain-soaked state, his shaft stood to attention. The memory of their trysts fired his blood.

She did not avert her eyes. In fact, her demeanor was bold. “You seem surprised to see me,” she said cockily.

Malraux stroked his beard. “You were not anxious for my company when we parted.”

She sidled up to him, thrusting her breasts provocatively. “You were being cruel. It was not my fault the dwarf escaped.”

He brushed his thumbs over her rigid nipples, then squeezed hard. “But someone had to be punished.”

She gasped, throwing back her head, but then she flounced away, a glint of mischief in her eyes. “That someone isn’t me. I have a better idea.”

“And what would that be?”

“The dwarf’s sister.”

He arched his brows. “The mute?”

She rolled her eyes suggestively. “The same.”

Malraux scoffed. “And where might she be?”

Letyce’s expression hardened. “I know where she is, but before I deliver her to you, I want your oath I will not be harmed, and a guarantee you will see me safely back to England.”

Malraux laughed. “And how can you be sure I will keep such an oath?”

Letyce smiled seductively. “You are many things, most of them evil, but you are not a man to forswear an oath.”

He chuckled inwardly. For all her whoring ways, Letyce knew him. “Very well, take me to her.”

Uncontrollable shivering racked Rosamunda. She thought she heard men’s voices calling her name, but had no will to rise from beneath the rock under which she seemed to be wedged. They would not hear her grunted pleas for help.

As her wits slowly returned she recalled being suddenly plunged into the cold, swirling water that had quickly swept her away.

But now she was on land, wrapped in what appeared to be Paulina's cloak. A woman had helped her.

Red hair. The woman had red hair. Paulina's hair was dark. The only person of her acquaintance with red hair was Letyce Revandel.

The memory filled her with dread. It was Letyce who had helped her. Letyce hated her. There was no good intent here. The *hore* had likely gone off to seek help, but who would she bring?

Malraux de Carnac.

Rosamunda dug her fingers into the rough surface of the rock, trying to ease out from its shelter. Sharp pebbles dug into her back, but she succeeded in sitting up. Pain sliced into her eye. She touched her forehead and her hand came away bloodied. The landscape tilted as she squinted into the misty gloom.

She did not see Letyce until the woman was upon her. She crawled away, but came up against the legs of a man standing beside her.

"In a hurry to go somewhere?" a familiar voice oozed.

There was no escape. Malraux picked her up, though not without some effort. "You're wet, and that's a nasty gash you have. We'll take care of it once we get to my *demesne*."

He threw aside the cloak tucked around her. "One less wet garment. I'll keep you warm."

Rosamunda struggled against him, but he held firm and

she was too weak to persist. She wept as the memory of being held safe against Adam's chest swept over her.

Malraux put her over his shoulder as he mounted, then settled her on his lap. "You should be thankful to Letyce. She saved your life. I am grateful."

She felt his hard maleness beneath her as they rode. Icy dread numbed her body. Malraux was not an honorable man. He would take from her what she longed to give to Adam.

PRAY WE ARE IN TIME

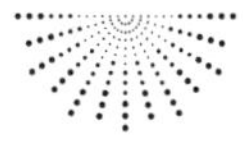

The village outside the walls of Carnac was seemingly quiet as night fell, but Malraux was confident a hundred pairs of eyes followed their progress, everyone anxious to learn if he had chosen his virgin of *Le Manio*.

They had ridden by way of the famed rock and he was satisfied all was in readiness—the scaffolding, the platform and the windlass with its pulley and rope.

He had hoped to put a fright into the mute, but she had passed out, and it was Letyce who shivered uncomfortably.

For effect, he reined to a halt outside the cottage of a village elder. "Brébeuf," he shouted.

The door creaked open and an elderly man appeared. "*Milord*?"

"Tell the rabble they can rest easy. I have my virgin here safe in my arms. Make the bonfires and other celebrations ready. We want to ensure this is the best All Hallows' Eve Carnac has ever seen."

Brébeuf brightened considerably, eyeing Letyce, then the girl in Malraux's arms. "I'll see to it, *milord*."

"Peasants are so predictable," Malraux observed as they made their way into the courtyard of his home.

Roget rushed out to meet them, taking Rosamunda from Malraux, who dismounted then regained his prize. "Follow me, *demoiselle* Revandel. You will watch over my virgin until the festivities. Otherwise I shall be forced to choose someone else."

Letyce stumbled from her horse. "But you gave me your oath."

He laughed. "An oath is only good if both sides keep to the bargain. You promised me Rosamunda Lallement as my virgin of *Le Manio*. You had best pray she fulfills her role."

The cave proved to be a godsend for the castaways. It had a natural chimney allowing them to build a hearty fire that one or other of the Bretons kept going all night. Its heat permeated the rocks, drying the clothing arrayed on them.

"Not completely dry," Adam declared, tossing Denis' doublet at him, "but wearable."

Denis sniffed the garment with distaste as he shrugged it on. "Stinks of smoke."

He pulled a strand of hair in front of his nose, flinging it back in dismay. "I reek of it."

He had not slept, and was aware Adam had not either. All Hallows' Eve had dawned, grey and damp.

Denis felt the need to make amends. "Anxious as I am

to get to Carnac's estate as soon as possible, I agree with you we should search for Rosamunda."

Adam's shoulders lost some of their tension. "The old Breton says there is another cove around the headland. We can search there. He knows the way to Carnac. That will save time."

Denis stretched. "I'm hungry. The hares the Breton lad snared last night were tasty, but I could have eaten more."

Adam rolled his eyes. "You and your appetite."

They doused the fire and set off in the wake of the sailor, picking their way over craggy rocks and tide pools. Denis spied a tiny crab in one, but it snapped its pincers on him when he pulled it out. "*Merde*," he exclaimed, sucking his finger. "I should have skewered it with my sword."

"Then what?" Vincent mocked. "Eat it raw?"

Denis screwed up his nose, deciding it might be better to remain silent and ignore the rumblings in his belly.

They reached the neighboring cove. Denis went down on one knee in the sand beside a rocky outcropping. "Someone has been here recently. The tide has not yet obliterated their footprints."

Adam hovered over him. "Small feet, a woman. *Non*! Two women. The imprints are different. They lead to the path."

Excited by the discovery, they followed the steep trail. Close by a rocky overhang, the tracks became confused. Denis walked further on, studying the terrain. "Horses. One ridden by a man, judging from the new footprints."

Vincent picked up something from the ground. "It's a child's cloak."

Denis hurried back to him and grabbed the garment, his heart in his throat. "This is Paulina's. I gave it to her at

East Preston." He turned it inside out. "There's a special pocket—for Topaz."

His voice cracked and Adam lay a reassuring hand on his shoulder. "If we follow the tracks we will find our ladies. I feel in my heart Rosamunda was here."

Denis blinked away the moisture in his eyes. "Pray we are in time."

It was early afternoon when Adam, Denis, Vincent and the Bretons flopped to their bellies to peer over a rise at Carnac's *demesne* and the village below it. Men tossed pieces of wood onto already large piles. People moved about busily. Laughter and happy chatter drifted on the air.

"Seems like any other village preparing for All Hallows' Eve," Vincent observed.

The old Breton shook his head. "Carnac is like any other village, except on All Hallows' Eve. People come from the surrounding villages and countryside. The lord of the *demesne* must have chosen a sacrificial virgin or the villagers would not be so happy. They live in fear of his choice each year."

Adam turned to face him. "Where is this rock he supposedly throws women down from?"

The man pointed. "Two miles from here, beyond the field of smaller rocks you see in the distance. No supposing about it, *milord*. I've seen it myself. It turns the young men into a pack of salivating wolves waiting below for the maiden to drop. Except wolves hunt together. Here they come to blows trying to be the one to save her."

Denis gritted his teeth. “And the one who does gets to claim her as his wife?”

The Breton wiped his sleeve across his brow. “If she is not too badly injured and after Malraux de Carnac exacts his *droit de seigneur*, the hero lies with the maiden. On occasion, they marry, but more often the girl is cast out of the village as a whore.”

Vincent’s anger showed on his face. “He demands *droit de seigneur*, in front of everyone?”

“He delights in it. For him it signals the success of the celebrations.”

Denis bristled. “Paulina is inside his *demesne*. We must get to her.”

Adam laid a hand on his brother’s arm. “*Non*, far wiser to locate *Le Manio* and make our stand there. He will not harm her before then.”

They slid down the slope and set off for *Le Manio*. Not one word was exchanged as they hiked quickly, steam rising from their heated bodies despite the chill in the air. The ancient monolith came into view. They edged closer, keeping out of sight, though there seemed to be no one about.

Shame flooded Denis as his shaft hardened uncomfortably, but a quick glance at the others made him feel slightly better. He was not the only one affected by the phallic shape of the enormous rock that towered twenty feet, an unmistakable symbol of male pride and power.

Even Adam was adjusting his breeches.

Oh, the bawdy jests that would have been flung back

and forth had they come upon this giant monolith under other circumstances. They would have been on their knees, indulging in male horseplay, hysterical with laughter.

However, the wooden scaffolding on either side of the rock brought home to them Malraux's evil intent. A servant stood on a platform at the top, spreading a canvas over some sort of mechanism. The structure swayed with his movements.

"It's a windlass," Adam said. "He plans to hoist her up."

Denis turned to his brother, his heart in knots. "We need a plan. If Malraux throws Paulina from that height she will not survive. I am not the best man to catch her."

Adam squeezed his bottom lip with his thumb and forefinger. As he and the others devised a plan, the servant climbed down and sauntered off into the woods.

Adam spoke at last. "I will catch her. If there is interference from locals, Vincent will hold them off with the help of the Bretons."

Denis bristled. "What am I to do?"

Adam looked into his brother's eyes, then up at the platform. He laid a hand on Denis' arm. "You must climb the scaffolding, hide under the canvas, and confront Malraux, or whoever takes Paulina to the top. We cannot all go up to prevent his throwing her. It will not take our weight."

Denis swallowed hard, dragging his gaze to the top of the giant rock. "Can we not confront him at the bottom, before he takes her up?"

Adam shook his head. "There is no cover at the base of the rock. We would be five against Malraux's men and the villagers. This way we hold the element of surprise. He will not expect another dwarf atop *Le Manio*."

Denis grinned half-heartedly. "And the drunken villagers won't expect anyone to rush forward to save a dwarf."

Vincent shaded his eyes to look up, his brow furrowed. "I suppose he means to raise her up with yon pulley. What does he think she is—a sack of grain? I will kill him for this."

Denis put a hand on his arm. "*Non*, that will be my pleasure."

The old Breton interrupted. "Forgive me, *mes seigneurs*, but everyone from the village and surrounding area will be wearing a disguise or costume. We must fashion masks for ourselves."

Denis chuckled as they sauntered off into the woods. "I'll help, but I won't need a mask. My face will be terrifying enough for Malraux when I spring forth from under the canvas."

Denis was the first to notice the glow on the near horizon. "They've torched the fires in the village. Best we leave now so I can get to the top of *Le Manio* before the procession arrives."

It was difficult to keep from smiling, despite his anguish. Adam and Vincent looked like uprooted trees. The Breton lad had woven thin branches from laurel trees into an elaborate crown for their heads, then twined more laurel and ivy around their tunics. Faces blackened with dirt completed the effect. Denis might have been fooled had he bumped into them on a dark night.

Adam scratched his ear with his fingertip. “Every insect in creation is crawling in my hair.”

The two Bretons put the finishing touches on their own disguises.

Vincent and Adam held the base of the scaffolding firm as Denis began his ascent.

The scaffolding had been designed by bigger men and he had to stretch to reach the next crosspiece, then heave his body up to it. Never had his short legs been more of a curse. Planks had been set across the horizontal poles, which were lashed to the verticals with rope, so he at least had a firm footing to stand on. Some of the horizontals had been tied loosely to the monolith.

He dared not look down, but knew Adam and Vincent stood ready to catch him if he fell. He was sweating profusely and panting hard as he gathered one end of the canvas and slid his aching body beneath it to wait, slumped against a crude wooden windlass. He felt like he had climbed to the top of Rouen cathedral.

ATOP THE MONOLITH

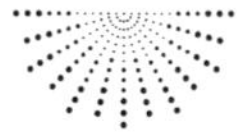

Adam and Vincent stole off to lurk in nearby bushes as torchbearers entered the clearing, followed by *shawm* and *bodhran* players. Behind them men and women danced and cavorted to the beat of the lively music, many seemingly already under the influence of intoxicating substances. Adam felt the vibration of the drums in his bones.

They crept from the shadows to mingle with the growing throng in the clearing. Behind the dancers marched a small contingent of Carnac's men-at-arms, looking anything but menacing with their halos of laurel leaves. Then came Malraux, mounted on an elaborately liveried gelding, waving to the cheering crowd, every finger richly jeweled. He wore a black velvet doublet, tight leggings, and shiny leather boots, the only man present not in costume.

The torchbearers lit the small bonfires around the perimeter. Smoke swirled in the wind. Adam blinked away the sting, reminded of the night of the fire at Kingston

Gorse when his life had changed completely. Rosamunda had brought hope and love back into his life. He longed to hold her again, to be assured of her safety.

He grunted and nudged Vincent. “Letyce Revandel rides next to Malraux. Let’s hope she does not see through our disguises. Take care her gaze does not fall on you.”

Vincent gasped. “Paulina.”

Behind Malraux, a servant led a palfrey atop which sat a maiden dressed in a voluminous white robe with a red cape that flowed from her shoulders to cover the horse’s rump. A black hood hid her hair and face. Her hands were tied to the pommel, but her head hung limply, her shoulders sagging.

Adam put a restraining hand on Vincent as he moved towards the woman. “Too soon.”

Vincent shrugged him off. “That’s my sister. She looks like she has been drugged. The macabre outfit makes her seem like a giantess.”

An uncomfortable churning twisted in Adam’s belly. “You’re right. Look at her hands.”

Vincent’s eyes widened. “They are too big. It’s not Paulina.”

The relief in Vincent’s voice was palpable, but Adam’s heart raced. “Then who is it?’

Vincent frowned. “Rosamunda?”

The voicing of his beloved’s name made the possibility real. Adam was certain it had been Rosamunda’s footprints on the beach and cliff path, and it was likely the male imprints belonged to Malraux. Few others in the vicinity would own a horse. Perhaps the other woman had been Letyce.

But then what had become of Paulina? He dreaded that

Rosamunda was indeed the hooded woman tied to the palfrey, but when Denis discovered Paulina had disappeared and had perhaps never made it to Bretagne… They had found her cloak, but no trace of her.

By now the clearing was crowded. Most of the women had withdrawn to tend barrels of ale set up on trestles near the trees. A steady stream of patrons plied their way to and from these improvised taverns as the women tucked coins into their aprons.

"Now I see what they get out of this," he remarked sarcastically to Vincent, but the latter seemed too intent on the hooded woman to listen.

Malraux dismounted and swaggered to the base of *Le Manio*. He made an expansive gesture to the crowd indicating they should continue their revels. The servant who had led the palfrey pulled open the red cape, slid it off and tossed it aside with a flourish.

A cheer went up from the crowd. Over a thin chemise, Malraux's sacrificial virgin wore a harness that criss-crossed between her breasts, clearly emphasizing the rigid nipples. Adam knew those lovely globes well and his heart bled with shame and indignation for Rosamunda. He wanted to rush forward to cover her. Vincent growled like a caged animal.

The servant attached the pulley to the back of the harness.

The crowd inhaled a collective breath as he started the climb up the scaffold.

The music stopped.

Malraux remounted his gelding.

"He wants to make sure the horde can see him," Vincent remarked sarcastically.

"Let's hope they keep their attention fixed on him and not on the top of the platform," Adam growled.

He wished there was some way to alert Denis, who believed it was Paulina about to be hoisted to the top of *Le Manio*. When the servant got to the platform, Denis would have to render him harmless or risk discovery. "Thank God for the smoke. At least it makes it difficult to see."

The *seigneur* de Carnac cleared his throat. A hush fell over the swaying crowd. "People of Carnac, and surrounds. Welcome to our annual All Hallows' Eve observances. I trust everyone has had an amusing time thus far."

Cheers confirmed his remarks, but Adam kept his attention on the servant as he neared the top.

Malraux scanned the crowd and coughed again, seemingly irritated that some among his audience were more interested in the man climbing the frame than in him. He raised his voice. "Soon comes the high point of our evening."

Murmurs of excitement rose from the crowd.

"You may be wondering whom I have chosen to be your virgin sacrifice this year. Not one from among you, but a beauty nevertheless."

He leaned over to slowly trace a finger over the front straps of the harness, and smiled. "As you see."

More bawdy cheers.

Raged boiled up in Adam's throat. He would cut off that defiling hand before killing the wretch. He glanced back to the platform, surprised to see Denis had dispatched the servant and taken his place by the windlass. If he had accomplished it without Adam's noticing, there was hope anyone looking up would see only a shadowed figure they would believe was hunched over to work the contraption.

Malraux raised his hand. “Our virgin sleeps now—a little tonic to settle her nerves.”

Laughter rippled through the clearing, churning Adam’s gut.

“But she will wake momentarily so we can appreciate fully her enjoyment of the proceedings.”

Vincent swore. “And I thought my mother was evil.”

Adam clenched his fists when Malraux produced a dagger from his belt. He slit the ropes binding Rosamunda’s wrists to the pommel.

She stirred.

“*Courage, mon amour*,” Adam whispered, dreading the moment she would awake and discover where she was. “I am here.”

Malraux raised his hand again. “At my signal, Roget will raise our angel. I myself will climb up to free her into your waiting arms. She may cling to the Manio as long as she can, but eventually she will fall.”

He wagged a finger. “However, in your enthusiasm, don’t forget my *droit de seigneur*.”

Many men licked their lips, no doubt conjuring an image of a maiden clinging for dear life to the giant phallus. Adam feared he might retch.

Malraux glanced up briefly, then dropped his hand. The palfrey moved restlessly as the maiden was lifted from its back. The jerk of the winch seemed to revive her, and she fumbled with the hood, dragging it off.

Adam must have drawn blood as he dug his fingernails into Vincent’s arm. Rosamunda’s wild blond hair stood up on end. Fear twisted her beautiful face into a grimace as she took in the wild scene around her, then mouthed her terror, kicking her legs.

Malraux chuckled as he put his foot on the bottom of the scaffold. "I forgot to mention, gentlemen, the virgin is mute."

For a moment the men stood dumbfounded, then raucous laughter rang out as jests were exchanged about the boon of a woman without a voice.

Adam put a hand on Vincent's shoulder. "Denis must be aware by now it's Rosamunda he is hoisting. Once Malraux gets up there—that's a lot of weight for the scaffold to support. I will stand ready to catch her if she drops. You and the Bretons keep the others at bay. We'll have to leave Malraux to Denis. At least he has the element of surprise."

Denis was perplexed. Paulina was much heavier than he'd anticipated. He tightened his grip on the handle of the winch. His back was breaking and she wasn't half way up to the platform. He knew the moment she started to struggle. His biceps strained like the devil to keep her moving. "Keep still, *mon ange*, I am bringing you to me," he whispered, bracing his legs.

He had heard Malraux's declaration of his intention to climb the scaffold. It was vital he free Paulina from the pulley before the monster reached the top. As her head came into view, he almost let go of the windlass. It was Rosamunda's disheveled hair. "Don't struggle, Rosamunda. It's me, Denis."

She glanced up at the platform. His heart broke for the terror in her eyes. Thank God it was not Paulina, but he had no time to ponder where she was. First, he had to save

Rosamunda from a dangerous fall. "As soon as you reach the platform, be calm while I unfasten the pulley. Adam is below."

She took a deep shuddering breath as she grabbed for the edges of the platform. Denis felt the scaffold sway as Malraux climbed nearer, urged on by the drunken sots below. He let go of the windlass handle, jamming the peg into the hole to brake it, then pulled in the rope hand over hand. He unhooked the pulley as Rosamunda scrambled to her feet. She clung to him so tightly he feared they might both pitch forward off the platform. "Easy. We must not give Malraux a hint there is aught amiss."

He drew his sword. "Get behind the windlass. Pay no heed to the body hidden there."

She stumbled in the long gown, but did as he bade.

Malraux paused in his ascent. The mob had gone strangely quiet. He looked down. One man, taller than most, stood alone in the centre of the clearing looking up at *Le Manio*. Like the rest, he was disguised as a tree. Peasants had no imagination.

Then he noticed three other men standing in a half circle with their backs to the man, two with daggers drawn, and the other with a sword. They were warning off all comers.

What in the name of the saints? Had some wretch connived to get the virgin for himself?

Though they were being held away by three armed men, the rest had their attention fixed on the platform. Something had gone awry.

He peered up, but saw nothing except smoke and the planks under the windlass. Roget would pay dearly if he'd had a part in any plot to let one man have the mute. He drew his dagger, clenching it between his teeth as he continued his ascent. He should have supervised the construction of the platform. Serfs never did a thorough job.

He sneered at the scene that confronted him when he reached the platform, the dagger in his grasp. "Denis de Sancerre! You came! I hoped you would. Perhaps we will toss a dwarf off *Le Manio* tonight."

He eyed Denis' sword, pointing to it with his weapon. "What do you hope to achieve with your pig stick?"

He lunged, anticipating a quick thrust to his enemy's heart, but the dwarf nimbly avoided his blade. He reached for the handle of the windlass to steady himself, noticing the mute crouched behind it. If he got his hands on her—

But Sancerre attacked. The runt had better sword skills than Malraux had anticipated. He avoided the blow, spun on his heel and thrust his dagger again, momentarily distracted by the loud creaking of the scaffold and the sweat obscuring his vision.

He rubbed his eyes, surprised to see Sancerre at the opposite side of the platform, apparently unhurt. He glanced down to see faces turned up to watch what was happening. What a fool he must look dancing around with a dwarf armed with nothing but a miniature sword. Time to finish this quickly.

He reached behind the windlass to grab the mute's arm. She struggled, until he threatened her with the knife. "Let go of the hoist," he commanded, dragging her back against his body, his free arm clamped around her waist, the dagger at her throat.

She shook her head defiantly.

The dwarf came closer, brandishing his sword, his ugly face twisted in anger. “Let her go.”

Malraux winced as the mute’s elbow connected sharply with his ribs.

The dwarf lunged, slicing open his bicep.

Malraux dropped the dagger and fell heavily against the windlass.

An ominous cracking sound caught everyone’s attention.

INTO THE VOID

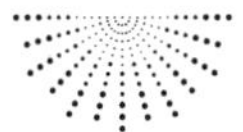

Adam rushed to the scaffolding when Malraux grabbed Rosamunda. He narrowed his eyes, peering up. "The planks under the windlass have given way," he yelled to Vincent and the others.

He backed away hurriedly as the hoisting mechanism teetered, then fell. People screamed and fled, but the windlass suddenly jerked to a halt in mid-fall, crashing against the scaffolding. Pieces of broken planking clattered to earth, not far from where Adam stood, but the windlass dangled precariously, apparently held in place by the rope and pulley.

His heart in his throat, he looked up again.

Rosamunda was clinging to the remains of the platform.

Denis struggled to pull her to safety, but most of the planking was gone.

Malraux had fallen and lay draped across a horizontal pole lower down the scaffolding, his bejeweled hands clamped tight on the wood, one leg inelegantly twisted around it.

The utter silence was broken only by the crackle and hiss of the bonfires and the ominous creaking of the swaying scaffolding.

Women held their hands to their mouths.

Men gaped.

No one breathed.

Trying desperately to devise a way to save his brother and his beloved, Adam cupped his hands to his mouth. "Denis. Keep absolutely still."

If they fell, he could not catch both.

Into the silence intruded the thud of hooves. Adam felt it in his feet. Many horses, approaching at speed. He looked to Vincent. "They will topple the tower."

Everyone turned to gape at the newcomers, a large contingent of armed knights reining their mounts to a halt. Adam immediately recognized Mathieu and Robert, but was not sure who the other diminutive knight was until she dismounted, screaming Denis' name.

Paulina?

Vincent ran to embrace her, but she never took her eyes off the scene atop the scaffolding. She broke away from her brother and shouted to Robert. "Bring the tent."

Puzzled, Adam watched his cousin direct his men, but he quickly understood the plan and took hold of an edge of the canvas.

"Carry it over to the rock and stretch it out. You must hold it as tightly as you can," Paulina commanded.

The last time Adam had seen Paulina she had reminded him of a timid mouse. Now she stood like the Conqueror at Hastings, issuing orders. The Boadicea of Kingston Gorse. He half expected to see Topaz perched on her shoulder.

She cupped her hands around her mouth. "Rosamunda, you must let go. We stand ready to catch you."

Nothing happened.

"I don't think she heard me," Paulina rasped.

Adam tried. "Rosamunda, you will be safe. I promise. Trust me. Let go."

Rosamunda looked into Denis' eyes. Her arms were being wrenched from their sockets and Denis would not have the strength to hold onto her much longer. The scaffolding threatened to collapse at any moment, dragged down by the dangling windlass.

"Trust him," Denis whispered. "He loves you. He will let no harm befall you."

"You?" she mouthed.

He smiled. "Now I see my Paulina is safe, I have no intention of dying on this rickety structure. I will jump after you."

Trusting her fate to God, she let go and fell backwards into nothingness.

Lying flat on his belly, Denis peered over the edge in time to see Rosamunda land safely in the canvas held by the men below. A cheer went up from the crowd that minutes before had been thirsting for blood.

Adam lifted her from the folds of the tent and carried her off to safety. Another man took his place at the edge of the canvas.

Paulina peered up at him, her face full of love and anguish, her arms outstretched.

For a moment his courage failed him. His spine and hips were not made like those of other men. What might result in a few bruises for them could cripple him forever.

But he'd be damned if he would die in a heap of broken wood. He slowly unbuckled his sword belt, then came to his feet carefully. But the scaffolding swayed alarmingly. He looked down. Malraux had managed to stand and was shifting his weight deliberately between two upright poles. He screamed at Denis. "I'll not die alone, dwarf."

It was now or never.

As the plank beneath his feet disappeared, Denis spread his arms wide and flung himself out into the void.

Paulina worried that catching Denis would not be the same as catching Rosamunda. As the scaffold fell apart, she shouted urgently to the men holding the tent. "Hold the canvas higher, but when he hits, let it sag a little with his weight."

As poles and planks clattered to earth, she prayed she would get the opportunity to tell Denis the things she should have confessed long ago.

He hit with a sickening thud. The men lowered the

canvas to the ground. Denis lay in the centre, his eyes closed, arms thrust out at his sides.

"Denis," she screamed, stumbling into the canvas. She fell to her knees at his side and threw her arms around his neck, kissing his full lips, his stubbled chin, his high forehead. "Please don't die, Denis. I love you," she sobbed.

Denis opened one eye. "You love me?"

She pulled back, rubbing the back of her hand over her eyes. "You're alive." She swatted his shoulder. "You made me believe you were dead."

He smiled mischievously. "I was enjoying the kisses and hugs. I thought for a moment I had landed in heaven."

He rolled to sit up, but she threw herself at him again, smothering him with kisses. He laced his fingers into her hair, forcing her to prolong the kiss. He coaxed her mouth open with his tongue and desire spiralled through her belly as he deepened the kiss. She felt his male part harden against her and brazenly pressed her mons to it. They broke apart panting for breath, his eyes wide.

"I have longed to kiss you," Denis growled.

She felt her face redden. "I don't know how to kiss."

Denis chuckled. "Yes, you do."

"Do you intend to lie there all night, or can I have my tent back?"

Denis scrambled to his feet, helping Paulina to rise. "Robert, cousin. I apologise. I owe you my life and here I am dallying with a maiden when I should be falling to my knees in gratitude."

The two men embraced. Robert laughed. "It's Paulina to whom you owe your thanks. She insisted we make the trek to Carnac, convinced your life was in danger. It was a courageous thing she did, escaping from Malraux."

Denis arched his brows as he looked at Paulina.

"And on horseback, believe it or not," she crowed.

Rosamunda savored Adam's warmth as he cuddled her to his chest. He had already used his dagger to slice off the offensive harness and covered her with Vincent's cloak. She had no memory of being garbed in the hideous white gown. The last thing she remembered was being picked up from the shore by Malraux.

She looked up at Adam and smiled as they watched Denis and Paulina stride off the canvas hand in hand and speak to Robert.

He kissed each corner of her mouth delicately, then nibbled her bottom lip. "I thought I had lost you," he rasped. "After the boat capsized, I believed you had drowned."

She put her forefinger on his lips. "Current strong," she mouthed. "Swept away."

He tightened his hold. "I will never allow you to be exposed to such dangers again."

She shrugged. "Life is dangerous."

Then she pointed to a solitary figure standing with the horses.

"My brother, Mathieu," he explained.

She frowned, hearing the sadness behind his words.

He inhaled deeply. "It's a long story. When we believed I was incapable of siring children, he insisted I forfeit my right to inherit Belisle."

She had never asked Adam about his family, or his

inheritance. What mattered was they be together. But she heard the bitterness in his voice. "Now?" she asked.

Mathieu glanced at them occasionally, averting his eyes quickly when he noticed them watching.

He stood and set her on her feet. "We will have to settle it. Now is as good a time as any. Stay here."

RECONCILIATION

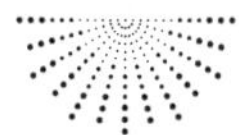

Robert de Montbryce was not the oldest living member of the family. His *oncle* Antoine had that honor. But as *Comte-in-waiting*, Robert was the acknowledged head of the clan in Normandie, since his father lived in England.

One reason the Montbryces had survived and prospered when many noble families had fallen by the wayside of Norman politics was their loyalty to each other under the strong leadership of Robert's father, Ram.

It grieved him that there was conflict between Mathieu and Adam de Montbryce. A house divided never prospered. He hoped there was a solution to whatever problem lay between them. He wondered what his father would do in the circumstances.

Mathieu had received the message pleading for help and joined Robert's contingent as they had ridden south.

Robert did not know why Antoine had elected to make Mathieu his heir instead of Adam, but sensed it had something to do with Adam's illness and subsequent deafness. Mathieu had refused to discuss it *en route*.

As Adam approached his brother, Robert deemed it wise to mediate whatever discussion might ensue. The determined glare on both men's faces did not bode well. The brothers had not embraced when Mathieu had first arrived, and it did not appear likely they would do so now.

Robert thanked the saints for the close relationship of trust he and Baudoin shared, but then only two years separated them. Adam was closer to Denis.

The three men came together in the middle of the clearing, now surprisingly empty. If the collapse of the scaffold had not convinced most of the revelers to scarper, the sudden arrival of a contingent of armed men had done the trick. Only a few remained, scavenging through the ruins of the scaffold from which the windlass still hung precariously.

Adam offered his hand. "I have not properly thanked you."

Robert gripped his hand and patted him on the back. "As I told Denis, you have Paulina to thank for urging us here. And I did not come alone. Mathieu was already on his way when we met on the road."

The brothers glared at each other, jaws clenched. Adam was first to proffer a hand. "*Merci, mon frère*. It's good to see you again."

Mathieu accepted the handshake. "You look a great deal better than when we parted, even with tree branches in your hair and muck on your face."

Adam rolled his eyes, fumbling in his hair to remove the remaining twigs. "I forgot."

Robert tried unsuccessfully to choke back laughter.

Adam smiled, but then became serious. “Actually, Mathieu, I am better. I am betrothed to a woman who loves me, and who wants to bear my children.”

It was only momentary, but Robert thought Mathieu looked stunned as he glanced briefly at Adam’s groin. What was going on?

The brothers stared at each other for long moments, neither moving a muscle. Robert grew nervous when Adam held out his hand. “Lend me your sword. Mine is concealed in the woods.”

Mathieu did not flinch as Robert reluctantly handed over his weapon.

Adam dug the point of the sword into the earth, resting his hand atop the hilt.

Mathieu hesitated only a moment before going down on one knee.

Adam turned to Robert. “I would ask you to bear witness to my brother’s oath of allegiance to me as rightful heir of Belisle Castle.”

Robert looked from one to the other, wishing he knew exactly what was going on. He asked Mathieu, “Do you, Mathieu de Montbryce, swear allegiance to Adam de Montbryce, as the rightful heir of Belisle Castle?”

“I so swear.”

Adam helped his brother rise, and gathered him into his embrace.

Mathieu sobbed into his shoulder. “Forgive me.”

Denis’ body ached in places he had never known could ache, but his heart was full as he watched his half-brothers embrace. Adam had regained what was his by right. The rift with Mathieu had been repaired. He too would need to rebuild his friendship with his youngest brother.

He kissed Paulina's cheek. "I am a wreck. How can you be in love with a man who stinks of sweat and smoke?"

She smiled. "At least you don't look like a tree."

He laughed, pressing her to his body. "I am in love with you, Paulina, since the moment we met."

"It was the same for me," she confessed. "I was too afraid to admit it."

He went down on one knee. "The last time I asked you to wed with me, I did it flippantly, though I was sincere. Now I want to ask you properly, as befits a beautiful and desirable woman. Will you wed with me, Paulina Lallement?"

She cupped his face in her hands and opened her mouth.

He held up his hand. "Before you answer, I have to warn you life with me will not be easy."

She smiled, her eyes full of love. "Why? Is there something you're not telling me?"

JUST DESERTS

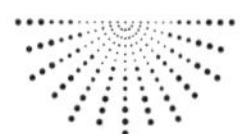

Letyce Revandel picked her way carefully through the wreckage of the scaffolding. She had remained hidden once it became obvious Malraux's plans had gone awry. Now she searched for her lover's body. He was a vain man who ornamented himself with expensive jewels.

At first she had thought to use them to aid in her escape back to England, but now she played with the notion of staying on at Carnac. Why not claim Malraux had wed her and become mistress of the *demesne* as a grieving widow? Who would naysay her? Certainly not the ineffectual Roget, wherever he had got to.

The Montbryces were camped in a nearby copse. The bonfires that had burned brightly were smoldering embers. There were few scavengers left now, but she was determined to find Malraux. His signet ring in particular would confirm her claims to be his wife. Midnight must have long since passed. It was All Hallows', an auspicious day to become mistress of a wealthy *demesne*.

"*Attention!*" a voice called. She peered into the darkness. A peasant stood a few feet away, pointing to the twisted remains of the scaffolding and the windlass dangling precariously above. "*Dañjer.*"

It was surprising how easy Breton was to understand, like English really. Did the fool think she did not know her mission was dangerous? But it was essential she secure the rings.

Clouds had obscured the moon for most of the night, but suddenly they parted. Something glinted beneath a tangled pile of wood. She struggled to heft one rough pole at a time, wrestling each aside with a grunt. Before long, sweat had soaked her clothing and her hands were raw as she made agonizingly slow progress towards what she was sure was Malraux's body.

Then she caught sight of his hand, white in the moonlight. A thrill of expectancy shivered through her as she reached for the rings. She drew her dagger in case she had to cut off his fingers to get the jewels.

Their fingertips touched.

Alarm surged up her spine. His skin was warm, not cold as she had expected. She pulled away, but Malraux's fingers tightened, holding her hand in his grip. Panic stricken, she raised her dagger but Malraux turned her wrist and the blade plunged into her own flesh.

She screamed.

"Do you intend to murder a dead man?" he rasped. "Stop your caterwauling and let me die in peace."

She could not see his face, buried beneath the wreckage, but she knew he was smiling his evil smile, and it terrified her.

"Let go," she wailed, pulling frantically, though her

hand throbbed like the devil and blood pumped from the wound.

He tightened his grip.

She struggled harder, bracing her feet on nearby poles. His evil laughter was the last thing she heard as the rope holding the windlass gave way, bringing the remains of the twisted wreckage crashing down.

BELISLE

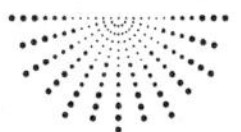

Two days after the turbulent events of All Hallows' Eve, Guillaume de Terrence and Lucien arrived with the horses and men at arms. Adam was overjoyed to be reunited with Nox, and Denis whooped with delight at first sight of Brevis.

When everything was in readiness for the arduous return journey, Adam and Denis took the women they loved to stand before *Le Manio*.

Paulina giggled. "It looks more impressive in daylight, even in the drizzle."

Denis squeezed her hand. "You are naughty, my love."

On the Feast of All Souls, they had seen the glow from the huge fire set by villagers who had crept back to *Le Manio*. The blaze had consumed the twisted pile of wood at the base of the now blackened monolith. Smoldering ashes remained after a night of heavy rain.

Adam inhaled deeply. "I suppose they deemed it fitting to dispatch their master's body on All Souls."

Rosamunda shuddered beside him as she gazed at the rock. "Letyce Revandel?"

"Long gone, I hope," Paulina said. "Poor Topaz. I wonder what became of her."

Denis brightened. "Last I saw, she was curled up under Henry's massive chair. Perhaps he will decide he likes cats."

Everyone shared the humor of his jest.

Adam tightened his hold on Rosamunda's shoulder, pulling her to his side. "We will soon be home in Belisle. Robert has given his permission for our marriages to proceed. He assures me his blessing is sufficient since he does not recognise Curthose's authority. If Henry approves, so does Robert."

"He even sent a squad of his men ahead to Belisle so *Maman* and Papa can prepare for our nuptials," Denis added.

"Will Robert be present?" Paulina asked.

Adam shook his head. "I asked him, but he does not want to be away from Montbryce Castle any longer than necessary in these uncertain times."

They stood for a few minutes more in silence, then made their way back to camp to begin their journey.

"You're possessed, Denis," Adam whispered to his brother as they bedded down in their tent for the fourth night on the road. "Try to get some sleep tonight instead of tossing and turning. You are wearing me out, and I am sure Robert is mightily relieved not to be spending another night in the same tent."

Denis turned over on his cot to face Adam. He drew the blanket up to his chin to ward off the November chill. "I'm sorry. I'm anxious to get home and get this wedding over with. Now I know Paulina loves me, I cannot wait to get my hands on her lovely little body."

Adam turned onto his back, grazing his knuckles back and forth across his forehead. "Think how I feel. I had given up hope of ever bedding a woman, now I get aroused simply looking at Rosamunda."

Denis snorted. "We're a pair of green youths."

Adam tapped his lips with his forefinger. "You'll wake Mathieu. And the ladies' tent is not far away."

Denis pouted. "Too bad the Lallement brothers suddenly became concerned about propriety, otherwise I'd have Paulina beneath me now. Ridiculous."

Adam yawned. "I don't mind. I was determined to wait until I was married before I planted my seed. I can wait a few more days."

Denis drifted off to sleep. His dreams were filled with images of Paulina. Her nipples were dark, haloed by wine-rich areolas. He brushed his thumbs over them, relishing her moans of pleasure.

He trailed kisses along her neck as she thrust her head back, raking her fingernails through his hair. He bent to suckle at her breast.

A grinning brindled cat appeared in his dream, startling him awake.

"*Merde*," he swore, pulling up his *couilles* to ease the ache at his groin.

~

Adam, Mathieu, and Denis rode into the courtyard of Belisle Castle. As they dismounted, their mother left the shelter of her husband's cloak to embrace each in turn. "Welcome home, *mes fils*, I am overjoyed to see you safely returned."

Antoine clasped forearms with each of his sons, thumping them heartily on the back. "We worried over Adam's message, then the riders came with news of your imminent arrival. Much has happened. You must tell us all."

He stopped suddenly. "But where are my future daughters-by-marriage?"

Adam braced his legs. "They are outside the walls with their brothers. We have things to discuss with you first."

Antoine frowned. "Is something wrong?"

Denis stepped forward. "Mathieu has ceded the line of succession back to Adam now that he is—er—cured."

"Cured?" Sybilla whispered, her eyes filling with tears as she looked at Adam.

Adam nodded, swallowing the lump in his throat.

Denis continued. "You must approve of this change before we can proceed further."

Adam did not envy his father his predicament. Antoine de Montbryce struggled to maintain his composure, but his face betrayed his conflicting emotions.

Mathieu spoke first. "Adam is the rightful heir. He has recovered his—" He reddened, avoiding looking at his mother. "His ability to—er—" He took a deep breath. "Anyway. I have withdrawn my claim, willingly, and have given Adam my oath of allegiance."

Antoine's breathing was shallow. He put his hand on his youngest son's shoulder. "You are a noble and honorable knight, Mathieu de Montbryce. I respect your decision." He turned to Adam. "As my eldest son, I recognise you as my heir. Now, bring in the women before your mother faints with anticipation."

"About my betrothed," Adam began. "Rosamunda is mute."

"And, in case you were wondering, Paulina is a dwarf," Denis added.

PILGRIMAGE

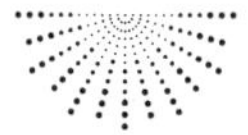

Sybilla de Montbryce tapped on the door of the chamber where her daughters were putting the finishing touches to the bridal ensembles of their soon to be sisters-by-marriage.

Appalled by what she had learned of Maudine Lallement, and amazed both girls had grown into such beautiful, generous women, she vowed to lavish on them the love they had never received from their own mother.

"My sons await their brides at the chapel door," she announced, "and I wish a word alone with my future daughters-by-marriage."

Bernadine and Florymonde kissed Paulina and Rosamunda on the cheek and left.

Paulina fidgeted with the sleeve of her dress. "Madame de Montbryce, Rosamunda and I thank you for these lovely gowns. Neither of us has ever worn anything as beautiful."

Sybilla smiled. "Please, call me *Maman*. It has been my pleasure to provide you with wedding gowns. What you are doing for me far outweighs what I have done for you."

Both women frowned.

Sybilla took Rosamunda's hand. "When Adam left home after his illness, I despaired for him. He had lost so much. I understand from what he has told me that you accepted to be his wife before you became aware he had recovered his ability to sire children."

Rosamunda smiled. "Love him."

Sybilla wanted to weep tears of gratitude. "I believe your love has aided his recovery, and I thank you from the bottom of my heart. It matters not a whit that you are mute. Be patient with us and we will learn to understand you as well as your sister."

"*Merci, Maman*," Rosamunda mouthed, her eyes bright with excitement.

No wonder he loves her.

Sybilla turned to Paulina and took a deep breath. "I have prayed daily that Denis would fall in love with a woman who loved him in return. He is a man who has triumphed over great adversity, but I have sensed his loneliness. You, Paulina Lallement, are indeed the answer to my prayers. I give my first born son over to your loving care."

Adam watched his wife charm the people of Belisle as she moved from table to table at the wedding banquet. He had to admit to a pang of disappointment when she had first appeared at the chapel door, her hair neatly bound up in some sort of tower arrangement, no doubt the work of Florymonde.

It pleased him that her wayward tresses had inevitably escaped the hairpins as the day wore on. Now she looked like his Rosamunda. He itched to run his fingers through her hair once they were alone in their bridal chamber.

He had worried on and off over the past few days, as excitement over the double wedding mounted in the castle and its environs, if he would be adequate to the task of bedding his wife. His malady might return. But the insistent urge as he watched her reassured him all would be well.

He glanced over at Denis who was practically salivating, his gaze fixed on Paulina's breasts. Like Adam, he watched his wife as she accompanied her sister around the hall.

Adam coughed loudly, drawing Denis' attention. "I'm for bed. How about you, brother?"

Denis grinned broadly. "I'll get the bishop."

Adam was only vaguely aware of what had gone on behind the screen where Rosamunda was being prepared for bed. He was too busy covering himself as Denis and Mathieu stripped him before the assembled well-wishers. His bride's blush warmed him as she was escorted to the bed, eyes downcast.

"You're fortunate I'll be occupied pleasing my wife, Denis de Sancerre, else I'd get my revenge when you are escorted to your chamber."

Paulina turned away, her face redder than Rosamunda's. Adam chuckled inwardly. Wait till she saw Denis naked. For a small man—

Rosamunda averted her eyes when Denis and Mathieu escorted him to bed, making a great show of tucking them in tightly.

The bishop intoned his blessing, sprinkled them with holy water, then the merry band departed for Denis' chamber. Antoine was the last to leave, with a wink and a smile.

Rosamunda lay rigid, hugging the linens to her chin. Her face was flushed, her rosemary-scented hair in its usual tempting disarray, despite what Adam supposed had been the efforts of his mother's maidservant to tame it with a comb.

They lay side by side. She must know he was naked beneath the linens. What had become of his adventurous bride who feared nothing?

Of course.

He had been so preoccupied with his own concerns, he had failed to give a thought to Rosamunda's fears. He turned onto his side and leaned up on his elbow, tugging the linens away from her chin. "May I see your bridal nightgown?"

She turned her enormous green eyes to him and let go of the linens. It was all he could do not to rip the flimsy chemise off her body and plunge into her virginal tightness.

He peeled the linens off her and pushed them to the bottom of the bed with his feet, revealing his own nakedness.

She stared at the ceiling.

"Don't be afraid, my love. Look at me."

She sniffled as a tear trickled down her cheek. "Nervous," she mouthed.

His heart skittered as her nipples hardened, straining against the fabric of the silky nightgown. He felt it important to be forthright, to tell her of his resolve to come virgin to his marriage bed. "I'm nervous too. This is my first time."

She swiveled her head to look into his eyes. "What?"

He took hold of her hand and placed it on his shaft, curling his fingers around hers. Waves of pleasure swept up his spine. "I have never entered a woman, Rosamunda. You will be the first."

His arousal grew beneath her hand.

Her puzzled gaze flickered to his groin. Doubtless she was thinking of Poling.

"You're remembering when I did this?" He bent his head to swirl his tongue over a distended nipple. She arched her back and increased her grip on his shaft.

He came to his knees, cradled her in his arms, lifted her off the bed, and set her on her feet.

She braced her hands on his shoulders, clearly wondering what he was doing.

He reached down to the hem of her nightshift and quickly peeled it off over her head. "I am naked. You should be too. It works better that way."

She giggled nervously, sending another wave of blood rushing to his groin. He stepped back to admire her. She was everything he had dreamed of. Perfect breasts with rigid pink nipples. Big areolas, a shade darker. Her waist was so tiny he could probably span it with both hands, then her body widened to shapely hips. He licked his lips imagining her flat belly swollen with his child.

The hair at her mons was darker, but he remembered its curly texture from Poling. With those long tapering legs, no wonder she was a great horsewoman. He almost spilled thinking of her riding him.

She made no attempt to cover her body. It thrilled him that she was obviously enjoying his perusal. His brave girl was back.

He hugged her to his chest and buried his nose in her hair. "I could spend the night making love to your hair."

She laughed, curling her fingers into the hair on his chest. "Soft."

He nibbled her earlobe until she scrunched up her shoulder. "Tickles."

When he had first removed her nightshift, her skin had felt chilled. Now her body had warmed and he caught the enticing aroma of female arousal. He picked her up and put her back on the bed.

She looked at him through half-hooded eyes.

He kissed one nipple. "I want to suck these lovely tits now, until you scream." He was instantly contrite. "I'm sorry, Rosamunda."

She thrust out her breasts, stroking his hair. "Suck. Like it."

He knelt, straddling her thighs, and cupped one breast with his hand. He suckled the nipple, gently at first, but then fully into his mouth as it grew more rigid.

She entwined her fingers in his hair, her breathing becoming more rapid.

He grazed his teeth against the nipple as her fingernails dug into his scalp.

She pushed her thighs against his, fisting her hands into the bed linens. "Adam."

His shaft throbbed as his *couilles* drew up between his parted legs. He switched to the other nipple, taking her hand and placing it on his sac. "Play with me," he whispered.

He groaned against the nipple in his mouth as she kneaded him with enough pressure he thought he might go mad with the pleasure. "Perfect," he growled.

She writhed beneath him.

He moved to kneel beside her.

She bent her knees and her legs fell open.

He kissed her deeply as his fingers drifted down her belly. His shaft bucked as he touched the wet warmth of her nether lips.

A ripple of need flowed through her as he slid one finger inside, brushing his thumb over her swollen nub. She arched her body into his hand as he slid in a second finger.

"Rosamunda," he whispered against her cheek as they broke apart for breath. His need to be inside her was urgent, but he wanted her to release as she had at Poling. "Come for me," he urged, sliding his fingers in and out, stroking the diamond of her desire.

When it came, her release nigh carried her off the bed. It shuddered through her, rocking him to his core. She mouthed his name over and over, and for the first time he regretted he would never hear his name on her lips. He withdrew his fingers, unable to wait any longer for her pulsating muscles to be clamped on his shaft.

He straddled her again, guiding his rigid manhood into the opening of her body and plunged inside quickly. He felt her maidenhead tear, but there was no stopping now as the white heat drove him on.

"Rosa, Rosa," he panted.

An errant thought flew into his brain. He made a solemn pledge to undertake an annual pilgrimage to the Shrine of Saint Alban.

Rosamunda lifted her hips to lock her legs around Adam's waist, awed by the passion that underscored the beautiful lines and muscles of his body. He clamped his arms around her thighs, pulling her to the edge of the bed, and came to his feet, bracing his knees against the side of the bed. He drew her legs up to his chest, leaning forward to plunge deeper.

She reached to brush her thumbs over his rigid nipples, relishing the flash of fire in his blue eyes. "I love you," he rasped, his words carrying her to an even higher level of ecstasy than the one to which he had brought her with his touch.

She dug her fingertips into his powerful thighs, feeling the urgency in his thrusts. The brief moment of pain had disappeared as warmth built within her. Her first timid glimpse of his manhood jutting up from its halo of black curls had been a bit alarming, and she had wondered how he could possibly insert it into her body, as Paulina had whispered he would.

Now she reveled in the fullness of him as quivering muscles pulsed in rhythm with her heart. Her own need built as he drove harder and harder, until his seed flooded her womb and her own body shattered again when he growled out his release.

He collapsed on top of her.

She trailed her fingertips through the sheen of perspiration on his shoulders as her mind wandered through the oft told tale of caves and secret passages, of dark, handsome heroes, rescuing maidens in distress. She had dreamed for years such a hero would come to rescue her.

He had saved himself for her. No other would possess him.

Now she lay beneath him, savoring his weight as she felt him soften and leave her body. Adam had not only rescued her, he had brought a hero for her beloved sister as well.

LET'S MAKE A BABY

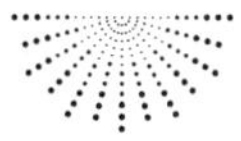

"Prepare yourself, my love. It's not a pretty sight."

Denis flung off the linens to reveal his nakedness, his heart in his throat. He knew the ugliness of his body.

To make matters worse, his unruly shaft stood arrogantly to attention. He had sometimes thought it a cruel jest of God that a small man should be endowed with such a member.

Paulina's eyes widened.

He rolled hastily to his side, gathering the linens to cover his groin. "Don't be afraid."

She shook her head. "I am no longer afraid, Denis. You have made me recognize the futility of fear. In giving me courage, you have given me back my life."

He took her hand, savoring her delicate fingers, so different from his own. "My life would mean nothing without you, Paulina. I love you, but how can you love a man like me?"

She shrugged, then came to her knees, quickly pulled

her chemise over her head, and whipped the linens away from Denis' body. She knelt before him naked, her arms outstretched. "All my life, I have hated my body, resented my size. But your eyes tell me you see only beauty."

Denis wondered how she could believe her breasts were not beautiful. The rigid nipples were exactly the color he had imagined, the areolas bigger. He licked his lips, longing to swirl his tongue over her pouting globes. "But you are beautiful."

She cupped her breasts, lifting them to her own perusal. His shaft turned to granite. Her eyes wandered over his body. Strangely, he suddenly felt proud of his masculinity. He clasped his hands behind his head and parted his legs slightly. Paulina looked like she might drool. "You want me," he teased.

She fixed her gaze on his shaft. "I am consumed with wanting. Can I touch you?"

He could only nod, sure if he spoke he would blurt out something incomprehensible.

She traced a fingertip along the length of his manhood.

Predictably, it bucked, and she smiled.

"You see the effect you have on me," he rasped.

She touched him again, this time circling the swollen tip of his phallus. "Silky," she murmured.

Much as Denis hated to put a halt to the progress they were making towards his ultimate goal, they had an important matter to discuss. He curled her hand around his shaft, then reached up to brush his knuckles across a nipple. Her eyelids fluttered closed. "We need to talk."

She opened her eyes and frowned. "Talk?"

"In a few short minutes, God willing, I will thrust this monstrosity inside your lovely heat."

She blushed, the flush spreading across her breasts as well as her face. He dragged his mind back to the matter at hand. "We must decide if I am to spill my seed outside your body—or inside."

"I don't understand."

He groaned inwardly, remembering their talk about cats and teats. Perhaps she did not know how children were created. He longed to fill her belly with his child, but did she understand the risks? Did he have a right to bring children into the world who might bear his affliction?

He swallowed hard. "It is from a man's seed that children grow."

Tears welled in her eyes. "I want to bear your children."

He came to his knees, pressing their bodies together, thigh to thigh, chest to breast, his shaft against her belly. He kissed her tears. "Even if they are dwarfs?"

She pulled away and looked into his eyes. "Will we love them any less if they are?"

He had been blind. This woman who had never known love from her own parents would of course cherish children. He had thought to deny her and himself that joy.

He kissed the top of her head, then broke them apart and lay back on the bed, patting the space beside him. "Come here and lay with me. Let's make a baby."

EPILOGUE

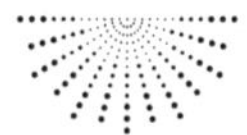

Alphonse Revandel seemed to lose his wits after his daughter's disappearance and his sons' incarceration. When news was brought to him that Winrod and Dareau had been murdered in prison, apparently by someone to whom they owed a great deal of money, he wandered off into the South Downs and was never seen again.

Antoine deeded Poling Manor to Denis with the proviso he never sell it. Denis spent summers there with his wife and children. Adam and Rosamunda and their brood usually accompanied them on the journey to England, the Montbryces staying at nearby East Preston.

Vincent Lallement succeeded as lord of a rebuilt and refurbished Kingston Gorse. Lucien married a wealthy heiress who brought him a sizable house in Hastings as part of her dowry.

Normandie became divided into two factions, those in support of the duke's claim to the throne of England, and those opposed. Having pledged loyalty to King Henry, the

Montbryces reinforced the defenses of all their Norman holdings, aware of the duke's anger at what he perceived as treachery. Everyone knew Curthose would eventually attempt an invasion of England.

King Henry continued to spend time, effort, and money increasing the size and grandeur of Arundel Castle.

Adam and Denis and their families often spent time there as His Majesty's guests. The two men were fond of boasting that the Giant and the Dwarf would be boon companions to the end. However, they made sure to return to Belisle Castle months before the king turned his thoughts to the annual celebrations of the Hallowmas Triduum.

Whenever he was in England, Adam took time to kneel in thanksgiving before the altar of Saint Alban. He became known as one of the abbey's most generous benefactors.

BOOK VI~ STAR-CROSSED

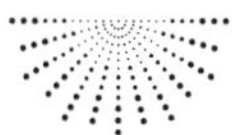

GIROUX CASTLE, NORMANDIE, SPRING 1101

Dorianne de Giroux had grown up in the bosom of a family filled with hatred and the desire for vengeance. Long before she was born, her late grandfather had been blinded and mutilated by another baron after a bitter argument over territory.

After the evening meal, she and Pierre joined their parents in the gallery, as was their family tradition. She tried to concentrate on her embroidery but, as usual, her father wanted to relive the reasons for the feud that consumed him. "Your grandfather sank into madness after his blinding and made life a living hell for his sons, Phillippe, Georges, and me," he complained. "Yet it was we who captured the Valtesse castle at Alensonne in retaliation. With the help of Valtesse's bastard son, we cast him out and exiled him, along with his daughter, Mabelle. Curses on fate that Arnulf would die and Valtesse regain his castle."

Dorianne had heard this story a thousand times and knew what came next.

"Seeking revenge, your uncle Phillippe went to England and plotted against Mabelle de Valtesse's husband, the *Comte* de Montbryce." He sighed heavily. "News eventually reached us Phillippe had been killed in Wales."

"Papa," she ventured with a tentative smile. "Can we not talk of other things?"

François de Giroux glared at her as if she had spoken in Greek and then carried on. "I'm not a violent man, but I can never forget the torments I suffered at the hands of my mad father."

It worried Dorianne that her older brother seemed to hang on their father's every word, encouraging his preoccupation.

"Well, Papa," Pierre said, "you almost succeeded in having one of the Montbryces convicted of adultery by the King's Court in Caen."

François smirked. "Much good that did. The Montbryces were in the Conqueror's pocket. Had I succeeded in getting Hugh de Montbryce condemned, Phillippe might never have embarked on his plan to aid the Welsh rebels who kidnapped Rambaud de Montbryce's wife and her brats."

Her father rarely showed affection for his children. Growing up, she had looked to Pierre for love. Their mother loved them, but she was a timid woman who wilted under the gaze of her husband and did his bidding in all things. Elenor now sat with her head bowed, as she did every evening, immersed in her sewing, contributing nothing to the conversation.

Dorianne dreaded the day her father would find her a husband. Having led a secluded existence in the Giroux castle, she had no friends, only her brother. A year older than she, Pierre was allowed more freedom and sometimes travelled with their father through their lands or to other barons' *demesnes*.

She harangued her brother for details of his travels upon his return, anxious to hear about the outside world. Pierre trained with the men-at-arms of the castle, and Dorianne sometimes stole up to the parapets to watch secretly as the men practiced their skills. Her Maman and Papa would be horrified if they were aware she'd seen men bared to the waist, sweating.

Young noblewomen of eighteen were not supposed to know of such things, and she would never divulge that she admired the strength God had given to men's bodies. So different from her own.

Occasionally, *seigneurs* from neighboring lands would visit, often bringing their sons. This was part of the game to find her a husband, but none of the unappealing young men seemed to satisfy her father's requirements, which probably had something to do with her dowry. She would have no say in the matter. She was past the age when most young noblewomen married. The only certainty was that her father would never betroth her to a Montbryce, though their lands were apparently but a day's ride away.

A few days later, her father took her by surprise at supper in the hall. "Dorianne, two days hence you'll accompany Pierre and me to the castle of the *Comte* d'Avranches."

"Two days?" she parroted, stunned she was being allowed to leave the castle, but suspecting more would be revealed and that it would concern a betrothal. She waited, noticing Pierre's nod of approval.

She grew more apprehensive and toyed with her food, watching her father chew leisurely on a chicken leg and then take a long swig of ale. Noisily sucking food out of his teeth, he confirmed, "We'll meet with the *comte* to discuss your betrothal to his son, Otuel d'Avranches. He maybe a bastard son, but your marriage to him will bring us strong allies in the coming war with Henry of England. The *comte* plans to host a Grand Council to discuss the political situation, and we'll be his guests. It's a perfect opportunity for them to meet my beautiful daughter."

Her eyes widened. This adventure might turn out to be a good thing, but a bastard? Encouraged by her father's unusual warmth, she ventured to ask, "Tell me about the c*omte's* son."

He cast her an indignant look. "I haven't met him. He's never attended any of the tournaments. He's but a boy of ten."

Her heart plummeted. "Ten! But father—"

He held up his hands. "Enough of this, Dorianne. He's a d'Avranches. That's the important thing."

She crossed her arms over her breasts, slid down in her chair and sulked for a while, then something else her father had said came to mind. "Coming war?"

Pierre scowled at her. "Don't you know anything? There'll be war over the throne of England."

She gritted her teeth and hissed back at him. "How am I supposed to know what's going on when I'm a prisoner here?"

Her father grunted something unintelligible, got up and left.

Elenor packed up her sewing and dutifully followed him, venturing a strange smile at her daughter.

Dorianne slumped back into her chair.

"What's wrong with you?" Pierre asked belligerently.

She wondered if continuing to share her feelings with him was a good idea. "In my wildest imaginings of my future husband I never dreamt he'd be a boy much younger than me."

Pierre shrugged as he came to his feet. "Dori, it's father's decision. You'll have to make the best of it. Be grateful he's not sending you to a nunnery."

She sat bolt upright, a cold chill chasing across her nape. "Why would he do that?"

Whistling, Pierre left without another word.

The future did not look promising.

ABOUT ANNA

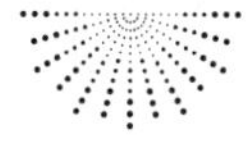

Thank you for reading ***BIRTHRIGHT.***

Reviews are always appreciated and contribute greatly to an author's success.

I'd love you to visit my website and my Facebook page, Anna Markland Novels.

Tweet me @annamarkland, join me on Pinterest, or sign up for my newsletter.

Be the first to know when my next book is available. Follow me on BookBub .

Passion conquers whatever obstacles a hostile medieval world can throw in its path.

Besides writing, I have two addictions-crosswords and genealogy, probably the reason I love research. I am a fool for cats. My husband is an entrepreneur who is fond of boasting he's never had a job. I live on Canada's scenic west coast now, but I was born and raised in the UK and I love breathing life into European history.

Escape with me to where romance began.

I hope you come to know and love my cast of characters as much as I do.

I'd like to acknowledge the assistance of my beta reader, Maria McIntyre.

Made in the USA
Middletown, DE
03 August 2018